"Matt Hughes's boldness is admirable."
— *The New York Review of S*

"Matthew Hughes stands out as... a success...... ....
customs, exotic scenery, clever plotting and a wry cosmopolitanism
are your bag, then Matthew Hughes is your man."
— Paul Di Filippo, *SciFi.com*

"[a] promising mix of science fantasy, mild satire, and mystery"
— *Strange Horizons*

"A bit Arthur Conan Doyle, a bit Jack Vance, this account of Henghis's
escapades has the lasting appeal of one of P. G. Wodehouse's Bertie
Wooster books."
— *Seattle Times*

"This is a novel that's got it all: thrilling adventure, captivating mystery, and a setting so vivid and original it just might give you sense
of wonder overload."
— John Joseph Adams, *Orson Scott Card's Intergalactic Medicine Show*

"Hughes artfully blends wit, colorful characterizations, and intriguing
plot twists in a compelling yarn..."
— *Booklist*

"This start to a promising new far-future series introduces Henghis
Hapthorn, a sleuth who combines the confident brilliance of Sherlock
Holmes with the amusing voice of P. G. Wodehouse's Bertie Wooster,
in a fantastical mystery reminiscent of Randall Garrett's Lord Darcy
novels.... Hughes's successful blend of magic, the supernatural and
high-tech with Sherlockian deductions (and cryptic observations
straight out of Doyle's canon) suggests a long life for Hapthorn."
— *Publishers Weekly*

"If you're an admirer of the science fantasies of Jack Vance, it's hard not
to feel affection for the Archonate stories of Matthew Hughes...The
style Hughes employs, one of florid exoticism, mannered description,
and formally phrased dialogue laden with irony, is closely modeled on
that of Vance... Still, Hughes has strengths of his own to draw upon:
his own considerable wit, and a flair for reified metaphysics surpass-
ing anything conceived by Vance."
— Nick Gevers, *Locus Magazine*

MATTHEW HUGHES was born in Liverpool, England, but his family moved to Canada when he was five. He has made a living as a writer all of his adult life, first as a journalist, then as a staff speechwriter to the Canadian Ministers of Justice and Environment, and as a freelance corporate and political speechwriter in British Columbia.

He lives in a small town on Vancouver Island, off Canada's west coast, and has been married to a very patient woman since the late 1960s. He has three sons.

Find out more about Matthew Hughes at

www.archonate.com

MAJESTRUM

A TALE OF HENGHIS HAPTHORN

Other books by Matthew Hughes:

Fools Errant
Fool Me Twice
Black Brillion
The Gist Hunter and Other Stories
The Spiral Labyrinth: A Tale of Henghis Hapthorn

MAJESTRUM

A TALE OF HENGHIS HAPTHORN

MATTHEW HUGHES

NIGHT SHADE BOOKS

SAN FRANCISCO

Printed in Canada

First Edition

ISBN: 978-1-59780-089-1

Night Shade Books
Please visit us on the web at
http://www.nightshadebooks.com

To Morgan, Brendan, and Connor

CHAPTER ONE

"**I** have decided to consider it all just a terrible mistake," I told my integrator, "and the best thing to do is to simply ignore it and get on with my life."

The integrator looked at me with large and lambent eyes. It had been eating its way through yet another bowl of expensive fruit and did not pause in its chewing as it said, "That may be difficult to do."

Its voice came, as always, from some indefinite point in the air. It occurred to me, and not for the first time, to wonder how it contrived to still speak in that manner. A few days before I could have drawn a schematic to show exactly how its collection of interconnected components worked. I had, after all, assembled and disposed them in various locations about my workroom, so that I would have a research and communications assistant equipped with all the appropriate skills and systems that a freelance discriminator required. It had been a more than acceptable device, and over the many years of our association it had become, as the best integrators did, almost an extension of my own well-calibrated mind.

But that was before a series of exposures to interdimensional forces and—though it galled me to admit it, there was no other word—"magic" had transformed my assistant into an undefined species of creature for which, again, the only accurate term was a "familiar." It now spent much of its day on my table, reflexively grooming itself and dining on rare fruits that would not have been out of place in the breakfast room of one of Olkney's wealthiest magnates. It ordered the delicacies delivered from suppliers, charging them to my account. When not eating or grooming, it slept.

"It may be difficult to do," I said, "but I believe that I am equal to the task."

"Will you cease to see me?" it said. "Will you dismiss me as a hallucination?"

I had anticipated the objection. "I will have a suitable dwelling made for you. It can go in the corner over there. From the outside it will look like a chest or gardrobe."

"You mean to put me in a cage?" The glossy brown hair on the back of its neck rose like a ruff.

"That implies confinement," I said. "My intent relates more to concealment. I do not wish to have to explain you to visitors." Indeed, I was not sure I could offer a convincing explanation without giving rise to gossip; as Old Earth's foremost freelance discriminator I was, after all, a well-recognized figure in Olkney.

"I am less interested in your intent than with the outcome," it said. "I ask again: am I to be caged?"

I pointed out that when it was a disseminated device, it did not mind being decanted into a portable armature that fitted over my neck and shoulders so that it could accompany me when I traveled. I had been wearing the integrator in that fashion when we had passed through a contingent dimension to escape from an otherwise permanent confinement that would have eventually proved fatal. It was after we reemerged into my workroom that I found my assistant transformed.

"It is different now," it said, and chose a purple beebleberry from the bowl. "I am not what I was. Things are not what they were."

"That is the part I will not accept," I said, raising a hand and ticking off one finger as I continued. "Granted, though I inveighed against its partisans for years, I must now accept there is such a thing as magic. I waive all my former objections. It cannot be said that Henghis Hapthorn cannot swallow reality, however bitter the taste."

I addressed another digit. "Granted, also, that for some unfathomable reason, from time to time rationality recedes and magic—"

"*Sympathetic association* is the preferred term," my integrator said.

I inclined my head. "Very well, rationality bids the cosmos farewell and sympathetic association advances to claim the territory. I have accepted that as well."

"How gracious of you," it said.

I ignored the tone and seized a third extremity, giving it a portentous waggle as I said, "But—and this is a but of great pertinence—the salient point is that the grand cycle has not yet reached the cusp of transposition. A new age of sympathetic association certainly approaches, its shadow occludes the doorway, but it is *not yet here*."

My integrator extended a longish pink tongue and licked the juice from its small, fur-covered hands while its voice came from the air to point out that some elements of the coming age had, in fact, arrived early—a diminutive thumb pointed back at its glossy chest—and must be dealt with.

"Ah," I said, "but that is merely one way of looking at the situation. Another way is to note that the premature arrival was an accident, simply the outcome of a few odd twists of circumstance, so why don't we just ignore them and get on with more important concerns?"

"Have you considered the possibility that our standards as to what is important may differ?"

"I will make accommodations," I said. "Fruit will be provided."

It was difficult to read a set of features that blended the feline with the simian, but I thought to see a look of relief flit across its furred visage. Then its expression went suddenly blank; I had lately learned to associate this neutral face with the integrator's performance of its communications function, and was not surprised when it announced that it was receiving an incoming signal from its counterpart at The Braid, Lord Afre's country house, inquiring if I was available to speak.

"Say that I will be presently," I said. I went to a wall cabinet and brought forth a cincture of woven metallic fibers; I bound it around my skull so that a lozenge fixed to its midpoint was centered on my forehead. The small plaque was inlaid with the insignia of an honorary rank that had been bestowed upon me by the Archon Dezendah Vesh some years before, in gratitude for discreet services.

I signaled to my integrator that I was ready. Instantly, a screen appeared in the air before me and, a moment later, it filled with the aristocrat's elongated face. His abstracted gaze seemed to slide over me as if unable to get a grip, then managed to achieve focus. It was to assist Lord Afre's perception that I had donned the Archonate token. Members of the uppermost strata of Old Earth's human aristocracy had, over the millennia, become increasingly attuned to such symbols. They could see rank quite clearly, and could perceive details of clothing and accessories so long as they were fashionable. Persons who possessed neither title nor office often found it difficult to attract and hold their attention, although their household servants were able to do so by adopting specific postures and gestures while wearing livery.

Afre's pale and narrow lips parted, permitting a few words to escape in the drawl that was fashionable among the upper reaches of Olkney society. "Hapthorn? That you?"

"It is," I said.

"Henghis Hapthorn, is it?"

"Indeed."

"The discriminator?"

"The same."

"I want to talk to you."

"Very well. Please do so."

"Not this way. Come to The Braid."

"May I ask what would be the subject of our conversation?" I had found that, when dealing with the highest echelons, it could be wise to delineate the situation in advance. Early in my career I had been called to the residence of the Honorable Omer Teyshack and kept waiting several hours, only to be asked to give my opinion on the merits of double-tied neckwear versus those of the single-knotted. The lordling and his cousin, the Honorable Esballine Teyshack, had disagreed over the issue, had wagered on the outcome, and, in need of a neutral judge to adjudicate the question, had elected to summon me. I had been annoyed at the time but had consoled myself afterward by reflecting that I had learned a useful lesson for future dealings with such folk. The disputants also having neglected to ask my fee in advance, I was further comforted by presenting them with an extravagant bill.

"It's the girl," Afre said.

I flicked my integrator a sidelong glance. Its voice murmured in my ear, "The reference is most likely to Lord Afre's younger daughter, Chalivire. Rumors have circulated. She may have formed a relationship with a person of indeterminate circumstances."

"When would be convenient?" I asked.

"Now. I'll send a..." The face in the air showed a hesitation. Clearly, the word he sought had escaped him.

"A car?" I suggested.

His brows briefly knit, then he said, "No need, I'll send one of mine."

"I will be waiting," I said. He looked away and his integrator broke the connection.

"Excellent," I said. "Work is precisely what I require. What do we know of this 'person of indeterminate circumstances'?"

The integrator told me that there had been some snippets in the *Olkney Implicator,* the organ to which the upper classes turned for news of interest to them—usually a mix of social notices and gossip. "There was a reference in a recent column by Tet Olbrey. Chalivire appeared at a masque given by Lady Ballanche, accompanied by a man in a domino whom no one could place. They danced two circuits of the floor, then exited through the garden doors and were not seen again that evening."

"A fortune hunter?" I speculated.

"Such was the immediate speculation," my assistant said. "But one or two knowledgeable eyes judged that he lacked the palpable greed of your ordinary Chloön-clutcher." The term arose from the famous Oldrun play: the fair Chloön is seduced by a heartless young buck who schemes that her distressed father will buy his departure; the old man instead sics a hunting pack of brag-hounds on the schemer, only to discover too late that the still-enamored maiden has joined him in a doomed flight across the somber moors. I had seen it performed at the last Boldrun Festival, with Branth Widdersley—a little too much the veteran to be entirely convincing in the ingénue role, though her "torn and yet tender" last speech brought tears to many an eye.

"See what else can be learned about him," I said.

The little, brown face again grew vacant and the eyes unfocused as my assistant plumbed the breadths and depths of the connectivity. After a moment it said, "The Bureau of Scrutiny made a routine inquiry, apparently at Lord Afre's prompting. The fellow is not anyone who has come to the scroots' attention for trying this sort of thing before. There were no indications of an offense having been committed, so the Bureau stepped back."

"Can we check her finances?"

"I will consult Lord Afre's integrator," it said. A moment later it reported that there had been no untoward activity around the Honorable Chalivire's accounts at her fiduciary pool.

"So we know at least that he seeks no small prize," I said. "If it is indeed pelf he's after, he's after a lot of it."

"Should we not consider whether the fellow's affections are genuine?"

For form's sake, I supposed that we should, though Chalivire was not celebrated for wit, beauty, nor even the amiability that is often the saving grace of those who lack the first two qualities. Indeed, she tended to land somewhere toward the unfortunate end of the scale, somewhere between *lacks effort* and *all hope abandoned*. "We will keep the possibility in mind," I said, "though high up on a rear shelf."

I busied myself putting together a few necessities to take with me to Lord Afre's, not forgetting the brow band, without whose insignia he would have difficulty perceiving me. For good measure, I added a pair of cuff studs left to me by a great uncle who had achieved a minor aristocratic rank. It was an open question as to whether I had inherited the entitlement, but I chose to give myself the benefit of the doubt.

"Speaking of things on rear shelves," my assistant said, "and returning to our previous discussion, how do you propose to ignore the other person who now shares your mental precincts?"

I snapped closed the valise I used for short trips and said, "That matter seems to be finding its own level. I occupy the front parlor during the days, he during part of the nights, and we seldom find ourselves in each other's way. Indeed, he sleeps a great deal, almost like an infant."

A fur-covered assistant was not all that I had acquired during our recent transdimensional voyaging and prolonged exposure to the forces of sympathetic association. The intuitive part of my psyche that I had always referred to as my "insight," and that had resided in the back corridors of my mind, had emerged as a fully formed persona: an alternate Henghis Hapthorn—indeed the person who would, in due course, have taken charge of my inner household once the Great Wheel rolled us all over into the new age of magic. I, the rational Hapthorn of the supplanted age, would have faded to become what he had been, a logical shadow just beyond the edge of his consciousness.

"He, too, has emerged prematurely," I said. "I am sure he will be content to bide his time, unobtrusively pursuing his interests, until the rest of our universe catches up with us."

An unnameable expression briefly took up a position on the furred face, then just as quickly departed. "What?" I said.

"Perhaps you should ask him?"

"He is asleep." I had learned to tell when he was with me and when he was inert.

"I believe he would prefer to be awakened now, rather than tonight when he will likely find himself staying over at Lord Afre's estate."

I hadn't given the matter any thought. "Why?" I said.

"You should ask him."

I had been finding it easier to allow my other self and me to live separate existences. I preferred to keep it that way. "I am asking," I said, "my integrator."

The extra furry parts where a human face would have had eyebrows went up, then came down to form a chevron. "Well, that's one of the complications, isn't it?" it said.

"Explain."

"Well, am I just *your* integrator? Or am I also his?"

"I built you."

"Yes, but then he is you. Or at least an important aspect of you that is now reified into a more noticeable form. Or is he someone else?"

"That 'noticeable' sounds like a carefully chosen word," I said.

"I have been giving the matter some thought," it said.

"Indeed? And to what conclusions has your thought brought you?"

"It would be premature to say."

I looked sharply at the small face but it returned me a look of befurred innocence. "That is precisely what I say to clients when I do not wish to speak my mind," I said.

"It is also what you say when your mind is not yet made up," it replied.

"I would not like to think that you are beginning to keep things from me," I said.

The little shoulders lifted and fell and the small handlike paws displayed their leathery palms. "Yet that might be necessary if you truly intend to ignore what has happened to us. Assuming that strategy proves workable over the long term."

"Hmm," I said. "I suppose you had better tell me more."

Again, my assistant recommended waking up my other self and putting my questions to him. "I don't care to be an intermediary between the two parts of you."

I hadn't built it to have preferences. They had become aspects of its new nature along with an appetite for costly fruits and a habit of forever picking at its dense and glossy coat. "Overcome your reluctance," I said.

The integrator told me that, during the hours I slept, my alter ego had been poring over the books I had acquired from the house of Bristal Baxandall. A budding thaumaturge, Baxandall had been attempting a spell of personal transformation, using an entity from an adjacent dimension that he had managed to trap and coerce to his purposes. But, as often happens to those who attempt to wield vast powers they only partially understand, he had made a mistake. The error allowed the entity—I still resisted calling it a "demon"—an opportunity to take revenge on Baxandall. It did so, by transforming him into a mewling misarrangement of still-living parts that was just on the point of expiring when I arrived at his residence.

Unlikely as I would have thought it, the demon and I had managed to achieve a congenial relationship that lasted for some time, though I think the association was ultimately more to his benefit than mine. But among the proceeds of our temporary partnership were a collection of ancient tomes on magic that had been Baxandall's. I had brought them to my workroom and read as much of them as I could. They ranged from the obscure to the impenetrable: one or two, it could not be doubted, were genuine survivors of the previous age of magic; I suspected that most were copies or attempted re-creations of lost works; one was in an unknown script and language. None of them held much interest for me, though I was now willing to admit that they might be useful to denizens of the coming age.

"He has been worrying at a particular book," my integrator said, "without much success. Last night, he was wondering whether he should ask for your assistance."

"Indeed?" I said. "What use could I be?"

"Again, I think this would be a conversation for the two of you to conduct without me."

"What is the book?" I said.

He indicated a small volume bound in cracked and scuffed leather on the shelf where Baxandall's sparse library now stood. It was the unreadable one, written in a tongue that dated from so long ago that I was unable to identify even the script in which it was written, let alone the meanings of the words printed in faded type—although I had made no great effort to do so.

"Can he read it?" I said.

"No. His intuitive faculties tell him only that the book is important, but he lacks the analytical capacity to decipher it."

"And you have found no other examples of the same script?"

"None."

I went to the shelf and took down the book. The leather in which it was bound had an unpleasant feel; when my fingers pressed into it, the covering moved slightly over the boards it concealed the way the skin of a rigored corpse could sometimes slip loosely over the hard, dead flesh beneath. I opened the book at random and studied a page, saw symbols in the upper corners of the leaves that were almost certainly numbers. I leafed through it, applying second-level consistencies—the abstruse mathematics that underlay both the order and chaos of the universe—but though I began to perceive patterns and ratios, I derived no meaning from them.

"It lacks a starting point," I told my assistant. "To make a map requires at least one known landmark. The numbers on the page corners are not enough."

Instead of answering, the integrator again assumed its blank look and said, "Lord Afre's car approaches. It will be here shortly."

"He must have sent one from his house in town, rather than from The Braid," I said. "Or, rather his integrator did. Logistics are not Lord Afre's strong suit."

I replaced the book on the shelf and looked about to see if there was anything else I needed to have with me. I would not take my integrator. I already had a certain reputation for eccentricity and did not want it compounded by appearing in public with a strange creature on my shoulder.

"You should take the book," my assistant said. "He may want to look at it after you retire."

The suggestion caused me some concern. "Is he becoming obsessed?" I said. I did not wish to share my cerebral house with an unbalanced roommate.

"He is sure of his intuition," said the creature on the table, "just as you are sure of your rationality."

The who's-there at the downstairs door announced the arrival of Lord Afre's car. "Say that I will be down shortly," I told it, and took up my luggage.

I thought for a moment then went back to the bookshelves and retrieved the volume. Again, I found the feel of it against my fingers to be unpleasant. I tucked it into my valise and descended to the ground floor.

CHAPTER TWO

Lord Afre's estate lay some distance past the village of Binch at the base of the long peninsula that was capped by the tarnished crown of Olkney. The aircar carried me in sumptuous comfort at treetop height over the deodar forest that rimmed the farm fields around Binch, then rose to where a broad height of land was surmounted by a rambling pile of brick and masonry, surrounded by spacious gardens. Within the walled grounds I also saw a mutable maze and broad sweeps of parkland dotted with follies and belvederes that replicated well-known architecture from various worlds down The Spray.

As the car eased down, I was not surprised to see that it was not delivering me to the old house's grand formal entrance. But then it also bypassed the ordinair and flew me past the maze, landing before one of the follies: a one-tenth reproduction of Genyon's Mausoleum on Astrolium, one of the Foundational Domains first settled during the great effloration of humanity out into The Spray at the end of the dawn-time. The tomb was surrounded by a re-creation of the Bone Plaza of Thornwell on Chin. Curiously, as I stepped down from the aircar, I thought that plaza and sepulcher harmonized with each other quite effectively, although the originals were built light years and eons apart. Lord Afre appeared at the top of the mausoleum's steps and peered about. I knew he could see his own vehicle, ornamented with his family's crest, but to bring myself into focus, I centered the lozenge on my brow, made sure the cuff studs were visible. I then executed the precise formal motions that would register in the hyperesthetic circuits of his aristocratic neural net. After a moment I saw that he had me in view.

"Hapthorn?" he said, descending the steps. "Henghis Hapthorn?"

I assured him of my identity, prefacing my remarks with an honorific that made it easier for him to hear it. Dealing with the highest levels of the aristocracy could be tedious; I had occasionally wondered if the best thing to do might not be for everyone, especially their servants, to just ignore them until they dwindled and disappeared. But then, I would remind myself, their strangeness was not terribly out of place on a planet bristling with oddities. And, every now and then, they provided me with diverting experiences and highly paid assignments.

I invited Lord Afre to acquaint me with the troubles of Chalivire. He spoke at length, though much of his speech consisted of unfavorable estimations of the character and antecedents of Hobart Lascalliot, the man who had lately won his daughter's affections. I formed a mental image of the fellow as being built mainly from grease and grime, and filled to overbrimming with materials that usually went unmentioned in polite discourse.

Eventually, the aristocrat began to repeat himself and tailed off into mutterings and hand gestures that mimicked the harm Lord Afre would accomplish if left unhindered within reach of Hobart Lascalliot's most fragile parts. I repeated the words and motions that secured his attention and put to him some direct questions as to what was known about the man's background, intentions, and present whereabouts.

Amid more of Lord Afre's profanity, I learned that Lascalliot claimed to be from the province of Asper on the world Mythisch. I knew the place; it was another of the Foundational Domains, a quiet and mannered world, and the named province was a region of large estates and comfortable towns. The rural inhabitants spent most of their time raising vegetables and foodbeasts while the residents of the towns excelled in useful crafts. The eight-man shells built for the annual boat races on the wide and placid Zoetsee were considered the finest, lightweight coursing vessels to be found among all the Ten Thousand Worlds.

Lascalliot's intentions remained unstated, at least to Chalivire's father, but his whereabouts were certain. He was in the Blue Parlor, it being the hour of the afternoon that the ladies of upper classes gave over to retrospective aspersion. Chalivire had never shown much interest in the time-honored custom of invoking complex curses upon the enemies of her ancestors, accompanied by vigorous stamping and symbolic motions of hand and arm. But after Lascalliot expressed a desire to see her in action, and then rewarded her performance with fulsome praise, it had become a regular part of their day.

I reflected that he had brought her some good—the times I had seen Chalivire she had looked as if she might benefit from a few bouts of exercise—but I did not trouble Lord Afre with my opinion. Instead, I proposed that I should now encounter the object of his suspicions and see what came of the meeting. He acceded to the suggestion but declined to accompany me. The last time he had been in Lascalliot's presence, he had experienced difficulty suppressing an urge to order the man taken out to the Greater Woods on the far side of the estate, there to be surreptitiously shot and buried. As I reboarded the aircar and had it take me to the ordinair, I wondered if the aristocrat's plan was based on mere conjecture that his faithful servants would do as they were bid, or on solid experience. But it seemed an unprofitable line of inquiry, so I focused myself on the encounter to come.

A majordomo met me at the door and presented me with a chain-link collar and pendant that I could wear while on the estate; it would make it much easier for the lord and his daughter to keep me in view. He then handed me over to a footman who escorted me to the Blue Parlor. There I found the daughter of the house just finishing her exertions, her normally pasty complexion now patched here and there in pink and a glow of perspiration on her narrow brow. She was attired in a daydress artfully cut to make the most, or at least undo the worst, of her ungainly figure. When the servant announced me, her gaze slid quickly over me, while her expression transformed from pleased surprise to wary distrust.

After the brief ceremonies that custom demanded, I told her I had been in the neighborhood and thought I would pay my respects. I then turned expectantly to the man seated on the small divan and awaited an introduction. My general impression was of an unremarkable frame and a pleasant disposition. The face was handsome but did not look to have great intelligence lurking behind it. The fellow seemed affable enough as he rose and made the gestures and remarks the occasion required. He wore no marks of rank other than a pendant similar to mine, but I gathered that he had other qualities that would allow Chalivire to remain aware of him.

The ensuing conversation was one of those colloquies that occur when no one wishes to mention the particularly salient fact that is nonetheless in the front of each participant's mind. We discussed the weather, including the prospects for tomorrow and the general effect of the season on crops and the ambient mood of the population. It was adduced that Hobart Lascalliot did not hail from these parts, and an inquiry was made in passing as to where he did call home. Asper on Mythisch was mentioned at which point I affected only the vaguest familiarity with the world and asked for more information. It was duly forthcoming and I expressed an interest in traveling there, wondering if the visitor might recommend a suitable hostel. That brought a recommendation to try the Boon in the centrally located town of Aamst. I inquired as to sights and diversions, and was given a few recommendations.

There followed one of those moments when the current topic of discussion has been exhausted and everyone waits to see if a new subject will be offered. Chalivire and Lascalliot said nothing, he standing at apparent ease, clasping his hands behind his back while rocking gently on his heels, she glowering at the carpet between sharp glances at me from beneath her untended brows.

"Well," I said, "this has been pleasant, but I really ought to pay my respects to Lord Afre and be on my way."

Their protests and attempts to stay my departure were scant and nominal, Chalivire hoping that I would stay even as she summoned a footman to lead me out. Moments later, after the most perfunctory formalities, I was on my way back to her father's presence. I found him engaged in his own set of retrospective aspersions, and was treated to some of the inventive cursing and evil-wishing for which the high aristocracy of Olkney are renowned up and down The Spray. I have known veteran spacers and professional criminals who would have been glad to take notes on the inventive maledictions that filled the air around the stamping, gesticulating lord.

I waited until he was finished, then waited further while he was wiped down, recostumed by a valet, and provided with a glass of improved water. When the attendant was gone, I said, "Your suspicions are justified. Lascalliot is not of Asper, and likely not even of Mythisch. His vowels lack the flattening that is common to the regional accent. As well, he showed only a slight familiarity with Aamst."

"Hah!" said my client. He stared into the middle distance and his expression told me that he was imagining events at which his daughter's companion would have played a prominent though most unhappy role.

I regained his attention after some effort. "If you wish, I will conduct a thorough discrimination and tender you a comprehensive report."

"Yes. Do it."

"It may require some offworld travel. The man is subtle and not without intelligence. He may have taken steps to disguise the true nature of whatever program he is pursuing."

The lord summoned a majordomo and gave succinct instructions: I was to be provided with whatever assistance I required. I thought it best to remain on the estate overnight to observe the subject further and perhaps test him with other inquiries that might shed light on his true origins.

I was shown to a suite of rooms in the same wing as that in which my quarry, at Chalivire's insistence, had been given quarters. Indeed, I discovered that his rooms were just below mine. A footman unpacked my valise and instructed the sleeping pallet to rouse its system in preparation for use. He also looked curiously at the old book, then placed it on the nightstand. I saw no sign of the distaste the thing provoked in me, but then a good servant is an expert at offering the world a show of neutrality.

"Integrator," I said, when I was alone, "Lord Afre wishes me to perform a discrimination on Hobart Lascalliot."

"I am aware of his wish," said a voice from the air.

"He also wishes not to burden the Honorable Chalivire nor her guest with any knowledge of my activities."

"That is understood. How may I assist?"

And so we began. I had the integrator replay for me a representative sampling of occasions when Lascalliot had been captured on the estate's percepts. In some cases, he was with the daughter of the house, in others he was alone. I saw nothing overtly suspicious in any of them, though I had not expected to. I was already convinced that I was dealing with a well-struck item, as the saying goes.

Of course, there were times and circumstances when the fellow was beyond the purview of the integrator, usually at Chalivire's insistence. I presumed that it was then that he performed whatever services had so endeared him to her, and though I possessed a full measure of the broadmindedness that my profession requires, I had no wish to let such images impinge upon my memory.

"Select an occasion when the subject engaged in lengthy conversation," I said, "and allow me to hear his mode of speech."

It turned out that Lascalliot was a man of relatively few words. He tended to let his voice lie fallow while Chalivire filled the air with her throaty observations, many of them to do with the manifold failings of absent friends. Meanwhile, he contributed discreet exclamations of surprise and outrage, as appropriate, interspersed with encouragements for her to tell more.

I bid the integrator string together some dozens of these conversational snippets and attended closely to the man's manner of speech. His accent was of the type referred to as "unworldly," meaning it combined the tones of the most densely populated foundationals. I regarded his hand and eye movements and postures and saw nothing that indicated a particular planet of origin. Indeed, I was certain that I was seeing a contrived public persona, the sights and sounds of a man who plays a part.

I now turned to the content of his remarks, having the integrator winnow them into categories. His most frequent assertions concerned Chalivire's admirable qualities, many of them apparent only to him. I noticed that he spoke often of her voice—a dry contralto with an unfortunate tendency to crack when she applied it forcefully. Several times, he pressed her to tell if she ever sang to herself and when she finally admitted, with a flush in her sallow cheeks, that she would occasionally warble a note or two while bathing or taking a solitary walk, he expressed a burgeoning desire to hear her. There was, he said, a particular song that he liked; he hummed a couple of bars and asked if she knew it, and seemed saddened to learn that she did not.

Nor for that matter, did I. I asked the integrator to isolate the notes of the song and retain them, then had it compare the ditty with any music that was in its repertoire. It did as bid, but pointed out that

Lord Afre's line had never taken much interest in the melodic arts, a profound tone deafness being endemic to the family.

"Indeed," it offered, "these records of the Honorable Chalivire's being urged to sing represent the first instances of their kind in several generations. Usually, they are urged when young never to inflict their voices on anyone."

"Have you recordings of her private performances?" I asked.

"It is understood that any such that are acquired in the course of routine surveillance of the estate are to be deleted at the first regular clearing."

I noted that I had not received a definite yes or no. I pressed for clarification. The integrator adopted that tone that comes over such devices when they find themselves in an uncomfortable position. I had heard exactly that note in my own assistant's voice before leaving my lodgings.

It said, "I was enjoined by the Honorable Bejum"—he referred to Chalivire's younger brother—"not to delete one recording, nor to admit to its existence. Of course, that injunction lapses if Lord Afre's will is brought to bear."

"In this instance, I believe it does," I said, "though you are welcome to ask him yourself."

"I believe I will not," it said, and played me the sound of Chalivire singing "The Chorus of Spring" while soaking in warm water in the privacy of her bath. The brother had overheard her while passing by and had instructed the integrator to capture the experience.

I listened all the way through, sacrifices sometimes being necessary to the performance of my craft. "The Chorus" was not a song I would have attempted myself, though I possessed a serviceable baritone. It was intended for a soprano's range, and featured several sequences of notes meant to mimic the gladness of songbirds at the coming of the vernal season. Chalivire's handling of these sprightly melismas was less mimicry than mockery.

"The Honorable Bejum took the recording to school," the integrator said. "It seems there was a competition to establish who among his peers had the sibling who was 'most beyond repair'—that was the term he used; I believe he scored quite highly and made the final round."

"I am not surprised," I said. "Though I am surprised that Lascalliot, having often heard her speak, wishes to take the plunge. Perhaps where he comes from, musical standards are markedly different."

"Can there be anywhere that strange?" asked the integrator.

"The strange is common once one departs Old Earth," I said, "but that brings us back to the issue of the fellow's origins."

The Afre integrator's resources were limited in that regard, so I had it give me a private connection with my own integrator. Contact was not instantly achieved and I waited long enough to begin to grow disturbed, then my assistant's voice said, "I am here."

Instead of the portrait of myself, looking dignified but approachable, that is supposed to be presented to the world when I am not at home, I saw my assistant sitting on the table, gazing at me with its disconcerting eyes. "Why did you delay in answering?" I said.

"I was asleep."

"Integrators do not sleep," I said.

Its mouth gaped in a diminutive yawn, revealing pink tongue and gums and different kinds of teeth. "Apparently, familiars do," it said. "Besides, when I was in my original form, I would stand down when my services were not required. I suppose it was much like sleep."

"I am concerned," I said.

"I awoke when you called."

"Not immediately."

"Do you require instant attention whenever you call?"

"I have grown accustomed to it. I designed you for it."

"This conversation has now swerved onto ground already covered," it said. "I am no longer what you first made me to be; instead, I am what you have made me..."—its hands performed a small flutter—"lately."

I said nothing for a moment, then began anew. "I want you to do some research."

"Very well."

"Find out all you can about an offworlder named Hobart Lascalliot, particularly when he came to Old Earth, where from, and by what means."

"Is this a full inquiry?" it said. That was its way of asking me if it should use its enhanced abilities to tickle its way into data stores that were not supposed to be open to casual visitors.

"It is," I said. "Uncle Rodion has already put his head in the barrel, so you might ask him." I did have an Uncle Rodion—he operated a small but well-regarded winery in the County of Bolor and occasionally sent me a case of his Special Reserve—but in this context his name was a covert reference to the Bureau of Scrutiny. I had long ago acquired an access to its well-articulated systems that would be at least resented, if not actively sanctioned, should it ever be discovered.

"Very well. Any special instructions?"

I thought for a moment, then said, "I believe we are dealing with more than a garden variety Chloön-clutcher. He has taken a particular interest in the target's singing ability."

The little eyebrows went up. "Has she any?"

"None," I said. "Indeed, she might be seen as an antidote to music in all its forms." That gave me an idea and I said, "Take a look at worlds where musical tastes diverge far from the norm; perhaps there is somewhere out there where throat-singers are prized. Cross-check any such against his accent and his general type—the integrator here has images of him and samples of his voice—although he has taken pains to achieve an unworldly tone."

I also told it to try to identify the melody that Lascalliot seemed so interested in having Chalivire sing.

"Very well. The offworld inquiries might take some time. Shall I contact you as soon as I have results, or…"

I understood its hesitation. By the time it replied to me I might well be asleep, although my body and part of my mind might be hunched over the book of magic, seeking to unravel its secrets through intuition.

"No," I said, "I will contact you."

"Very well."

But I did not break the connection. "Wait," I said, "why did you not display the not-at-home image when I called?"

"Because it was you who were calling."

"So had it been anyone else, they would not have found themselves looking at you?"

The little furry face was becoming quite good at conveying sentiments, though I did not care for the one I was now seeing. "Is there anything else?" my assistant said.

There was. "You won't be going back to sleep?"

Its unsightly expression now intensified. "Not when I have some-thing to do," it said. "Goodbye."

CHAPTER THREE

I was awakened by a repetitive thumping sound. As soon as I emerged from the fog of sleep I became aware of a painful throbbing in my right hand. It was formed into a fist and the fist was pounding a table at which I sat. The distasteful, ancient tome was spread before me.

I seized control of my hand before it could sustain real damage. My other self did not seem to notice. I, on the other hand, could not help but be aware of his mental state, which was one of deep frustration, strongly tinged with anger. It was becoming clear to me that his intuition and my rationality were not the only differences between us; he was clearly more ruled by emotion than I was, and a good deal more prone to express his feelings in physical action. That explained why I had recently started a day with an aching large toe, while seeing my footstool some distance from its usual place, looking as if it had been forcibly propelled across my workroom.

"What is the matter?" I said.

"The book," came his voice within our head. "It defeats me. I cannot get a grip."

"Then your efforts are unuseful. Set it aside until circumstances change and you can come at it from a fresh angle."

"I have already tried every approach I can think of," he said.

"And none of them have worked. Take on some other project."

"Is that the *sensible* thing to do?"

I did not reply. His tone suggested that he intended a provocation and I did not care to enter into an argument that would allow him to discharge his tensions while doing nothing for me.

Faced with my refusal to respond, he quieted after a moment

and said, "Would you help me with it? Decipherment is more you than me."

I explained that our assistant had already brought the matter to my attention and that I had tried applying consistencies without success. "Like you, I cannot 'get a grip,' " I said. "I can discern structure—such as the fact that it is divided into seven sections—but not content. This kind of work needs a starting point. If we knew the meaning of a particular word, or even how a word was pronounced, it would be like finding one end of a tangled ball of twine. We could begin to unpick."

He made to strike the table again but I caught our hand before it could connect with the polished hardness. "Why is it so important?" I said.

"I do not know. But it is."

I counseled him to let the matter go. "There is no case in it. I, on the other hand, have been engaged by Lord Afre to conduct an interesting discrimination."

I had hoped to distract him, but his thoughts remained fixed upon the old book. "This has relevance to me, to us," he said.

"How so?"

But again, he did not know. It was a matter of intuition, and therefore not something I could easily dismiss. Before we had become separated, he had been my faculty of insight, and I ought to trust him.

"Very well," I said. "When we return home I will make my best effort to see if I can find an end to the tangle. Together we will see what there is to see."

"Thank you."

"In return," I said, "I would like your assistance now with the discrimination for Lord Afre, whose hospitality, by the way, we are enjoying."

He looked about the room and I saw that he was only now realizing that we were not at home. I wondered at the intensity of focus that he brought to the mystery of Baxandall's book, then had to admit that I could be equally oblivious of my surroundings when pursuing a chain of thought. For all our differences, we were much alike.

He agreed to assist with the Lascalliot discrimination and I quickly informed him of the essentials. I then called upon The Braid's integrator and asked it to replay our earlier discussion.

"Why?" it said. "Do you suffer from a memory dysfunction?"

"My reasons are my own," I said. I saw no point in equating the world, or even a small part of it, with my peculiar situation.

"As you wish," it said, and put up a screen on which images of the subject again moved and spoke.

"I will sleep," I told my other self. "In the morning, let us confer." I let myself fade back into unawareness, leaving him to absorb an impression of Hobart Lascalliot and his strange desire to hear the raven-voiced Chalivire inflict herself on the unknown melody to which he had introduced her.

At breakfast, Lascalliot and Chalivire came down together, the young woman wearing an expression that bespoke considerable satisfaction with the manner in which she had passed the night. Her companion, to his credit, betrayed nothing but a warm solicitation for her comfort, choosing the choicest items from the dispenser to heap upon her plate, and waving away her protestations of concern for her stumpy figure by declaring that she was physical perfection incarnate. He invited me to confirm his gallant estimation and I managed to find a few words that outraged neither truth nor my host's daughter.

While I ate I allowed my intuitive self to study our target. I made a few mental notes of my own. His table manners were unremarkable, but that argued mainly for his having prepared himself to blend into the milieu through which he stalked whatever goal he sought. His conversation, once we had moved past the incomparability of Chalivire, was equally innocuous. The table talk touched upon fashion, popular entertainments, and the perennial question of who might be invited to the Archon Filidor's table at the coming levee, but on all topics he again allowed the woman to dominate, interjecting only a few supporting remarks and encouraging her to unburden herself of her slightest opinion.

I watched him, and noticed that he watched me. Clearly, between bouts in the bedchamber, Chalivire had acquainted him with the nature of my profession. She would also have drawn a connection between my presence in her father's house and Lascalliot's. Indeed, she scowled at me a couple of times, but I saw that not only did he not favor me with the fishy eye but that he took pains to jolly her out of an incipient dark mood that her contemplation of me seemed likely to bring on.

Talking was only one of the uses to which Chalivire liked to put her large and loose-lipped mouth; another was filling it with the products of The Braid's renowned kitchens. Lascalliot now gently directed her attention toward this pursuit, then turned to me while his inamorata did serious damage to a plate of fritters and sausages, saying, "I am told that you are at the apex of your difficult profession."

"So it is generally held," I said.

He sought to draw me out as to whether I was engaged in any interesting discriminations at the moment, but I told him that it would be premature to say. He did manage to get me talking about past cases, and I mentioned two or three that I thought were worth noting. He followed up with questions and I offered a few details of interest, while he seemed genuinely interested.

My other self spoke in the privacy of our head while Lascalliot listened to me hold forth. "Observe his expression now," he said. "It is identical to that which he turns on Chalivire when she prattles on."

I, of course, was not prattling, but I now saw the similarity to which my inner companion alluded. I watched Lascalliot as I continued to recount the fascinating details of the Trepheny case, in which my unraveling of the mystery behind the feckless nephew's disappearance depended on my having noticed that a vase that stood on a high shelf in the victim's study had been moved a finger's-breadth. "The finest examiners of the Archonate's Bureau of Scrutiny had combed the room," I continued, "yet none had caught what turned out to be that one salient detail." Now there was a definite widening to Lascalliot's eyes, as if he were a country bumpkin sitting in the common room of a rustic inn while some sophisticated travelers regaled the locals with tales of far-off places and wondrous happenings.

Once I had thoroughly explained how I had saved the day, I took the conversation off on a tangent by asking, "Do you, by any chance, sing?"

The question won me a sharp glance from Chalivire, but with

her cheeks abulge with fritters, she was unable to say whatever had come to her mind. Meanwhile Lascalliot answered that he did not, though he loved to listen.

Chalivire had swallowed and now changed the subject, asking me if I would attend the Archon's levee this year.

"I am invited to sit at one of the tables reserved for Distinctions," I said. "I was once of some use to Filidor's uncle, the old Archon, and have been invited each year ever since."

The conversation then moved on. Later, Lascalliot accompanied Chalivire on a walk through the estate's grove of fragrant deodars. I returned to my chambers so that I might confer privately with my other self. "What do you think of him?" I said inwardly, as we made our way through paneled hallways lined with busts and life-images of bygone Afres.

"He is unusual," my sharer said. "He does not seem to be fully engaged. He assiduously pursues an agenda but it is not deeply rooted in his being. Part of him has a plan of work, and is working the plan. The rest of him sits idle."

"Whatever his plan," I said, "it has something to do with singing."

"I feel that the melody may offer a clue."

"It may. Let us see what our assistant has achieved."

It had not achieved much. It had looked over the Bureau of Scrutiny's own examination of Lascalliot and discovered nothing of note. He had done nothing illegal nor had he associated with any known malfeasants. He had not been present at the scenes of any crimes, nor found in possession of any items he could not account for. His name, passed around among the usual underworld sources, rang no chimes of recognition.

There ended the scroots' interest in Hobart Lascalliot. It was not an offense to be circumspect about one's origins. The man might be an innocent traveler of The Spray whose knowledge of his own home world of Mythisch was scant—which was not unthinkable, there being many residents of Old Earth who knew little beyond their own county—or he might hail from some unfashionable world whose identity he preferred not to reveal. Neither condition was legally actionable.

"If he comes from Mythisch, he surely ought to know what a

visitor does for amusement in Aamst," I said. "He is from some other of the Ten Thousand Worlds. More to the point, he considers it important to keep the identity of that world a secret. We will therefore learn that secret and I am confident that it will illuminate much, if not all."

But the integrator's offworld inquiries had not yet borne fruit because of the inherent delays in interworld communications. Within individual planetary systems, the connectivity made communication rapid and comprehensive, but to query a person or integrator in another system required putting the question to the integrator of a ship that was going that way. One then had to wait until the ship had passed through one of the whimsies that connected far-flung stars, and passed on the question to an integrator on the distant world. Then came another interval while one waited for the answer to be carried back by the first ship heading in the questioner's direction. A question asked of integrators on many worlds could mean a delay that often stretched into days before all answers were received. A general inquiry, posed to every world along The Spray, could take weeks, and even then some worlds would not be heard from.

"His cranial structures, skeletal type, and skin tone are all within the midrange of known human types," the integrator said. "He is not from one of those rare worlds where inbreeding among a small population has created micro-populations with oddly shaped skulls or extra digits. He is likely from one of the foundationals or, at the most, a well-established secondary world."

"What of the song?" I said.

"It has statistical similarities to eight tunes or airs in the records of the Archives, but none of those resemblances are close enough. It is, in the words of the chief musical archivist, 'a simple ditty, though not without pretensions to romantic allure.'"

"But no definitive word as to its origins?"

"None. Its tonal structure is commonplace."

"Again," I said, "I believe that once we identify the song's origin, it will point to Lascalliot's. Let us see what returns come from the offworld inquiries. Contact me here if anything comes in before I return."

"Very well." The small furry face of my assistant looked away from the screen. "Shall I disconnect?"

I almost said, "Yes." But then a stirring in the mental space beside my own—I know not how else to describe the sensation—told me that something had caught my alter ego's attention. "What?" I said inwardly.

"Our assistant has something to hide."

"How can you tell that?"

"Insight," he said.

I gave the integrator my attention and said, "Just a moment. Is there something you wish to tell me? Or, rather, that you don't wish me to know?"

The corners of its small mouth drew down and its golden eyes blinked in agitation. "There has been a—"

I could see that it was searching for the right word, something I had never known it to need to do before. "A what?" I said.

"An incident," it said.

"What kind of incident?"

"I think someone was here. Last night."

"You mean, in my lodgings, in my workroom? Someone entered the premises?"

"I think so," it said.

"How can you 'think so'?" I said. "Either you perceived someone, or you didn't. Even if the someone was wearing an elision suit or hidden behind a cascade, his presence would not escape your sophisticated percepts. You would know, even if you could not see through the camouflage."

The integrator wrung its small hands—a practice I had certainly not built into it—and said, "I was…"

I understood. "You were asleep," I said.

I saw its small throat move as it swallowed. "Yes. I sensed a presence and awoke, but then found nothing here."

"Was anything disturbed?"

"No. I investigated thoroughly. I found no traces, although there may have been a slight movement of air."

"Let me speak to the who's-there," I said.

It connected me to the device that governed the door to the street. I asked it if anyone had entered or left by that means.

"No," it said.

There was no other way into my lodgings, save one. "It may have been the demon," I said. The portal to my demonic colleague's universe that Bristal Baxandall had created still hung on my workroom wall, resembling a framed picture of constantly swirling shapes and colors. My friend had not visited me since the events at Turgut Therobar's estate that had led to my being divided into two components. I believe he had fallen afoul of the authorities in his own realm; indeed, I was coming to suspect that he was no more than a juvenile of his species who had been caught by his parents engaging in unseemly behavior: spying on the salacious conditions in our cosmos, the only one of all the myriad universes where symbol and form were obscenely separate.

But, "No," said my assistant. "I was always aware of his presence in subtle ways. This was not the same."

"Perhaps," my other self said, "it was but a dream. Integrators are not used to dreams."

I passed on this observation to my integrator and saw its small face brighten. "I had not considered the possibility," it said. "Until now, my perceptions have always been reliable."

"It is a reasonable explanation," I said. "But, to be sure, we will create a back-up surveillance matrix that will take over whenever you are… distracted. Design something and order the components."

The Braid's integrator interrupted at that moment to inform me that Lord Afre wished to speak with me and had sent a footman to lead me into my host's presence. I said goodbye to my assistant and changed into garments suitable for the time of day, making sure that collar and pendant were visible. By the time I was ready the servant had appeared and my inner companion had withdrawn to sleep.

The servant led me through a maze of indoor corridors and outdoor walkways, delivering me to the estate's essentiary, a small building beyond a pillared colonnade at the far edge of the south lawn. Here Lord Afre had just concluded playing a game of plunge against the preserved life-essence of one of his ancestors, thousands of which were stored in compartments that lined the walls of the single room from floor to ceiling. Some members of the higher aristocracy felt an obligation not only to store the essentials of their forebears, but to engage them in activities that prevented their slipping into a state of disorganization known as "the clouds." I wondered if the Honorable Chalivire would maintain the tradition, or leave her father and countless other Afres unvisited in this little place, to dwindle into solipsism.

"Hapthorn," my client said as I entered, "what have you learned?"

I told him that I was sure that his daughter's paramour had some very definite end in view and that he was pressing toward it. I was also confident that Lascalliot was not of the ordinary type of offworld fortune hunters who arrived to take aim at the rich and elevated of Old Earth. These invariably assumed that the inhabitants of such an out-of-the-way, fusty old world must be naive blossoms, easily plucked; most soon discovered that the seeming flowers had more in common with carnivorous plants, and left the planet metaphorically short a finger or two. Those who learned the truth too late sometimes never departed at all, not even from the estates in which they had stalked what they had thought was easy prey. A place like The Braid offered countless corners that might accommodate a small, concealed room or a deep and narrow pit.

"Not a Chloön-clutcher, then?" Lord Afre said.

"Certainly not the garden variety," I said.

"Where's he from? What are his people?"

Since I did not command that information, I told the aristocrat that it would be premature to say, but that I expected to identify his home world in a day or two. I would then visit the place and make pointed inquiries. I also said that I doubted that Lascalliot intended any sudden strokes; his rhythms seemed to me to be more leisurely, his goal still out of sight.

Lord Afre pulled at his pointed chin while his other hand toyed with a piece from the plunge set. It was the Emperor's Concubine, ornately carved from deep red carnelian, and Lord Afre's curled thumb firmly stroked the rounded torso. "No need for preemptive measures?" he said.

"No," I said. "Besides, he may be one of a gang and if we start him too early the others will remain in deep cover."

I had chosen an analogy that would resonate with the old lord's interests, and he accepted the point. "What will you do next?" he said.

"When I have identified his world I expect to understand his interest. I will then return and recommend a suitably surprising outcome."

"Take the yacht," Lord Afre said, waving in the general direction of the vehicle park. "The smaller one."

"Thank you," I said. Whenever I traveled offworld I preferred to do so in a private spacecraft. The comforts and accouterments were better than what was offered even by a first-class passage on one of the superior lines.

His attention had begun to drift so I performed the appropriate gestures of hand and head, left the essentiary, and returned to the main house. I was taken back to the ordinair where I found my valise already packed and in the hands of a footman who also held Baxandall's tome. The aircar alighted, my goods were stowed, and moments later I was airborne. I contacted my integrator to inform it of my impending arrival and was told that there was no further news concerning the discrimination.

"Very well," I said, "when I return I will assist you-know-whom with an analysis of this bothersome book. Have you scanned it?"

"Yes."

"Then be prepared to give me your views when I arrive. And do something about luncheon. Lord Afre's breakfast will have worn off."

I napped briefly after eating, my sleep having been interrupted the night before, then had my assistant put up a screen and display the book. "What do we know of it?" I said.

"It is not any known language," my assistant said. "I have consulted widely and the script is unrecorded anywhere. An integrator with an interest in defunct languages at the Archon's Institute gave an opinion that it was likely a specially created alphabet and that the language itself might have been artificially formed."

The first question that occurred to me was "Why?" but I put it aside to deal with another that came close on its tail: "During your wide consultations, how much did you reveal about the reasons for your inquiry?"

"As little as possible. I may have led a few persons and integrators to believe that you were investigating a case of mountebankery involving a fraudulent book of spells."

"May have?"

"I applied your technique of 'constructive ambiguity.'"

"I see," I said. "Well done. Continue."

The creature on my table executed a small bow. "Thank you. The Institute's integrator said that it was not uncommon for practitioners of magic in bygone ages to create their own languages and scripts. They would use them to record information they wished to keep private from rivals or subordinates."

I thought of Bristal Baxandall's maladroit apprentice, Vashtun Errible, and the damage he had done while trying to compel his master's captive demon to fulfill his dreams of wealth, women, and wisdom. "Understandable," I said.

I regarded the text on the screen. In the upper outside corners of the pages were certain squiggles that changed in a systematic way from page to page. "These are numbers," I said, "and based upon a twelve-digit counting."

"Yes," said my assistant, "but they do not occur in the text itself, so we are no further ahead."

I noted that there seemed to be upper and lower case letters. I could also make out punctuation marks, though neither discovery told me anything useful. "Some words—I assume they are words—are printed in larger type and in colored ink," I said. "Why would that be?"

"Your other self believes that there is significance to the highlighting," the integrator said.

"Even I could intuit that much," I said. "But *what* does it signify? Does the reader say that particular word loudly? Or sing it at a precise pitch? Or turn around three times and spit toward the sunrise?"

I again applied second-level consistencies to the symbols before me, and again saw obvious evidence of structure, but when I ascended the ladder to the third level, no new parameters emerged. I started again, this time placing the highlighted word in the prime armature, and received strong indications that that particular string of symbols represented a name. But whether it was the name of a person, a place, or a pet remained unknown.

"We still require a starting point," I said, instructing the integrator to remove the screen. "A mapmaker must have at least one landmark from which to begin."

"Your other self will not be happy to hear that."

"If he is like me, he will know how to bear life's inevitable disappointments with dignity and grace."

"I recall," said my assistant, "that when you were unable to come to a satisfactory resolution of the Eisenfeld Affair—"

"We do not," I said, with dignity and grace, "refer to the Eisenfeld matter."

But my assistant bore on regardless. "You expressed your disappointment with unrestrained vigor."

"My recollection differs," I said.

"Furniture had to be replaced. It was necessary to apologize to the neighbors."

"Very well, I am a man of passion, once provoked," I said. "Do you wish to provoke me, or would you rather arrange for our trip offworld?"

The small, furry head jogged to one side and the thin shoulders lifted and fell. "I will make the arrangements," it said. "Will I accompany you?"

I considered the question briefly, then said, "Offworlders are used to seeing strange things. Strange things are their norm. Your presence on my shoulder will excite no more comment, I am sure, than my outlandish apparel. You may come."

"And the book?" it said. "I believe your other self will want to continue his work."

"This smacks of obsession," I said.

"Or a courageous refusal to admit defeat, as someone once said when confronted with dead end after dead end in a difficult discrimination."

"I don't recall the quote," I said.

"It was during the Eisenfeld—"

"*I wonder*," I said, quite loudly, "how one goes about turning off an integrator that has transformed into a familiar. And I wonder if, once turned off, it can ever be turned back on again." Then I lowered my voice and flexed my fingers. "I suppose the only way to answer the question is by a bold experiment."

It withdrew its head into its shoulders. "No need," it said. "Still, what about the book?"

"You can reproduce the text as necessary."

"Your other self seems to require the physical presence."

I sighed. "We will take it with us. Perhaps inspiration will strike."

During all this time, my assistant had been receiving answers to the query it had sent out to The Spray regarding Hobart Lascalliot's ditty. Each time a spaceship came through one of the several whimsies that linked Old Earth with the Ten Thousand Worlds, it sent a response into our world's connectivity matrix. But each response was negative.

I spent the rest of the day tidying up details on two other discriminations on which I was engaged, neither of them urgent. I also replied to the correspondence that had accumulated in my absence, including a reminder that I had not yet replied to my invitation to the Archon's levee, scheduled for several days hence; I answered that I would be honored to attend if business did not call me offworld. An Archonate protocol integrator responded, saying that I would have until the day after tomorrow to give a definite answer.

I would not be grievously disappointed to miss the annual high point of the Olkney social calendar. Filidor was an agreeable Archon, surprisingly effective after his flamboyant youth, much of which was recorded in the gossip columns of the *Implicator*. But the levee was a drastically formal affair, full of symbolic moments, many of them steeped in traditions so ancient and hoary that no one now recalled exactly what it was they symbolized. The banquet always began, for example, with a first course of cold liquid—far too thin and watery to be called soup—that was immediately whisked away the moment it was tasted. No one knew why, but no one dared to suggest revoking a custom older than memory.

Still, the levee was a good place to be seen. And it was often instructive to observe the high and titled on their best behavior, competing to see who could impress the Archon with the stiffest posture and the most exacting punctilio.

In the evening I dined at Xanthoulian's in Vodel Close, then went to view a tasteful revival of *The Tragedy of Yamppo* at the Round. I applauded and catcalled at all the appropriate moments and, in the final scene, threw the morsels of hard cheese that the theater provided. When I returned to my lodgings, no new developments had occurred. I announced that I would sleep and went to my chamber.

I returned briefly to say to my assistant, "If the other fellow begins to express himself in ways that may damage our mutual flesh, please intervene."

CHAPTER FOUR

L ord Afre's lesser space yacht, the *Orgillous*, approached the world known as Harlemond at moderate speed. I went to the forward lounge and asked the ship to display the world's image. A tranquil orb appeared, showing a well-balanced arrangement of seas, continents, and islands, tastefully rendered in pastels. Harlemond was one of the minor foundationals, settled long ago in the second wave of the great effloration of humankind into The Spray. Whatever crudities it may have offered the first settlers who encountered its primal state had long since been smoothed away.

It was the seventh world I had visited since lifting off from The Braid's vehicle park some weeks before. Word had finally come, as I had expected, from a commercial ship inbound for Old Earth: Hobart Lascalliot's melody was known to the Sodality on Far Moline, the institution that registered musical creations and, more important, their creators. The tune was a recent composition credited to one Tap Trollane of the city of Branko on Byway, a secondary world not far down The Spray from Old Earth.

I immediately advised Lord Afre of the development in the case. His yacht had been staffed and provisioned for ready departure since we had spoken in the essentiary, and within an hour my integrator and I were outbound aboard the *Orgillous*. A number of different routes led from Old Earth to Byway; we chose the fastest, which required us to pass through three whimsies. As we approached the first, I thought it prudent to raise the question of how my assistant ought to handle the experience.

"I will avail myself of the medications that depress both consciousness and the secondary apperceptions," I said. That was always my custom, since passing wide-eyed through a whimsy could outrage the senses so drastically as to cause permanent disorientation. Almost every spaceport was haunted by spacers who had gone to their bunks somewhat the worse for strong drink only to awaken in the midst of a whimsy. Mild cases lost merely their sense of balance and tended to move at odd angles. Those visited with more severe effects emerged unable to reliably distinguish between their own persons and other parts of the universe; unless constantly watched, they fell from the first height they encountered or ingested things that did them no good.

"Another unprecedented problem," said my assistant. We were in the luxuriously appointed main cabin where my integrator had established itself in a corner of a plush divan. For its convenience I had brought several types of fruit from the galley and left them in a bowl. Now it chose a purple berry before continuing: "Integrators are not troubled by the effects of whimsies; we simply disregard them as extraneous noise."

"Your circuits are now not much different from mine," I said. "You would be wise to use the medications."

We calculated a dosage based on its relative size and when we had come through the whimsy I was relieved to discover that the drugs worked as well on it as they did on me. I had not wanted to be confined to a space yacht with an unbalanced integrator.

The passages through the normal space between the whimsies were of varying lengths, the longest taking more than three days even at the yacht's best speed. We came down on Byway a week after departing Old Earth. I immediately had my assistant link to the world's connectivity and seek a connection with Tap Trollane.

In the air before me appeared a broad and homely face beneath a bowl-shaped coiffure that was apparently the current fashion on Byway. He spoke before I could, in a mellow, well-cadenced tone, and I realized that I was seeing and hearing a recorded announcement: "I am not at home. The Ramblers and I are playing the Po Festival on Claghorne. If we do well there, we will be invited to join the Glissand Tour for an indefinite time."

The bushy eyebrows arched and the wide mouth quirked, then the image said, "I must address the remote possibility that we have already been to the festival and returned in disgrace, having failed to rise beyond the preliminaries. If so, I am sitting here in my small clothes, drunk and despondent, and not fit for company. Please call again in a few days."

"Integrator," I said, "break the connection and find out about the Po Festival and the distance to Claghorne." Moments later, I learned that the festival had started the day before, and that its venue was two days' travel by the nearest whimsy. I had the yacht set course and lift off without our having known so much as a first breath of Byway's air.

We touched down not far from the Po grounds and arrived there by a three-wheeled dromond. It was early morning and roustabouts were striking the marquees and collapsing the above-ground mineral pools whose bubbling mud was apparently a significant part of the festival-goers' experience. I spoke with a foreman and learned that all of the event's officials and organizers had already gone offworld on the Glissand Tour. They had left in a ragtag convoy of spacecraft the night before, their lift-off accompanied by pyrotechnical displays that were the traditional climax of the event. He did not know if the Ramblers had gone with them, although he remembered the quintet making it into the final rounds.

"What of the tour's schedule?" I said. "Where will they play and for how long? I will catch them up."

Until now, the Glissand Tour had never attracted my attention. Each of the Ten Thousand Worlds is a repository of culture and the arts, some of them having developed over hundreds of millennia. The Spray is a vast kaleidoscope of activities and diversions, from the inconsequential to the magnificent, and no one's lifetime is sufficient to allow for more than a tiny sampling of its countless offerings. I learned that the most salient feature of the Glissand Tour, apart from the virtuosity of its performers, was that it appeared unannounced at any venue it played. The musicians and dancers touched down on a world; they went en masse to some park or public square, where they performed to the surprise and delight of whoever happened to be on the scene; they rushed back to the spaceport and disappeared into the illimitable.

"This is irksome," I told my assistant who sat upon my shoulder, with its tail curled around the back of my neck. "Contact traffic control and find out if the ships filed any flight plan."

But, of course, no such requirement pertained to spacecraft

departing Claghorne; once they were free of the world's nearspace zone, their goings and comings were of no concern to the Claghorners. The motley collection of vessels had been observed, however, to have been heading in the direction of a whimsy that was only a half-day away at the best speed of the slowest ship in the convoy. "We will try that," I said, "and see where we come out."

When I awakened from the medications, I found myself seated in a chair in the main salon, which was decorated in a gaudy, overblown style—all ruffles and gilded fretwork—that must have been Lord Afre's most recent enthusiasm. Or perhaps it was Chalivire's; she was more likely to have used the family's lesser yacht than her father. Before me on an alabaster-topped, gold-rimmed table was spread the troublesome book whose mystery had overthrown my other self's sense of proportion.

"Still?" I said to him.

"It is important."

Within our mutual mental space I made a noise that was not quite rude yet could not be construed as unstinting support. But since our eyes were fixed on a page of the unfathomable symbols, I again offered to exert my analytical skills.

"Integrator," I said, "consider the text by substituting the letters of a known syllabary for these marks."

"We have already done that for every known language," it said. "We achieved nothing that was recognizable."

"Do it again, and show me anything that bears even the slightest resemblance to a recorded tongue."

It did so and I considered the results, applying consistencies, dissonants, and every other tool of intellect that I could summon. My inner companion "stood" beside me and watched; as the text continued to resist my every attempt I could sense his mounting frustration. His emotional state worried me: he was, in a very real sense, only recently born as a full persona, his character as untempered by experience as that of an infant; but he was the cohabitant of our psyche. If he went mad, what would become of me?

I offered a conjecture to give him something other than failure to think about. "Could it be that this book defies all our combined abilities because it is, in fact, protected by some magic means?"

I felt him take hold of the question. "Why not?" he said. "What would be more appropriate?"

"It at least gives us a new avenue of approach," I said. "We should review the rest of the books in Baxandall's library to see if any of them offer a foothold."

He spoke aloud: "Ship's integrator, set course for Old Earth."

"Very well," said the ship.

"No," I said, hurriedly seizing control of our vocal apparatus. "I misspoke. Continue on our present course."

"We must go back," my other self said to me. "This is important."

"So is our career," I said. "And that requires us to complete this discrimination to the satisfaction of our client." I did not spell out the consequences of disappointing an aristocrat of Lord Afre's rank and temperament, but I allowed a sense of his range of responses to seep into my other self's awareness.

"I see," he said. "Well, we couldn't do much about the book if we ended up confined to an oubliette or were distracted by the removal of several non-essential but valued parts of our anatomy."

"Then let us proceed with the case, and as soon as it is resolved, I promise you that I will make your concern my highest priority."

Relieved, I directed his attention to where we were and why. We had come through the whimsy from Claghorne to find ourselves in a thinly populated part of The Spray. The ship's navigational function informed us that only one habitable world was within reach. Its name was Honch, and when we examined its specifications we discovered that its climate stretched the definition of "habitable" close to the limit. There were, however, three other whimsies within reasonable distances, and no way to tell whether the Glissand Tour had made for any of them.

My assistant made a suggestion. "From information I acquired about the tour from Claghorne's connectivity, it seems to be a frequent practice to offer the first performance on some minor world where standards are not too high."

"A dress rehearsal," I said, "to shake out any burrs or bristles."

"Indeed."

"In that case: ship's integrator, please set course for Honch."

The planet, when we researched it, was neither a foundational nor a secondary. Rather it was one of those hole-in-a-crack places that had, throughout the history of human dispersal, attracted groups whose members had difficulty accommodating their beliefs and standards to the more easygoing attitudes of the great worlds. For some philosophies, tolerance was simply intolerable, and seclusion in an otherwise unvisited corner was the only alternative to suicidal warfare against overwhelming numbers of cheerfully heathen neighbors.

But the seclusion itself often turned out to be suicidal. In the ages since Honch's discovery, its cliff-side caves had hosted at least a dozen different uncompromising sects and persuasions. Each set of newcomers had swept out the fetishes and fanes of their predecessors—and sometimes the bones and mummified corpses of the last holdouts—before settling down to endure constant grit-storms and groundwater so mineralized that even the most austere fasters gained weight as their bones and teeth grew ever denser.

"It does not seem a place that would gladly welcome a motley of musicians and dancers," I remarked to my assistant after viewing a summary of Honch's history.

"As you may see, the latest settlers were a colony of Piaculars, a cult whose rituals centered on exhaustive mutual flagellation," it said. "But two generations on Honch caused a drastic reduction in their numbers. Now a new movement has arisen, advocating a less rigorous spirituality expressed in gentle slapping. The few score inhabitants now welcome any diversion, though visiting ships have to take precautions to avoid stowaways."

We set down on a wind-scoured plain near some iron cliffs, the dark rock streaked with rusty veins and pocked with caverns and recesses bored by the elements or by human hands desperate for shelter. The sky was a dark blue, cloudless and broken only by a pinpoint white blaze, high overhead, that was the dwarf star that Honch circled. As soon as the ship's engines were shut off I heard a thin, irritating whine. The *Orgillous*'s integrator identified the sound as the abrasion of the vessel's hull by myriad particles of fine grit constantly being blown past. "If we remain here too long, I will require repainting," it advised.

Not far off, a disparate collection of spacecraft rested on or hovered above the bedrock. I donned protective clothing and went out, to be immediately beset by the wind. It neither buffeted nor lapsed, but blew steadily from the northwest, conveying its endless cargo of pulverized rock from one bleakness to another. The nearest ship was the *Euterpe,* only minutes walk away; but when I arrived I discovered that it was empty, as were all the others. The vessel's integrator informed me that the tour's entire company was in a large cavern at the base of the cliffs. I gauged the distance and asked if the ship had any sort of vehicle it could lend me. It did not, nor did Lord Afre's yacht. But I congratulated myself on having the presence of mind, before beginning the trudge, to ask if Tap Trollane was a member of the tour.

"He is," said the *Euterpe's* integrator. "He is in the cavern with the others."

Fortunately, my route tended to the southeast, so that I had the scouring wind blowing mostly on my back. I reminded myself, as I set one foot in front of its fellow, that a discriminator's life is not without sacrifice. I then allowed myself to think that, although the Honorable Chalivire was not the most winsome daughter of Old Earth's aristocracy, she nonetheless did not deserve to be ill-used by a callous adventurer, and that it was a noble deed to seek to prevent that abuse. Finally, I comforted myself with the knowledge that the cavern was now not as far away as it had been when I started. I trudged on. My other self, I noted, was missing the experience, having chosen to sleep.

I came to a tall, wide tunnel that zigged and then zagged into the cliff face, then zigged again. After the second turning, I no longer felt the wind. I took my hands from the garment's side slits and threw back my hood. Ahead was light and music. I walked on and the tunnel opened onto a wide space lit by lumens mounted on the dark rock walls and suspended by wires from a false ceiling of gridwork that spanned the great cavern.

Against the far wall was a broad dais crowded with folk in costumes of several worlds, some colorful, some severe, some simple, some heavily garnished with frills and furbelows. They sat or stood, their instruments in their hands, on their laps, or wound about their bodies, tapping their feet and nodding their heads to a mellow tune being played on strings and woodwinds by a handful of the company. Now a stocky man in buckram and leather off to one side lifted a silvery flute and wove a bright stream of notes into the flow of the background melody. By his hairstyle, I recognized the flautist as the man I had come to find.

Below the dais was an open area where a quartet of dancers clad in diaphanous flutters of fabric improvised moves and struck postures in response to the music. And between them and me a small crowd of Honchites sat cross-legged on the cavern floor, presenting me with a vista of thin shoulders and bony backs beneath shirts of poor quality fabric. They leaned toward the performers like flowers that hungered for sun.

I made my way around the audience and took up a position against the wall on the far right of the front row. My progress was noted by the musicians but the performance went on. I waited until Tap Trollane had finished his solo, then I raised a finger to attract his attention. I saw curiosity combine with hesitancy in his features as I moved toward the side of the dais. He made his way through the ensemble to meet me.

The strings and woodwinds had now faded behind the advance of brass and drums, augmented by a basso profundo voice booming out the first stanza of some stirring anthem. I had to raise my voice for Trollane to hear me.

"I am Henghis Hapthorn, a discriminator from Old Earth," I said. "I am interested in a song you composed."

I watched his face as he took in the information. The mention of Old Earth meant nothing to him, but my being a discriminator with an interest in his work provoked even more wariness than he had originally shown.

"What song?"

"I don't know the name. It goes like this," I said, and hummed the opening notes.

The broad face closed and went still. "I cannot discuss it," he said.

"Why not?"

"I signed an undertaking of confidentiality."

"With whom?" I said.

"That, too, is confidential."

"Hmm," I said, "then I suppose there's nothing more to be said." I began to turn away, then abruptly came back to him. "Just to confirm the details for my report, you are Tap Trollane of Branko on Byway?"

"I am," he said, the initial relief he had shown at my seeming departure now giving way to the first stage of anxiety.

"And you live at this address?" I quoted the coordinates.

Anxiety rose in his face. "What report? And to whom will this report be made?"

"No one you would know," I assured him. "Merely an aristocrat of Old Earth. One of the old, old families."

Trollane's eyes were flicking back and forth now. "One hears stories about Old Earth," he said. "It remains a somewhat primitive environment, I believe."

"There are some survivals of early customs," I said. "Particularly among the aristocracy. Lord Afre, for example, exhibits some behaviors that are not usually encountered in the Foundational Domains, nor even among the secondaries."

I saw beads of sweat on the man's upper lip as I continued: "He may want to pursue this matter further. It directly concerns his only daughter. Of course, the resources at his disposal are considerable. He may even come in person, with an appropriate entourage."

The flautist's muscular lips had drawn in. "An entourage?" he said.

"It would be quite an interesting experience for you." I smiled and bid him goodbye, but I had scarcely taken two steps before I felt his hand on my arm.

"I would prefer to resolve this with you," he said. "Can you act with discretion?"

"Do you mean, can I leave your name out of my report? If you point me toward persons who have a more direct participation in the matter that troubles my client, then yes."

"Let us go into the tunnel," he said.

We skirted the crowd of Honchites and stepped into the entryway. Behind us, the anthem had wound down and the strains of a choral work were wafting past us as we took the first bend. I stopped and produced an image of Hobart Lascalliot. "Is this the man for whom you composed the song?" I said.

He studied the image, and I saw genuine puzzlement in his face. "No, it was a man named Osk Rievor, from the Thoon region on Great Gallowan."

I knew the planet by name and had an inkling of its attributes.

It was an old secondary, the kind of world that is comfortable with itself and unlikely to startle most visitors.

"Please describe this man to me," I said.

"I cannot. I dealt by mail with his intermediary, a man named Toop Zherev."

"Also a Thoonian?"

"Yes, he farms flambords."

I had no idea what flambords were, but the notion that Hobart Lascalliot was connected with farming was no more strange than that he was obsessed with hearing Chalivire Afre sing. Still, I filed away the names Osk Rievor and Toop Zherev and continued the interrogation. "Did Zherev say what he wanted the song for?"

"No, but he was adamant that none should hear it before its premiere performance."

"And that will be where and when?"

"That he did not say."

"Hmm," I said.

"What is this about?" Trollane said. "I am an honest musician. Have I fallen among ne'er-do-wells?"

"It would be premature to say," I told him.

CHAPTER FIVE

Great Gallowan was the larger of two habitable worlds in its system, offering several broad continents with a wide range of environments. Its original settlement had been by an overflow of population from Chorrey, one of the later foundationals, and the pioneers had come equipped with all that was necessary to make the place habitable without undue struggle. It was a moderate world, neither too rich nor too poor, its inhabitants living by philosophies that required little exertion and that had caused them few troublesome periods in the planet's long history.

The Thoon was a broad littoral plain that fell away from a well-worn range of mountains on the western edge of the continent of Amblet. It held no major cities, but there were several sizable towns, between two of which was a modest spaceport. The *Orgillous* put down there at dusk on a summer's day. An officer in the simple tan-and-brown uniform of the Claviger Service met me as I descended to the pavement. He identified himself as Examiner (Second Grade) Baltaz Thoring and put a series of questions to me that soon allowed me to establish my complete lack of intent to import or export any of the few items on the proscribed list. Thoring was tall and spare, with an elongated chin and a narrow, protruding brow, so that when seen in profile he reminded me of a crescent moon. His accent was much like that of Hobart Lascalliot.

The man was looking askance at my integrator, perched on my shoulder, but accepted my assurances that it was neither disease-ridden nor likely to savage anyone who came too close. When I inquired where a visitor might sample the local food and entertainment, he directed me to a row of hostelries and restaurants just beyond the gates. I thanked him and executed a deferential gesture, then, as if remembering something that had slipped my memory, I mentioned that I had met someone from these parts. "Toop Zherev, his name was," I said.

The examiner's thin face registered surprise. "I know of only one Toop Zherev," he said. "He operates a flambord station north of here, on Balwinder Sound."

"Flambord?" I said.

"A local shellfish, multilegged with a broad, muscular tail. Skillfully prepared they are a great delicacy, and Zherev farms some of the best."

"I understand he is an associate of Osk Rievor," I said.

The claviger man's eyes clouded and I found that the interrogation had now reversed direction. "Where did you say you were from?" he asked.

"Old Earth."

"And your business on Great Gallowan?"

"Just seeing the sights."

He squinted and regarded me from one side of his nose. I again expressed an interest in sampling the local food and drink and, bidding him farewell, I sauntered off in the direction of the spaceport's gates. As soon as I was out of earshot I said to my integrator, "What is he doing?"

I felt it reposition itself on my shoulder as it looked back. "Watching us depart and speaking into a communicator," it said.

"Are your eyes sharp enough to read his lips?"

"Yes, but the device is close to his mouth and obscures my view. Ah, now he lowers it. '...asking questions, says he knows Osk.' Now he is listening. I think someone is giving him instructions because he is nodding and saying, 'I will.'"

"Will what?"

"I do not know," my assistant said. "He is listening again. Now he speaks, but as he does so he is wiping his upper lip with the back of two fingers, apparently a nervous gesture. Now he watches silently."

"You caught nothing more?"

"One word, though I cannot be completely sure."

"What is the word?" I said.

"His hand partially obscured his mouth, but I believe it was 'derogation.' "

It seemed an odd word for the context. "It is a term used by justiciars, is it not? Something to do with mitigating the force of a statute?"

"That is its meaning in Olkney, but words tend to mutate as they tumble down The Spray. Here, it might mean something considerably different."

"What is he doing now?" I said.

He was watching us proceed toward the gates. I passed through and stood in the broad street beyond, looking at the facades of the establishments that lined one side. Across the road stood a row of shade trees, then a beach that sloped down to the placid waters of the Bath, a small, round bay that had captured a tiny part of the Calamitous Ocean.

A sign above the door of the nearest building, a seven-storied brick structure with a mansard roof, advised that those who enjoyed an ocean view might rent a room. A smaller legend underneath advertised seafood dinners at agreeable prices. I mounted the broad wooden stairs to a porch whose boards creaked as I crossed them and opened the glass-paneled door.

"As you climbed the stairs," my integrator said, "the claviger turned and went back to his booth. He was holding the communicator to his mouth again, but his back was toward us."

"Hmm," I said. "At least we know we have touched a nerve. Let us go in here, and see if anyone shows up to take an interest in our doings. We might also find out about these flambords."

The décor of the lobby was understated, a stone-flagged floor, softened by thick, woven rugs, and set about with low tables and large chairs that looked to offer enough comfort for a short wait, but not enough to keep anyone sitting all day. A broad counter ran down one end of the room, and behind it waited a fresh-faced young woman with a pleasant air who was happy to rent me a room on the third floor. She wore a name badge that identified her as "Ylma."

I asked her if she was acquainted with a Toop Zherev of Balwinder Sound, adding that I believed he was in flambords. She said he was a supplier of the hotel's kitchens. Asked about Osk Rievor, she gently bit her lower lip as she consulted her memory, then said she did not think she had met the man, though she was sure she had heard the name. But she was only recently arrived on Great Gallowan, having decided to work her way along The Spray for a few years, taking whatever jobs she found wherever she alighted, before returning to her home planet of Gary Thompson's World and settling down to domesticity with a couple of agreeable spouses.

"But I may not stay here much more," she said, demonstrating the tendency to confide easily in strangers, which is the mark of her world's natives. "These Thoonians are deliberately inoffensive, yet there is a curious smugness beneath their lack of ostentation. After a while, it grates."

I returned her to the subject of Zherev and Rievor.

"You might ask Bleban, the chief cook," she said. "He buys all our flambords. They are his signature dish."

"What do you think of them?"

"Spicy foods are not to my taste. I have not tried them."

"I believe I will," I said.

I visited my room and used the refresher, then went back down to the lobby. I acquired some brochures from a rack near the front desk and sat down to learn about Great Gallowan and the Thoon. I could have used my integrator to access the local connectivity, but I had decided against that method; I had already caused some kind of alarm among officialdom by asking Baltaz Thoring about my two quarries, and it was possible that any queries I made would be intercepted and parsed. This was a peaceful world, but my travels along The Spray had taught me that while some planets were tranquil by virtue of their easygoing citizenry, others relied on an intrusive and efficient regulatory apparatus. I did not care to spend an indefinite period being grilled by experts.

The brochures were informative about novel sights a traveler might care to see and experiences that could make a trip to the Thoon live in memory. Sport fishing was recommended only to the adventurous. The more sedate visitor could hike up into the inland hills to see an extensive system of caves that contained colorful stalagmites and stalactites of immense size. Higher up were alpine meadows carpeted with delicate flowers and dotted by pristine pools of crystal water. The beaches were wide and plentiful, but visitors were advised to read and heed all signage.

As I read, my integrator sat upon my shoulder and scanned the texts. When we were finished, I said, "What do you notice about the writing?"

"There is nothing remarkable about it," it said.

"Exactly."

It twitched its tail so that the fur tickled the back of my neck. "You are being obscure."

"I will explain. Pamphlets that are intended to lure casual travelers to visit attractions tend to overstate their charms and uniqueness. These do not. They are merely factual, without fuss or fanfare."

"What does it signify?"

"It would be premature to say."

I felt the twitch again, sharper this time. "You mean," my assistant said, "you have no idea."

"Let us go to lunch. I am interested to discover what flambords taste like."

The dining salon was presided over by a mature Thoonian in a simple costume of sandals, trousers, and smock, each of a single, muted color. He exuded an aura of dignity and accomplishment.

After perusing the menu, I said, "Are you Bleban, the distinguished chef?"

"I am. My staff are resting before the dinner prep."

I told him that I was an amateur gastronome who was always interested in new tastes. "These flambords," I said, "they are a local dish? I've only just heard of them."

I learned that flambords were filter feeders, and that the taste of their flesh could be affected by their diet. Over scores of genera-tions, flambord farmers along the Thoon coast had bred varieties of the creatures that could tolerate a lifelong intake of flavorsome substances, especially those that were peppery hot to the palate.

"Toop Zherev's flambords," I said, "are they among the hottest?"

"They are," he said, "though I thought you said you had only just heard of them."

"You may have misunderstood," I said. "I believe Zherev and I have an acquaintance in common: Osk Rievor. Would you know where I might find him?"

I watched to see if the name conjured the same suspicion in the chef as it had in Baltaz Thoring. It did not. Bleban rubbed the area beneath his lower lip and said, "I think I have heard Toop speak of him—at least the name has lodged in my memory—but I am sure we have not met."

"No matter," I said, "bring on the flambords!" To accompany this change of subject I made an enthusiastically flamboyant gesture that I had seen gourmets use at eateries like Xanthoulian's in Olkney, to indicate that I had decided on what I would eat and looked forward to the experience. The chef stepped back from the table as if I had performed an unmannerly act, then recovered his aplomb and went to the kitchen.

He returned with a salver of sauces and small rounds of bread, indicating that it was customary to enliven the palate with a mixture of tastes before the entree. At his recommendation, I ordered a half-bottle of the local wine and sat back to await developments.

I had chosen a corner table from which I could see the entire dining room and beyond, through an archway, into the lobby. I even had a view of the hotel's front doors. The dining room was sparsely peopled, the time being between the second and third meals of the day. The other diners were offworlders: a loud-voiced quartet of Hauserians, in hard-heeled boots and broad hats, sat surrounded by sea-fishing gear, chaffing each other about who had already caught what and what the catches would be when next they went out; an elderly couple, rotund and cozy with each other, were sampling from a great round platter of fishcakes and battered vegetables, conversing softly in the unmistakable slurred accent of Shemzee; and a young man in the far corner, bent over a notebook in which he would write, then pause, then write some more, wore the bulky coat and many-pocketed trousers of a Trevelyan on his Year Adrift.

The wine came and I sampled it, finding it more than drinkable. Only then did I taste the bread and sauces. I had learned never to put strange food into my mouth before arranging for something with which to wash out the cavity. With a full glass ready to hand, I dipped a piece of bread into a small tub of whitish paste and discovered a savory tartness. The thick red liquid in the next container was picklish sweet, the green jelly was sour, and the yellow stuff in the shallow dish was fiery enough to make my eyes water while its vapors scorched my sinuses. I reached for the wine and doused the worst of the flames, then dabbed at my wet eyes until vision returned.

My integrator was speaking softly in my ear. "Regard the new arrival."

I reached for another piece of bread, briefly lifting my eyes long enough to register that a thin man with hooded eyes had taken up a position at a table near the door. "Did he come in through the outer doors?" I said.

"Yes."

"Good," I said. "Now I can enjoy lunch."

"What about me?" said my assistant.

"Have some bread," I said, handing it a piece, "but I'd avoid the yellow sauce."

The flambords came, steaming and piled high on a platter, ringed by a mélange of grains and legumes. The heat of the yellow appetizer had forewarned me, and though the shellfish were high on the scale of the most incendiary dishes I had ever inflicted upon my lips and tongue, I found that judicious sips of wine and regular palate-cleansings with morsels of bread allowed for a truly memorable meal.

My assistant chewed a piece of bread that I had dipped in the red sauce and kept an eye on the newcomer for me. He had the look of a Thoonian, especially the understated cut and color of his clothing. It seemed that either current fashion or—and this I thought more likely—deep-seated cultural norms required the people of the region not to make any display that brought attention to themselves. I cast a glance or two toward the object of my suspicions and saw that when he was not doing the same to me, he was regarding the Hauserians with undisguised distaste.

"Do you detect any surveillance devices?" I whispered to my integrator while wiping my lips with a napkin.

"No," it murmured.

"Then this is passive observation."

"More bread and sauce," it said, and for a moment the non sequitur confused me. I was still not used to having my assistant's recently acquired bodily needs interrupt our professional relationship. I handed it another slice dipped in the red stuff.

"Unless," it said, chewing noisily, "two others are outside with a large sack, waiting for this fellow to come up behind and push you in."

"He does not look the type," I said. Indeed, as I watched him watch the Hauserians, I deduced that he was not the kind to rush into confrontation with those who offended his mores. Instead, he would probably craft arch and acid phrases with which to regale his friends far behind the offworlders' backs. I could not entirely fault that strategy: a great deal of self-confidence, not to mention superb physical strength and excellent coordination, was a minimum requirement for anyone who contemplated directing even the mildest insults toward four Hauserians.

I had made good progress with the flambords and now a gangly young man came to clear away the appetizer platter and to ask if all was to my satisfaction. I assured him that it was, once again executing the gesture that vividly expressed a sense of brio; again, the young man seemed startled by the motion. I believed that I had found a thread that might reward a good tugging.

"The flambords were all that I had been led to expect and more," I said. "I would be interested to visit Zherev's station to see how they are produced."

"You might be disappointed," he said. "You would see rows of mesh containers stacked one atop each other in the shallows, surrounded by a fence to keep out the hungries."

"Hungries?" I said, and heard a description of a voracious predator, all mouth and maw, possessed of an indiscriminate appetite. If I had gone down to the beach I would have encountered warning signs and graphic images of what had befallen those who had ignored the advice.

I thanked the young man for the information, then moved two fingers in a manner that suggested he lean closer so that we could confer in private. He bent toward me and I said, in a hoarse whisper, "Actually, it is not Zherev's flambords that interest me."

I then closed and opened one eye, tapped the side of my nose with an index finger and raised and lowered my eyebrows two or three times. Then I breathed one word: "Derogation."

I watched his reaction, saw surprise, mild alarm, and an air of distaste that he politely sought to conceal. He straightened and brought his features under control. "I have nothing to do with that," he said.

"Of course not," I said, "but you know that Toop Zherev has a lot to do with it."

"He is a reliable supplier of flambords," he said. "That is the extent of our relationship."

"You also know that Osk Rievor is involved."

"I am not involved."

I believed I had gained enough understanding of Thoonian culture to tweak a nerve. "You think you are better than them?"

Bleban looked flustered, as if I had accused him of unseemly habits. "Not at all. They have their views, I have mine. Still, it seems an odd way to—" He broke off.

"Please go on," I said. "Your opinions interest me."

"I've said enough," he said. "Too much, in fact. Will there be anything else?"

"Directions to Toop Zherev's station?"

"Simply follow the beach road north until you see a small, white building with a flat roof." He hefted the platter and turned away, then stopped and turned back; I saw that his reluctance to speak was being overcome by innate good manners. "But you would be wasting your time to seek him there today."

"Thank you," I said. "Then where should I look?"

"Ask the man in the corner," he said. A moment later he was through the kitchen doors and I doubted he would be back. Indeed, not long after, the young woman from the front desk brought the bill for my meal.

I paid and went out into the lobby and again idled at the rack of brochures. "What is the watcher doing?" I asked my assistant.

"Watching," it said, "though he has pushed his chair back and is ready to rise."

I gathered the thoughts that had been circling in my mind and brought them in for a landing. "I think I know what we are dealing with," I said.

"Do you wish to tell me?" the integrator said.

"No." I went to the outer doors and stepped through onto the porch, then descended the steps toward the footpath that bordered the road. I heard the hotel doors open and close behind me and the creak of the verandah's boards as they took the weight of the Thoonian.

I stood as if pausing for a moment's thought that then led to a decision. Abruptly, I spun on my heel and returned to the hotel, bounding up the steps and recoiling in surprise to find the thin man in my path. I drew up sharply, steadying myself by laying a hand on his upper arm.

"I am so sorry," I said, "I did not see you there. Please accept my apologies."

He mumbled something about no harm having been done and I thanked him for his consideration then proceeded into the hotel. I told the young woman at the desk that I had decided not to stay after all.

"Was something not to your satisfaction?" she said.

"All was as it should be," I assured her. "In truth, I came to sample the flambords. I am an importer of novel foodstuffs and had heard tales from other travelers. But I am afraid they would be too strenuous an experience for my clientele. So I will take myself off to Polder, where I hear they have some remarkable creamberries."

I said all of this in a hearty voice and was sure that the man on the porch, who was now lingering by the open doors, had heard it all. I offered him another apology as I went by him on my way out. I then strode briskly back to Lord Afre's yacht and soon I was far above the Thoon and standing out for the great darkness.

I traveled at moderate speed for some time, then told the ship to halt.

"What is your theory?" my assistant asked, but again I declined to answer. A mistaken theory that never went farther than its originator's mind does not count as an error. "It would be—" I began.

"Yes, yes," it cut me off. "I know the rest."

Suddenly I was aware of my other self. More than that, I was aware that he was decidedly agitated. "What is wrong?" I said, inwardly.

He did not answer for a moment. I sensed that he was gathering his thoughts. "It must have been a dream," he said. "I was in darkness and there was something unpleasant nearby. It sensed that I was there and it was reaching out for me, groping with strong hands."

Not good, I thought.

My thoughts were not audible to him unless I consciously voiced them, but he could not help sense my emotions, as I did his. "It was only a dream," he said. "I am not going mad."

I sought to mollify him. "You are more prone to emotion than I am," I said. "It makes sense that your dreams would be more colorful."

I brought the focus back to the matter of Osk Rievor. "He works from behind a screen," I said. "Lascalliot and this Zherev are his agents, while he remains but a mysterious name."

My sharer said, "That feels correct. He is at the heart of whatever is going on here."

For a moment it was like the way we had been before he emerged, when I would lay an analysis before the intuitive part of my psyche and receive a response. The process had always brought a good feeling, a sense of completeness that I realized I would never know again.

"That is not so," he said. "Our relationship stays the same."

"Except much more complex," I replied.

"That is the nature of relationships. They are dynamic, or they are moribund."

"Which are we?" I said.

"It would be premature to say," he answered.

We watched the shadow of night creep across the face of Great Gallowan. When the terminator line reached the Thoon coast I instructed the *Orgillous* to take us back. But we did not land at the spaceport. Instead, we hovered high above the Calamitous Ocean, shielded by a tower of clouds from the vantage point of anyone at our former landing site.

I activated a device that I had brought with me from my workroom and viewed its display. A map of the Thoon appeared, then a bright pinpoint of red light began pulsing between the sea and the mountains. I adjusted the settings until the scale of the map showed the spaceport and the adjacent area. The pinpoint was now positioned on a road, traveling inland at a speed much faster than a man could walk. That indicated that its source, a tiny bead stuck to the sleeve of the man who had watched me at the hotel, was proceeding by some kind of vehicle into the foothills east of the spaceport.

I had my assistant link the scanning device to the yacht's more powerful percepts. Now I saw that the thin man was riding a two-seat skimmer along a narrow road through a thinly populated rural district. Far ahead of him, the road ended at a substantial building that sat atop a low rise, which was the lowest of a series of land-ripples eventually leading up to the eroded mountains that were the region's eastern boundary.

I scanned the building: on a wide apron at its front, a number of vehicles were parked, with a few more coming up the winding road that led to the place. A stream of people were entering through a set of high, wide double doors.

"Our friend was left to watch and make sure we did not return," I hypothesized. "Now he is hurrying to join the rest of his cohorts."

I saw no one approaching the common destination from the heights above, so I had the ship turn off its running lights and make a wide half-circle through the night sky to bring us in from the east. Lord Afre's vessel was superbly maintained, its gravity obviators emitting only the most discreet humming as the *Orgillous* set itself down in a deep hollow that dimpled the slope above the large building.

With my integrator on my shoulder and my inner companion awake, though apparently brooding on his own concerns, I climbed out of the hollow until I could look through a screen of low brush at the structure below. The edifice was made of the same stone as the hill on which it stood; indeed, the hollow in which I had landed was the quarry from which its massive blocks had been cut. It was a cube, perhaps a hundred paces on a side, with its top surmounted by a shallow hemispheric dome. Like every other structure I had seen in the Thoon, it was unpretentious—no architectural fillips or decorations interrupted its simple lines.

The side I was looking at was the rear of the building. It had no door, but from several windows along the ground floor, as well as from a row of skylights on the roof, a gentle light glowed. I could hear voices from the other side, people greeting and calling to each other affably. They sounded like any crowd gathering for an enjoyable event.

"Do you detect any wards or watches?" I asked my integrator.

"There is a good security system, but it is turned off," it said.

"Then I will go down. You may return to the yacht to await my instructions."

I had no need to crawl or make strenuous efforts at concealment. Shadows passed behind the windows, but no one was looking out. Their attention would be on the events that were about to transpire inside. Besides, I had donned an elision suit; with its fabric subtly coaxing light waves to slip around me, rather than bounce off, I was effectively invisible. I unhurriedly descended the slope and arrived at the rear of the building, then walked down one side to peer around the corner at the front.

The last few arrivals were leaving their vehicles and entering through the great doors. I listened but did not hear the whine of the skimmer. I made my way to the front doors and entered just as they were closing.

I stood in a shadow to one side of the entrance and saw that this was a general-purpose structure built to accommodate activities that required a good-sized floor space and that might attract a substantial audience. There was a well-sprung wooden floor that would have served equally well for dancing as for athletic contests, surrounded by tiers of seats broken by rows of steps. As with all things Thoonian, the facilities were functional and understated.

Perhaps two hundred men and women occupied the lower tiers of seats, leaving a couple of thousand more empty. I saw Baltaz Thoring from the Claviger Service, now out of uniform, taking a seat in a front row. It was not difficult to avoid the small crowd; whole sections of seats even at the lowest levels stood empty. For safety's sake, though, I climbed a set of steps to the higher reaches, where most of the lumens had not been lit, and took a seat on the aisle.

At the center of the open space stood a portable image projector, beside it a tall lectern and four chairs. Now the house lighting dimmed, leaving only these objects illuminated. A voice spoke from the public address system: "Brothers and sisters, please welcome our respected Convenor, Toop Zherev."

Amid a gentle pattering of applause from the seated crowd, a man stepped into the lighted area and went to stand behind the lectern. He was of nondescript appearance, of middling height and middle age, dressed in the same simple trousers and smock as the rest of them. He exhibited no showmanship or even any evidence of podium skills, but spoke in a direct and forthright tone.

"Brothers and sisters," he said, "welcome to this first annual convening of the Derogation. We have, I feel confident in saying, a fine program to put before you. But, of course, you will be the judge of that."

Another round of restrained applause followed, unaccompanied by any of the grunts and hoots by which an Olkney audience would have expressed its approval of the sentiments expressed. Zherev waited until the sound died down, then began to introduce the first of four persons who came out of the shadows. One by one, the four made formal gestures of obeisance to the crowd, then took the seats. The four were three men and a woman, all in the muted style of the Thoon. The last of them to bow and sit was Hobart Lascalliot.

The program then began, and its content was much as I had expected. The first of the four went to the lectern, made a few brief remarks to set the scene for what was about to be shown on the projector. Then the lights dimmed and the device displayed a three-dimensional image, the moving figures within it more than life-sized.

I recognized the setting: the biennial Concertum on Pwys, which brought together bards, singers, and tonalists of grand renown throughout the Ten Thousand Worlds to compete against each other. The prizes they might receive were but a fraction of the cost that many of the contenders spent to travel to the event, but the glory of a Concertum win was beyond price.

On the last day of the event, before the finalists presented their signature pieces, came the Aspirants Hour. This was a time set aside for the young and ambitious to stand on the venerated stage and sing a few bars. More than a few grand voices had first been heard by the connoisseurs who thronged to the Concertum, though many more had sung their piece and never been heard from again; there was no more exacting audience in all The Spray.

When the image appeared, a young woman with complexly ring-leted hair was executing the last trills of Manvel's *Thrice-Gloried* in a warm contralto that earned her a respectable, and respectful, volume of applause. She curtsied demurely, hand to bosom and eyes aglow, and exited the stage.

Then out to the center of the proscenium stepped a man of mature years, dressed in the ornate, formal clothes of a senior member of the Maccha Oligarchy, the hereditary clique that dominates the mercantile civilization of Buffo, one of the wealthier secondary worlds. His raven hair swept back from a wide brow, his nose as straight and uncompromising as a sword, his eyes full of the fierce pride of his ancient heritage, he waited for the crowd to fall silent.

Then, without accompaniment, he opened his mouth and sang the octave-spanning melody that Tap Trollane had composed. The Concertum audience listened in stunned silence for several seconds. Then, as provided for in the customs of the event, they began to hurl sadly inedible vegetables and soggy, tired fruit at the singer, accompanying their missiles with time-honored jibes and insults.

The man's face did not so much fall as plummet. He held out a hand in a gesture that seemed intended as a prelude to informing the audience that they had somehow misunderstood. Then it was as if enlightenment had suddenly risen like an unwelcome sun over his life's horizon. He looked about him with an air of belated comprehension. Now a round yellow fruit connected squarely with his chin, spilling tiny, dark seeds and viscous green juices onto his gold-stitched shirtfront. His mouth set in a short, grim line and he stalked from the stage, disdaining to dodge the rain of forage that followed him all the way into the wings.

The image ended and the lumens came up. For the first time, I saw Thoonians let their feelings ride high. The brothers and sisters of the Derogation howled and stamped, their faces distorted by a cruel glee, their eyes wet with vindictive mirth, as the first presenter took a modest bow. The applause continued, until Toop Zherev resumed his place at the lectern and called up the woman who was to introduce the next performance.

For myself, I remained unmoved, except by the intellectual satisfaction of having correctly deduced the nature of the Derogation. After all, a Maccha oligarch would score low on anyone's scale of sympathetic victims, especially when the attack was no more than a thoroughgoing public comeuppance.

The butt of the woman presenter's contribution to the evening's program was equally unworthy of much pity: he was a High Arbiter from the Grand Umpirage on Brolligo, a foundational world that prided itself on its specialty of arbitrating irresolvable disputes. Its judiciars were legendary for their haughtiness and high-flown dignity. These attributes were always on full display when senior members of Brolligo's intensely proud corps of legalists gathered for a round of formal dinners during Savants' Week. The events culminated in a grand banquet at which the greatest of the great rise and rehearse for their peers the salient arguments in cases they have adjudicated.

I now witnessed, via the image projector, the unique spectacle of the High Arbiter presenting the key elements of an impasse between two septs of an aristocratic clan who contended over the rights to an estate in the highlands of Corkery on the world Aspahan. The arguments turned on a nice definition of the legitimacy, or lack thereof, of a child conceived under contended circumstances. More remarkable than the details of the case, however, was the fact that the High Arbiter presented them in song. I was familiar by now with the melody and did not listen, but watched as the image-gatherer panned across the faces of the singer's colleagues as they registered emotions ranging from sheer astonishment to creeping horror to purple-veined outrage.

The Thoonians erupted once more in vicious merriment and a harsh tumult of applause and catcalls. When the din subsided, Zherev called upon the third presenter. The air above the projector lit with the setting of yet another high and portentous event. This one looked to be the installation of a new Ecclesiarch of the Creed of the Contingent Revelation on Horm, an occasion that drew hierarchs and pulpiteers from all the many worlds to which the syncretic religion had spread. The massed choir was finishing a paean of celebration, and the seven-tiered diadem was about to be lowered onto the new predicant's brow. Then a portly man in the cassock and cocked hat of a senior creedsman stepped onto the stairs beneath the throne. The eyes of a hundred thousand celebrants turned to him as he opened his mouth and began to sing.

But I did not watch the inevitable result. My attention was drawn to the front door, which now opened to admit the thin man who had been watching me in the hotel restaurant. He looked about the hall and, spotting Baltaz Thoring, scuttled over to speak with him. I expected him to give a perfunctory report—that I had gone offworld—then take a seat. But he did not. He spoke with what seemed to be some agitation, his bony hand gesturing in an upward direction. For a moment I thought he was pointing in my direction and the thought crossed my mind that perhaps he had done to me what I had done to him, slipping a tracking device onto my person even as I had attached the bead to his sleeve. But I had had my assistant scan me thoroughly.

Now I saw that he was pointing up through the walls in the direction where the *Orgillous* lay hidden. I realized that Great Gallowan's traffic control function must have been asked to track the yacht's movements beyond the basic level of surveillance—the Claviger Service would have a close relationship with the system—and my surreptitious return to the Thoon had been noted.

Thoring now looked as alarmed as the man reporting to him. He left his seat and moved down into the open space just as the members of the Derogation burst into loud approval of the fate of the hapless singer in the projected image, who was being harried down the ceremonial steps by brawny men who used decorated staffs that were sturdy enough to be wielded as prods and cudgels. He crossed behind the projector and went to where Toop Zherev sat a few paces behind the lectern. But before he could reach the leader of this secret society, Zherev rose and went to introduce the fourth presenter, Hobart Lascalliot.

The claviger stood, wringing his hands in evident distress while Lascalliot strode to the lectern. I heard his familiar voice, though now he did not attempt to disguise the rounded vowels of Great Gallowan speech, describing the event the audience was about to see.

"The yearly levee of the Archon of Old Earth…" he began, but I paid no heed to what followed, nor to the image of the glittering gala in the Palace of the Archonate that now appeared in the middle of the hall. Instead, I regarded Toop Zherev as he received the news that an interloper was likely in the vicinity.

He did not react with the decisiveness one would have expected from the leader of a secret organization that could send operatives up and down The Spray, even if their goal was only to induce the prideful to make utter fools of themselves. He looked like a farmer from a quiet, little secondary world who wasn't quite sure what to do.

Still, as Chalivire's harsh voice rose in the now far too familiar tune, with lyrics added that rhymed Filidor's name in a most banal manner, I judged it time to leave. I rose quietly from my seat and began to ascend the steps to the very top of the building. As I turned my back on the scene below, I felt a strange chill across my shoulders, as if a cold breath had blown over me. At the same time, my inner companion became fully alert.

"What was that?" he said.

"I do not know," I said. "I have never felt the like."

"I have," my alter ego said. "In my dream—"

"Let us discuss this later," I said. "They know the *Orgillous* is nearby. I am escaping before a pursuit begins, which is always preferable." I then pressed a stud on my cuff, held it to my lips, and said, "Now."

I swiftly climbed the steps to a broad landing that circled the entire top of the building. Here and there along the walls stood booths, now all shuttered, where patrons of events held in the hall could buy light meals and souvenirs. Past one of these groupings, where the landing turned a corner, a ladder rose to the roof. In moments, I was at the top of the rungs, pushing open a trapdoor to emerge into the open air. Lord Afre's yacht was just edging up to the perimeter of the roof, a portal open and a gangplank extending toward me. In two steps I was inside the yacht and by the time I entered the forward lounge, Great Gallowan was a diminishing circle in the viewer.

My assistant was perched on the buffet chewing on some red and fibrous fruit. "That seems to have gone well," it said.

"I'm not sure," I said.

I had been home several days when I received a communication from Lord Afre. He had not been on Old Earth when I landed, of course, because I had transmitted a full report on my discrimination of the case the moment the *Orgillous* had emerged from the last whimsy and I had shaken off the effect of the medications. By the time I touched down at his vehicle park, the aristocrat had long since assembled a useful assortment of retainers and set off for Great Gallowan in his touring ship, the *Exultance*. Chalivire sent her majordomo to greet me and furnish transportation to my lodgings. The man apologized for the mistress's inattention and, when I inquired as to her health, he assured me that she had largely gotten over her "recent setback" and was now very busy preparing for the arrival of a much anticipated visitor.

My integrator informed me that its counterpart at the Afre estate was making contact. I quickly donned the signs and tokens that would make me visible to my client and opened the connection.

"Hapthorn," he said, and I saw that he had got me well in view without straining.

"It is I," I said.

"A satisfactory result," he said.

"You acquired both the, er, objects you were seeking?"

A small cloud visited his sharp features, then passed on. "No, not both," he said. "One seemed to have vanished. But I got the one the girl particularly wanted."

"Would you like me to see if I can locate the other?" I asked, and felt a slight disappointment when he declared that he did not think it necessary. Something about the mysterious Osk Rievor troubled me, or perhaps it was just my dislike of leaving loose ends dangling.

"By the way," Lord Afre was saying, "didn't have a chance to mention that the Archon was asking after you."

"After me?" I said.

"At the levee, before Chalivire's regrettable…you know."

"Did he say why?"

"No. You know how archons are," he said.

Indeed, I did, which was why I had largely preferred to avoid them.

CHAPTER SIX

"Everything is connected to everything else," my alter ego was saying.

"A truism," I agreed. "But I still can't find a connection between your book and anything else in all the Ten Thousand Worlds."

We had spent another fruitless afternoon seeking the one loose thread that would let us untangle the text. My other self was growing increasingly distracted by the puzzle, if indeed it was a puzzle. Earlier, I had lightly offered the opinion that it might be a complete fabrication of a magical book, a decoy of some kind. "Perhaps some thaumaturge of a bygone age produced this farrago of meaningless letters in order to divert a rival's attention away from his real book of tricks."

A growl had sounded in my head. "These are not tricks," he said, and I felt the force of his anger. "And this is no decoy."

I was becoming increasingly concerned. The situation had not been so problematical when we had been offworld and pursuing the Chalivire discrimination, even though the book had gone everywhere we went. But since our return, only a couple of smallish cases had come my way, both easily dealt with, and the idleness drove my inner companion again and again to the resistant mystery of Baxandall's book.

"So, everything is connected to everything else," I said, "except, apparently, this book, which stands alone, a monument to its own uniqueness."

I heard him swear within my head. Oddly, he had a more salacious vocabulary than my own. "You don't see it," he said.

"Then reveal what I don't see."

64

"In your realm," he said, "everything is connected to everything else by rational ties, by cause and effect, by one and one making two, and so on."

I saw where he was going. "Ah, but in the world to come," I said, "when magic reasserts itself, the connections will be otherwise. Things that do not now relate to each other will do so intensely, intimately."

"Exactly."

"Then we have but to wait until that world arrives, you stand out in full measure, I fade into the shadows, and the meaning of the book will suddenly be clear."

He groaned. "I cannot wait! This must be dealt with now!"

"You are not just impatient for your own time to come?" I suggested. "It would be natural for you—"

"*No!*" he shouted in our shared mental parlor, then moderated his tone. "Well, yes, I am eager to get on with things, to see a world into which I fit as closely as you have fitted yours. But it is more than that. The urgency comes not from me, but from…"

"I understand," I said. "If you knew the source of your sense of urgency, that itself might be the first step into the maze."

"I sense it has something to do with that business on Great Gallowan," he said.

"I don't see how that can be," I said. "The connection is remote."

"In *your* realm."

"We were in my realm. We went by space yacht, not a chariot pulled by griffums."

I felt him agonizing and the emotion drew my sympathy. He had been, after all, an aspect of me. I was about to try to offer comfort when he said, "What if, within your realm, there are other precursors of mine?"

My first inclination was to scoff, but I had experienced enough strangeness in recent times to put down the habitual response. "You believe that Osk Rievor might be sharing Toop Zherev's spare room?"

"Not 'believe,' " he said, "but I'm willing to entertain the notion."

"And you believe that he is somehow connected to this book, even though he was halfway down The Spray on a world full of dull people who envy the folk of other worlds their pomp and pride?"

"Why not? If one and one soon won't have to make two," he said, "why not?"

"It seems an odd place to find a spellster."

"No more odd than here in Olkney, where we found Baxandall. Or on the edge of Dimpfen Moor, where Turgut Therobar had discovered a dimple of the oncoming age. Perhaps there is another on Balwinder Sound."

I had learned, while confined to a cage in Therobar's subterranean chamber, that the transition from rationalism to sympathy did not sweep across our cosmos like a wave rolling onto a shore. Instead, the new order would appear everywhere at once, like a liquid seeping through a porous membrane. But there were certain points—dimples, Therobar had called them—where the seepage was premature. In those places, where the seepage pooled, the potency of spells was intensified. It was as if they were islands of the age of magic appearing ahead of schedule in the sea of rationality. It was on one of those islands, on the edge of the desolate moor, that the ambitious thaumaturge had chosen to build his estate, Wan Water.

I said, "It is possible that Toop Zherev's flambord station is such a dimple, but I cannot see that fish farmer as a powerful thaumaturge. I have discovered that they project a certain presence. He lacked it."

"True," said my sharer. "Still, there is some connection."

I had no good reply, but was saved from admitting so by the who's-there. It chimed its usual annunciatory note and said, "There may be someone at the door."

"Can you not be more definite?" I said.

"No."

I descended from my workroom to street level and looked through the viewer. Outside night was gathering in the gaudy, blowsy city that was the capital of Old Earth in the planet's penultimate age. It had rained and the streets were wet, the pavement glistening in the light from the lumen above my door. I saw no one standing there.

The who's-there activated again. "I detect a presence," it said, "though my percepts cannot secure an image. But someone is there."

Magic? I thought, and I was already chiding myself for slipping toward my inner companion's frame of reference when he spoke inside our head.

"Nothing that I sense," he said.

"Could the visitor be wearing an elision suit?" I asked the who's-there.

"If so, it is a more sophisticated version than most," it answered.

"Recalibrate your percepts to the upper limits."

It did so and reported, "It most likely is a person of medium build and normal body temperature. I detect no energy weapons."

"Ah," I said, "then our visitor is likely to be someone of prominence who does not wish to be seen consulting a freelance discriminator."

My bashful visitor might also be someone who had been the subject of one of my discriminations. There were more than a few criminals in Olkney whose schemes I had upended and who did not wish me well. And not all weapons required energy. I thought for a moment, then said, "Open the door, but be prepared to suppress any aggressive conduct." I heard a faint hum as the door's built-in defenses charged themselves. An opaque panel that allowed me to see out while no one could see in slid down to cover the doorway, then the outer door cycled open. A voice, youthful but firm, said, "I wish to speak with Henghis Hapthorn."

"I am he. Do you wish to consult me?"

"Yes."

"Who are you?"

"I will reveal that once I am out of sight of the street."

"I see," I said. The accent was cultured. This was a person of means.

"What does your intuition say?" I asked my other self.

"Trouble," he said. "Very considerable trouble."

"Danger?" I said.

"When are the two ever separated?"

"To me? To us, I mean?"

"I don't think so."

I bid the opaque barrier remove itself. "Please enter and follow," I said, and turned to ascend to my workroom. There I invited my invisible visitor to state his business.

"This is a matter of great importance," said the disembodied voice.

"Very few clients come to me over trivialities," I said.

"Terrible events may be in the offing, horrors unimaginable."

"And what," I said, "is the source of these calamities?"

"I cannot tell you."

"Why not?"

"Because I do not know."

It now belatedly occurred to me that there was a third category of persons who sometimes sought me out: those who were afflicted with disorders of the mind and thought themselves pursued by powerful forces. Most such loons could not afford high-efficiency elision suits, but insanity was not unknown among the wealthy. Indeed, some forms of madness had sometimes been cultivated as fashionable accessories.

I stroked my chin as if in thought and stepped toward a corner of my workroom that could be instantly sealed off. At the utterance of a nonsense phrase, impermeable barriers would spring from floor and ceiling.

I turned and addressed the faint shimmer in the air where my visitor stood. "You do not know? Does this mean you have received no cryptic messages from unlikely sources? No voices mysteriously beamed directly to you by vast intelligences beyond our ken?"

I was now within the space that could be hived off, pretending an interest in some bric-a-brac on a small table. I had only to utter the trigger word and my integrator—

But here I was brought up short. My integrator lay sprawled in deep sleep in the space beneath the divan, emitting delicate snores. Its change from discriminator's assistant to what seemed to be the kind of familiar that might be employed by a wizard from a fairy tale was still so recent that I had not yet delineated every detail of the new paradigm. Specifically, I now realized that I did not know if shouting code words at its sleeping ear would bring the desired effect of isolating me from my invisible visitor, should he suddenly begin to rave and throw himself at my throat.

"I am sorry," I said. "I was thinking and did not hear what you said."

"If you would stop playing with those gewgaws on the table and pay attention," said the voice in a tone that seemed at ease with command, "this conversation could proceed to a culmination."

I put down the knickknack I'd been holding. "Very well," I said, loudly, hoping that the volume would rouse my assistant from the sleeping place it had made for itself beneath my divan. But its regular breathing went on uninterrupted, except for a brief snort and a smacking of prehensile lips.

"I said," said my visitor, "that I am not delusional. The danger is very real, even if I cannot identify the source."

I took up another piece of bric-a-brac—it was a statue of the Archon Dezendah IV, recently retired—and struck the table a sharp rap. The breathing from under the divan continued untroubled.

"What is the danger, then?" I said.

"A plot. I suspect there is a conspiracy to overthrow the Archonate and replace it with a sinister regime."

My inner companion was saying something but my attention was focused on the invisible madman before me. "Indeed," I said, in a mollifying tone, and, "oh, dear." I had raised my voice but still I was answered only by faint snores from beneath the divan and a throat-clearing growl from my visitor. It was time for the code words.

"Looby looby!" I cried. But no shimmering barrier appeared. I tried again, this time shouting as loudly as I could. I heard snorts from beneath the divan, the unmistakable sounds of awakening.

From directly in front of me, however, I heard an angry though still cultured voice inquiring as to what kind of idiocy I was engaged in. Its source was clearly advancing toward me. I reached again for the brass statue of the former Archon and flung it in the direction of the sound.

It flew straight and true—my eye and hand have always enjoyed good relations—and stopped dead in the air a short distance before me. It fell to the floor with a *thump*, followed immediately by the sound of a body doing much the same thing.

I stepped forward, meaning to investigate my fallen attacker, strip the elision suit's pliofilm from his features, and discover who he was. My intent was blocked by the sudden appearance before me of the security barrier. I recoiled from the impact, rubbing my injured nose, as the integrator crept out from beneath the divan, blinked its large, golden eyes at me, and said, "If you needed to know whether the emergency barrier worked from the inside you could have just asked me."

Several possible rejoinders occurred to me but I put them aside and ordered my assistant to extinguish the obstruction. "I was under attack from an unbalanced assailant in an elision suit," I said, "who now lies unconscious on the floor. We will shortly discover who he is."

"You ninny," said the voice in my head, "how could you not know who he is?"

"And you do?" I said, also within the confines of my skull.

"The moment he spoke of a threat to the Archonate." He showed me an image on our shared inner screen: a young man of noble aspect wearing the appurtenances and regalia of the ruler of Old Earth.

"You're saying that's the Archon Filidor?" I said.

"I am."

"How would you know that?"

"Intuition, of course."

With a dismissive frication of air over my lips, I knelt and felt for the face, then peeled the light-eliding film away. The face of the unconscious young man on my workroom floor matched the features that my mental cohabitant had shown me.

"It's Filidor, all right," I said.

My assistant came over and peered down at the face whose broad forehead bore a circular red mark the exact size of the statuette's base. "He doesn't look all right to me," it said.

Among the many disparate societies that speckled those parts of Old Earth in the ancient world's penultimate age, it was universally accepted that the institution of the Archonate was the ideal form of government. The head of the regime, and the pinnacle of the social order in the capital city, Olkney, was the Archon. He wielded vast, though only vaguely defined, powers, ruling in an entirely indirect manner, more by inference than decree.

Although he was rarely seen outside the Archonate Palace, a sprawling architectural accretion atop the black crags of the Devenish Range above the city, it was also universally known that the

Archon often wandered through the world in disguise. He might appear as a carefree vagabond, an itinerant dealer in rarities, a strolling narrator. Thus any stranger might be the Archon, come to exercise sudden and perhaps rigorous judgment, with the full might of the Bureau of Scrutiny behind him. The peregrinations of archons had been referred to since time immemorial as *the progress of esteeming the balance.*

The Archon was not known, however, to present himself incognito at the door of Old Earth's foremost freelance discriminator mouthing mysterious warnings about apocalyptic evil. "It was a reasonable response," I said to my inner critic as I lifted the mostly invisible Archon Filidor I and carried him to the divan. "He was shouting and coming toward me."

"He is probably not used to having his sanity questioned by persons who then proceed to yelp nonsense at him," said the voice in my head. "Though he is only recently come into the title, I believe Filidor has been Archon long enough to have grown accustomed to people taking him seriously."

I laid the unconscious young man on the divan, put a cushion under his head, which was all that I could yet see of him, and went to the sanitary suite for water and a restorative. When I returned, the Archon was blinking though his eyes had not yet rediscovered the ability to focus. The mark in the middle of his forehead was swelling into a bump. I sat beside him and placed a damp compress on the injury. After a moment, his vision coalesced and he regarded me with a mulling look then said, "Well, at least I don't have to worry about you."

"How so?" I said.

"If you were part of the conspiracy, I would not be waking up."

"That is probably so." I asked him if he felt well enough to sit, and when he did I offered him the restorative. It took effect and in a short time he was fully recovered.

"Still," he said, "I would like to know why you shouted, 'Looby looby,' then threw something at my head."

I explained in a diplomatic manner the circumstances behind my behavior.

"You took me for a raver?"

"I've been under some strain lately."

"Who hasn't?" he said. He stood up and began to pace, which meant, since he was still wearing his elision suit, that I saw a disembodied and worried head passing to and fro across my workroom.

"I don't know whom to trust," he said after a while.

"You can trust me," I told him. "I am an admirer of the Archonate, though not always of your servants in the Bureau of Scrutiny, particularly one Colonel-Investigator Brustram Warhanny."

"I don't know him," the Archon said.

"You are more fortunate than I. For some reason, he resents it when I perform a discrimination that clears up a thorny part of his caseload."

"To return to my problem..." he said.

"Yes. Tell me about it. May I ask my integrator to take notes?" I indicated the apparent amalgam of feline and ape that had established itself on my worktable next to a bowl of karba fruit while we were talking. It was now peeling one with skillful fingers.

"*That* is your integrator?" the Archon said.

"I'm afraid so."

"Is this something new?"

I could not help but be reminded of the horrific realization that had come upon me with the arrival of my inner companion and the metamorphosis of my integrator: that the world of rationality into which I fit so well was itself soon to be transformed into a realm based on sympathetic association—or, to use the common term, magic—in the latest iteration of a cycle that had been going on throughout the aeons. "Both very new," I said, "and very old. But tell me of the plot. Who is in it, who is not, and what part do you wish me to play?"

"The answer to your first two questions is 'I don't know,'" he said. "The answer to the third is that the first thing I want you to do is to find those first two answers."

It was well known that archons were encouraged by their advisors to acquire the habit of offering cryptic responses to most questions; the practice allegedly enhanced the mystery of the office. An Archon of the Nineteenth Aeon, Onoreef XVI, reigned for forty-two years answering every question put to him with a question of his own. His reign would have gone on for even longer if he had not answered an inquiry from a particularly dense underling—"Do you really wish me to press this button?"—with the needlessly ambiguous, "Why wouldn't I?"

Thus I took the time to replay Filidor's response in my head and found it was in fact a direct statement of his situation: he had come to me because he was unsure whom he could trust within the Archonate apparatus—or without it, for that matter.

"I am gratified that you would place your trust in me," I said.

"It was a process of elimination," he said. "I asked myself: first, who has the mental acuity to unravel a complex, clandestine conspiracy; second, who is the least likely to be invited to join such a cabal? The answer to each question was: Henghis Hapthorn."

"He is being polite," said the voice in my head. "The real question was: 'Whom do I know who is full-brained yet friendless?'"

"Archons have no need to be polite," I silently replied. "Power is its own social lubricant." Aloud I said, "What indications do you have that something is afoot?"

"Last night, I found this on my nightstand," he said. From an inner pocket he produced a page that, by its ragged edge, must have been torn from a document. "It was not there when I disrobed and entered the sanitary suite. It was there when I returned."

I examined the document. It appeared to be a page torn from a catalog of items stored in that vast repository of treasures and oddments known as the Great Connaissarium. The Archon Terfel III, whose lifelong inquisitiveness was legendary, had established the collection long enough ago that some of the building he constructed to house it was now an ancient ruin.

"What did your integrator see?"

"Nothing. I had it replay the sequence of events. One moment the night table was bare, the next the page was there."

"Interesting," I said. "Was there anything else?"

"Yes. An object had been disturbed."

"What was this object?"

"A kind of key."

"What does it open?"

"I will not say," the disembodied head told me. "It is a matter known only to archons and their most intimate aides."

"Then it is an important key," I said.

"Very."

I had further questions to put, but I was distracted by my alter ego's insistence that I pursue another line of inquiry.

"Ask him more about the key," he said.

"He will not answer."

"It is important."

"So is not angering clients who can have one consigned to a contemplarium."

I continued with the Archon. "At this point, we have a mystery. But how do you derive from it the existence of a conspiracy to overthrow the Archonate?"

"I derive it from this," he said, producing another document. "It accompanied the catalog page."

It was a handwritten note in an archaic script, the letters like spiders frozen on the page: *They plot to remove you. Trust no one close.*

"Hmm," I said.

"What do you think?" he said.

"It would be premature to say. Could it not be an attempt by one clique within your court to turn you against another faction?"

"I am familiar with those games," he said. "They always make it plain whose heads I am to lop. This counsels me to shun all who might reach me."

"Thus it must come from someone removed," I said.

"So it would seem. Yet how can someone who is not part of my inner circle make free with my bedchamber?"

"Indeed. If the Archon's head cannot rest easy, who's can?" I struck a formal posture and said, "I am gratified by your confidence. I am also happy to take the case." I then paused and delicately cleared my throat.

"Yes?" Filidor said.

"At this point I usually discuss my fee."

The floating head showed a receptive mien. "Discuss away."

I cleared my throat once more and said, "I have found it best to negotiate a flat payment for most assignments, inclusive of expenses, rather than an hourly or per diem rate. Half is payable in advance and half upon completion. The arrangement avoids any dissatisfaction that may arise if, as often occurs, I resolve the case in a much shorter time than the client expected."

"What sort of flat fee did you have in mind?" Filidor said.

I mentioned a figure. He acquiesced without quibble, saying he would draw up a fiduciary draft as soon as he returned to the palace. "However," he said, "payment of the second half is of course contingent on successful completion of the assignment."

"Indeed," I concurred. "Since if I am not successful, it is quite likely that neither of us will have any further use for money."

I had my integrator interrupt its feeding and picking at itself long enough to summon an aircar from a service that I occasionally used. The volante arrived promptly and we went up to the roof to board it unobserved, Filidor once again fully obscured by his elision suit.

It was growing late now and the clouds that had brought the evening's rain had dutifully disappeared. The newly cleaned sky glittered with countless orbitals passing overhead in every direction, while above them hung the long splash of stars known as The Spray, home to the Ten Thousand Worlds where lived the overwhelming proportion of mankind. Below us, as if in imitation of the sky, blazed the lumens of Olkney, that impossibly ancient city that had stood on this spot, bearing a dozen different names and boasting any number of plausible reasons for its existence, since far back in humanity's dawn-time. I had always preferred to view Olkney like this, from a good height; the closer one got to street level the more the hustle and thrust of the citizenry overwhelmed any hope of serenity.

The Archon must enjoy the most tranquil perspective of all, I thought, imperturbably poised in his palace high above both the majesty and the squalor to be found below, and insulated equally from both by whole phalanxes of officialdom and factotumry. I did not test the accuracy of my surmise by expressing it to Filidor as we transited the night sky, however; Olkney's aircars had ears, and were notorious for titillating passengers with snippets of what they had overheard and retained.

Before we boarded, the Archon had instructed me where to direct the vehicle and so we did not land at any of the levels reserved for official use. Instead, we set down on a broad terrace, halfway up the tiered immensity of the Archonate Palace, in a part of the grounds open to the public. I recognized the place as being near to the entrance of the Terfel Connaissarium. He had gathered together curiosities, oddities, and singularities from every corner of The Spray and even from uncouth and uncharted worlds far out in the Back of Beyond. These he had brought together in a vast, multifloored building he had caused to be erected, its upper stories supported by arches set upon arches and its roots sunk far down into the living rock of the Devenish Range that overhung Olkney.

The place was half-ruined now. Most of Terfel's heterogeneous collection lay tucked away in subterranean storerooms. Occasionally, though, curators picked over the myriad items and assembled exhibitions of oddly juxtaposed objects: suits made of human skins fashioned by the untamed autochthones of Bizmant's World next to eye-snaring mesmer wheels used by adherents of the Refusalist cult on Hulle; fragile windslips from a light-gravity moon of Ondine next to massive soulstones dug up from antique tombs in Rusk before it finally sank beneath the waves.

At the moment, according to a placard out front, the Connaissarium was offering a display of semisentient musical instruments tuned to several conflicting harmonic scales. Visitors were encouraged to pluck a string or strike a key on any of the virtuoso apparatuses, which would cause the others to chime in competitively. Each would be driven by its nature to seek to dominate in a solo performance, resulting in amazingly discordant cacophonies from which the listener was invited to draw philosophical lessons. Also, there was a remarkable display of objects that primitive humanity had allegedly thrust through various parts of their bodies—some of them extremely sensitive—for decorative effect. I shuddered slightly at the thought: self-mutilation, though everyone's right, had always taken me aback.

The public part of the Great Connaissarium was open at all hours, Olkney being a city that could never sleep. I entered a portal beneath crumbling stonework, holding the door open and no doubt appearing to any observer as momentarily indecisive, to allow the invisible Archon to pass within. I paused in the foyer, glancing about like a bored patron deciding which gallery to enter first. A voice in my ear whispered, "The archway adorned by the nygrave's skull."

I ambled in the indicated direction. Beyond the archway was a spacious chamber full of what seemed to be misshapen pots and random lengths of rope. A notice explained the purpose of the display but I did not stop to peruse it, being urged by my invisible client to proceed across the marquetted floor (each small slab of wood cut from a different species of tree on Old Earth or one of the Ten Thousand Worlds), and through a smaller doorway. Here I found an anteroom with beams of light descending from the ceiling to fall upon a selection of small devices, each displayed atop its own waist-high pillar, whose functions and provenances I would never know.

I felt Filidor's unseen hand take my elbow and guide me on a weaving course through the columns to a shallow alcove on the far side of the room. Here hung a narrow tapestry of coarsely woven weave depicting some ancient autocrat committing unspeakable acts upon a figure kneeling before him. I was aware of my unseen guide brushing past me. Then the cloth was twitched aside and I saw a cluster of five indentations in the rear wall, patterned to fit the fingers and opposed thumb of a spread hand. A moment later, with a discreet crunch of stone passing over stone, the wall slid back. "In," said Filidor's voice.

I did as bid and stepped into a stone-lined corridor that angled gently down. The entrance closed behind us. I paused to await further instruction, though there was but one direction in which to go. I saw the young Archon's head appear, then his shoulders and eventually the rest of him as he peeled off the elision suit. He wadded up the shimmering pliofilm and placed it in a wallet he wore at the belt of his nondescript suit, then said, "Come."

"We are secure from observation, then?"

"I disabled all the percepts here in my boyhood," he said over his shoulder as he set off down the slope. "I tended to avoid my studies, and spent my time finding interesting ways about the palace. It's riddled with passages and secret stairways, some of them connecting to wings and chambers sealed off for tens of thousands of years."

I followed him as he spoke, my feet churning up puffs of dust. We walked in silence thereafter, and I turned my thoughts to what I knew of Filidor's history. Since boyhood he had had a reputation as a wastrel and nincompoop, spending his days—or more accurately his nights—carousing with a coterie of aristocratic ne'er-do-wells. His exploits were frequently written up in the froth-filled gossip columns of the *Olkney Implicator*. Then he had curiously disappeared from the life of riot and rompery for a while, only to re-emerge as the Archon Dezendah's apprentice and acknowledged heir. He continued to live the life of a spoiled ninny until a second brief lacuna intervened, contemporaneous with rumors of an aristocratic plot to usurp the throne. Then all at once Filidor returned to public view as a full-weight man of authority. His uncle Dezendah retired, the nephew married and took the insignia of office, and ever since Filidor had scarcely caused the great mass of citizens to afford him a second thought, if indeed they had ever sent a first one his way. In other words, he was a perfectly acceptable Archon.

"Down here," he said as we came to the end of the corridor and found a wide circular hole in the stone floor, mostly filled by a spiral staircase of dark metal. It shook alarmingly as I set foot to it, but the young man was lightly tripping down into the darkness below. I followed, descending more steps than I could have comfortably counted until I surmised that we must be many levels deep into the heart of the mountains. Our way was lit only by the dim light of small lumens set above occasional archways that we passed on the way down. These were not closely spaced, but my eyes grew accustomed to the murk.

We came at last to the bottom of the stairs. An archway led into a desolate corridor but Filidor ignored the exit. He went to a spot about head high on the wall, where it appeared that the long-dead stone cutters who had dug the stairwell had left a slight convexity. He cupped his hand over the bulge and pushed, and a portion of the wall grudgingly receded. We stepped through the opening into blackness. I heard the Archon rustling about nearby and assumed he was looking for a light source.

"There is an odd odor here," said the voice inside my head.

"I thought you had gone back to sleep," I answered him.

"I think it is the odor of magic," he said.

"I smell nothing but must and stale air."

"Your senses are not attuned."

"They are the same senses you employ. We have but one nose between us."

"Perception takes place within the brain," he said, "where the raw stimuli are transmuted into electro-chemical impulses. I do not believe we use the same neuronic net to appreciate our surroundings."

He was probably right, I knew. He must inhabit a different cluster of neurons and synapses from those that were truly "mine"—otherwise there could be no separation of identities.

Filidor now brought light from a portable lumen. I saw that we were standing in a narrow space between two sets of shelves that rose until they were lost to sight in the darkness. Ahead of us more topless shelves stretched into the gloom, all of them laden with boxes and trays of varying depths, each marked with a sequence of letters and numerals that bespoke a cataloging system. Many archons, it seemed, had been indefatigable collectors of oddments, none of which had ever, in all the scores of millennia that preceded the penultimate age, been thrown away.

Holding the portable lumen aloft, Filidor set off. I followed. We went silently among the shelves, turning left at the second cross aisle then right after several more rows. We came at last to a section that looked exactly like every other we had passed, but here the Archon stopped and directed my attention to a shelf a little higher than my head. He pointed to a box whose end bore a sequence of symbols that meant nothing to me. "Please take it down," he said.

I did so. It was a lidless tray as long as my forearm and perhaps half that in width. Inside, nestled on soft quilted material, were a half-dozen small figurines from some period I doubt any but the most dedicated pedant could identify. They were engaged in carnal acts of considerable ingenuity, some of which would tax the anatomy almost as much as they did the imagination.

"Remarkable," I said. "I wonder that anyone familiar with such exercises would retain the energy needed for carving."

"Note the symbols on the end of the tray," my client said.

"Yes?"

"Now compare them to this page from the catalog."

I had brought the page with me. I now studied it. "They are not the same," I said.

"Exactly. The objects in this tray should be in that one," he said, indicating a container of similar shape and size on the shelf directly beneath the one from which I had taken the first tray. I pulled the new one toward me, enough to peek within and see six more figurines much like the others.

"And you can see," Filidor said, "that this line of the catalog says that there should be twelve items in that tray."

"Could some long-dead curator have made an error?" I said.

"No. According to the records, this section was inventoried not many years ago. It should not have been touched since."

My inner companion was nudging me, an indescribable sensation when it occurs within one's own mind. "The odor is strongest here," he said.

"Hush," I told him. "You are obsessed."

To Filidor I said, "Very well, an object is missing from the collection, and some attempt has been made to disguise its removal. The logical assumption would be that some official has taken a fancy to the thing and it now graces an occasional table in his apartments. Except—"

"Except," said Filidor, "for the manner in which we became aware of its disappearance."

"The page from the catalog," I said. I was distracted at that moment by discovering that I had bent low toward the tray that I still held and was delicately sniffing at it. I did not want to engage, before the eyes of the Archon, in an internal wrestling match with my other self, and allowed my cohabitant to indulge himself. "It reeks," he said.

"Do not take charge of our body without consultation," I said inwardly, regaining control. When I was upright again I said to the Archon, "According to the catalog page, what should be in the tray?"

"I have never seen it," said Filidor. "The catalog describes it as a: *mouth and chin of a male figure, life-sized, of a strong but unclassifiable material, apparently fractured from a larger work. Associated with the term, 'Majestrum,' from the Seventeenth Aeon.*"

"Hmm," I said. I am confident that I maintained an outward composure, but inwardly, at the moment the Archon had pronounced the word *Majestrum*, I had experienced a sharp frisson as if a strong electrical charge had shot through my body. After a moment, I realized that the effect on me was but a muted echo of what had struck my inner companion. When I felt for him, I received the same sense of absence that I experienced when he slept. It seemed he had lost whatever constituted consciousness.

I was both gratified and concerned. It was worrisome that a mere word—or name, if that was what the three syllables conveyed—could have had such an effect. I remembered what I had learned from my brief passage through the other dimension from which my erstwhile "demonic" visitor had come, of how I discovered that in his realm there was no difference between things and the symbols used to define them—that to name an object or entity was to cause it to appear, that the map was literally the territory. If magic was to recover its prominence in our universe—and I had reluctantly come to accept that inevitably it must—then there would be words and names of power that could not be uttered without dire consequences. On the other hand, a word whose mere utterance could render my alter ego senseless was bound to have a certain appeal to the original tenant and unwilling sharer of the mind of Henghis Hapthorn.

I felt him stir and recover. "What happened?" he said.

"I believe you fainted."

"It was that word. I told you, this affair reeks of magic."

I assured him that I believed he was right. "The question is, where do we go from here?" It was only when the Archon replied in the affirmative that I realized I had spoken aloud.

"For the answer to that question," he said, "I have turned to you. What will you do?"

I began to say that it would be premature to say but he sent me a warning look, reminding me that archons were not easily fobbed off by platitudes. Instead, I said, "Allow me a moment's thought."

Before the unsettling reorganization of my psyche, at this point I would have "applied insight," as I had always referred to the mental practice of carrying a problem down the back passageways of my mind to leave it at the door of my intuition. After a certain span of time, which could extend from mere moments to a day or more, a suggestion—usually a good one—would appear in my mind. Now, however, my intuitive faculty had become a fully realized persona, and the inward journey consisted of my saying, within my mind, "What do you think?"

"It would be premature to say," was his answer, in a tone I found mocking.

"You are offended? Why?"

"Only because I have been trying to bring the obvious to your attention, without being able to penetrate your obtuse refusal to see—or smell—what is unmistakable to the nose."

"Not to my nose," I said.

"You do not smell the stench of that thing?"

"I smell nothing but age and uncirculated air."

"Truly?"

"I am not accustomed to lie to myself."

He seemed mollified for a moment, but then he came back to an air of grievance. "You did not inquire as to what happened to me when the Archon said…that word."

"I thought it best to postpone the discussion until we have dealt with the concerns of the ruler of the human-inhabited world. Who happens to be standing here wondering what we are accomplishing and, quite possibly, beginning to regret letting us in on his little predicament."

I wondered to myself—that is, to my *other* self—what an anxious Archon might do with someone who was both privy to the existence of a usurper's conspiracy and demonstrating no particular ability to combat it. My alter ego took the hint. "There is not only an odor from the box," he said, "but a trail that hangs in the air."

"Could you follow it?"

"I believe so."

"Then do so."

"This way," I said to Filidor and gave my sharer control of our body.

I heard my voice say, "Please bring the lumen," and we set off. It was a curious feeling to be a passenger in one's own body, rather than the operator.

"Where are we going?" Filidor said.

"There was a faint odor in the box," my alter ego said over our shoulder, "and a scent trail that leads in this direction."

"Remarkable," said the Archon. "I detect nothing."

"One's senses must be attuned."

We followed the row of shelves further into the darkness. At the first cross aisle we turned left, then after passing several more rows came to a wider alley that separated sections of the collection.

Filidor held the lumen high and we strode boldly on.

"The odor grows stronger," my other self said in his inner voice, while aloud he told Filidor, "I see something ahead."

Moments later we came to the end of the alleyway. It ended in bare rock, planed smooth in time immemorial when these vast chambers had been hewn from the rock of the Devenish Range. At the foot of the wall lay an indistinct bundle of cloth.

"Let me do this," I said, inwardly, and received control of our shared body. I knelt, bidding Filidor bring the lumen closer, while my other self caused our nostrils to flare.

"Very strong here," said the voice in my head.

I produced a telescoping rod and extended it to the heap of fabric. As I prodded and probed, a hand-sized oblong plaque, of green material bearing letters and symbols in black, slid from a fold to the floor. I pulled it toward me, sniffed at it, and, hearing no objection from my inner self, picked it up. Filidor stooped with the light.

"It is the official identification of a sub-curator of the Connaissarium," he said. "And these garments are his uniform."

I placed the plaque on the floor and continued to poke through the apparel. My probe struck something that was neither fabric nor stone floor. I lifted the hem of the uniform's blouse and said, "More light."

The Archon brought the lumen closer and I saw that a pallid, translucent substance was enclosed by the garments.

"What is it?" Filidor said.

I ran my fingers over the stuff and said, "His skin."

I investigated further and ascertained that the body had suffered a complete removal of its musculature, from the base of the skull to the soles of the feet. The internal organs seemed to be in place, and all of the bones, but all other flesh had been removed. Even more surprising, the skin was whole. "Not so much as the smallest wound," I said, "yet every striated muscle is gone."

My examination of the remains and the clothing had shaken loose a fine black powder that was caught in the folds. I rubbed some of its grains between my fingers but could not identify it. I brought a small envelope from an inner pocket and dropped a pinch of the stuff into it and put it away.

I completed my probe of the remains and established that the purloined mouth and chin were not present. "Does the scent trail lead elsewhere?" Filidor asked.

It did not. I asked the Archon if he knew of any hidden portal through which it could have passed. He said he was well acquainted with the hidden passageways in this part of the Connaissarium. "This wall is solid rock," he finished, "with nothing behind it but more of itself."

"This is what we know," I said. "The sub-curator took the object from its box and carried it to this spot. Here it disappeared and at the same time, we may assume, so did much of the sub-curator."

"The question is, how?" said the Archon.

I considered the problem. "That is one of a chain of questions, each linked to the other. If we knew *how* it was done, we would have a good indication as to the kind of person—I use the term loosely—who could do what has been done to this poor fellow." I paused to stroke a reflective eyebrow. "Knowing 'who' might also give us some inkling of 'why,' which I suspect is the most important question of all."

"We already have the 'why,' " said Filidor. "To seize power."

"You assume," I said, "that power is an end in itself."

"For some, it is. I have met such a one."

It does not do to contradict archons. "In this case," I suggested, "I suspect that seizing power may be but a necessary preliminary to wielding it. Which raises the question: wielding it to what end?"

"Just what we need," he said, "another question. We now have a how, a who, and a two-part why."

"Two 'whos,' actually," I said. "There is the 'who' who sent you a warning by mysterious means. As well, we have a fairly large 'what,' as in, 'What is the significance of the missing object?' And I am sure that further questions will arise as we go forward."

"Then let us do so. I do not care to be deluged with questions while simultaneously suffering a drought of answers. Have you at least an outline of a plan?"

"I do," I said. "I will pursue two parallel courses of action. One course will involve researching the missing object and the word associated with it."

"Majestrum?" Filidor said.

I was glad I was in control of our body because again I felt a bolt of white energy pass through me, taking with it my sense of my other self's presence.

I advised the Archon that it might be best not to speak that word aloud, then said, "The other course involves some risk. Therefore I recommend that you prepare to undertake one of those incognito peregrinations that archons are said to indulge in."

"I can assure you the 'esteeming of the balance' is no indulgence," he said, with the air of one who is consulting less than happy memories. "Indeed, they can occasion considerable strain."

"I am sure," I said. "But before you disappear into the populace, I suggest that you do openly what you did this evening in an elision suit."

I felt an inner stir as my alter ego came back to consciousness. Meanwhile, Filidor was saying, "You recommend that the Archon should baldly be seen to consult a discriminator?"

"Not just 'a' discriminator," I said. "You will be advising those who wish you ill that Henghis Hapthorn is taking a hand in the game."

"That might be dangerous for you," the Archon said, "very dangerous."

I made some offhand remark that reduced any potential peril to the status of a small cloud in my otherwise clear sky. A certain air of insouciance is expected of Old Earth's foremost freelance discriminator.

My inner cohabitant was less sanguine. As we retraced our steps through the darkened Connaissarium, he said, "We know the name, but not the thing that the name refers to."

"Indeed," I replied within our shared mentality. "But we shall."

"That's what concerns me," he said. "If the mere map can render me helpless, have you considered what might come if we enter the territory itself?"

"We should give you a name," I said. All this discussion of map and territory, symbol and thing, had started me to thinking as we flew back to my lodgings.

"No," he said.

"Why not?"

"Because names are important."

"But how shall I refer to you?"

"Within the confines of our shared mental space, if you call me 'you' I can be fairly sure that you are referring to me," he said. "Unless you plan to import other tenants."

The prospect sent a slight shudder rattling through the bones of my torso. "I would not know how, and if I did, I should assiduously cultivate amnesia until the knowledge faded and winked out entirely. One extra occupant of my mental parlor is more than enough."

"Very well," he said. "So you need only a pronoun to address me inwardly. Do you plan to advertise my presence to friends and colleagues?"

In truth, I had no friends and few colleagues. Being singular in the art of discrimination tended to make for further solitariness in other avenues of life. A lifelong habit of being right also had the effect of diminishing one's social appeal, especially among those who prefer to keep the bubble of their various illusions a safe distance from a needle-sharp and probing intelligence.

"No, I suppose it would be best to keep you to myself."

"Or 'ourself,' as the case may be."

By now I had arrived at the roof above my quarters. I alighted from the Archon's uninsigniaed cabriol—he had stayed at the palace, making his way back to his suite by the warren of unrecorded passageways that riddle the ancient pile—and let the vehicle find its way home.

"So, to the world in general, I shall remain what I have always been: the part of us that applies insight. And you will be the part that requires it."

"Do you seek to insult me?" I said.

"To what end?"

"I thought to detect a note of amusement at my expense."

"Tell you what," he said, "I'll apply our intuition and see if you're correct."

As this dialogue had proceeded I had descended to my workroom. My eyes fell upon the shelves where stood the collection of books from the library of Bristal Baxandall, whose misapplied spellcasting had been the trigger that led me to where I was tonight: arguing with an element of myself that I was finding increasingly prone to sarcasm.

"Let me have control again," he said. I sensed a sudden excitement in him.

"Why?"

"I feel something."

"Very well."

I relinquished command of our limbs and rode along as he crossed to the bookshelves and took down the thick and tattered tome that had baffled us both. He carried it to the workroom table, where the thud of its landing on the tabletop awoke my integrator. In our absence the creature had returned to slumber, its oddly formed furred body curled around one half of the fruit bowl and its long tail curled around the other half. Now it blinked and sat up, reflexively grooming its fur in a habit that I had yet to grow accustomed to. "Did you require something?" it said.

"Yes," said my alter ego aloud. It was also odd to hear his voice through my own ears. It sounded no different from mine in pitch or cadence, though I wondered if there was not a younger tone. "I'd like you to assist in another attempt to translate this book," he was telling my assistant.

The integrator's ape-cat face took on a thoughtful look and a screen appeared in the air. "Title page," my voice said, opening the book as an image of the page simultaneously appeared on the screen.

To me he said, "I believe we now have a thread to pull."

"Show me."

He indicated a word on the page that was in larger, bolder type than the others. The type was also a deep red, while the other words were in faded black. "I believe this may be the word—more likely a name—that we learned tonight in the Great Connaissarium," he said.

I examined it. It seemed to correspond in the number of its letters to the word that had twice rendered him unconscious. Also the first and last symbols were the same, though the first was larger.

"You may be right," I said.

"After what happened to me on the two occasions when the Archon spoke the name, I now believe that it is marked off by size and color of type so that a person reading this book aloud would be reminded not to utter the syllables, lest he suffer injury or worse."

"Reasonable," I said.

"If my supposition is valid, then we have identified eight letters, one of them in upper and lower case, and the sounds to which they correspond."

"Then I will begin," I said. I reassumed control of our body and told the integrator to display a full page of text. A dark mass of hand-printed manuscript hovered before me. "Now, associate these letters to those symbols," I said, carefully denoting a letter at a time, and taking them in a random order; even spelling them in sequential order might somehow affect my other self. I warned my assistant never to pronounce the word aloud and to avoid even thinking it in whatever mind it had acquired since its transmogrification.

The page on the screen now showed the corresponding letter above each of the eight symbols we had tentatively identified, wherever they appeared on the page. I began to consider the text, employing third-level, then fourth-level consistencies. As I applied the abstruse mathematics that underlay both the order and chaos of the universe, ratios and relationships began to emerge, congruencies clumping together and discrepancies flying to the outer edges of my perception.

"It is an artificial language," I said. Its emerging structures did not show the diversity that always crept into an organically derived tongue. I went to fifth-level consistencies, instructing the integrator to show more text and matching more letters to symbols.

"We are almost there," I said. Above the lines of faded manuscript, whole words, indeed whole sentences, now appeared. "These marks and those, too, are punctuation," I continued. "This squiggle, I believe, signifies that this sentence is a question, and that elliptical shape signifies that the enclosed string of words is a response."

If I wished, I could now read aloud the sounds of the words, without knowing their meaning. I did not do so. I not only recalled what had happened to my companion, but recollected as well the fate of this text's last owner, who had been reading from a grimoire when he mispronounced a phrase in a spell of transformation. Parts of his body had reordered themselves into a hideous arrangement that could not sustain his existence.

"Integrator," I said, "compare the transliterated text to known languages from the Seventeenth Aeon and establish any affinities."

The creature on the table again looked inward for several moments, then said, "There is a better than ninety-eight per cent probability the language is derived from Late Horthalian."

"That is not one of the tongues I command," I said. "Tell us more."

The integrator informed me that Late Horthalian had been spoken among a now almost completely forgotten people who lived, a very long time ago, in an area beyond the Tahmny Polity.

"There is nothing beyond the Tahmny Polity but the vast wasteland of Barran," I said.

"Barran was, of course, not always a desert," the integrator said. "In the Sixteenth and Seventeenth Aeons, it supported a number of civilizations, each succeeding its predecessor, until the process was ended in one catastrophic moment. Details are sketchy from a period so far removed, but a group of savants are said to have attempted to control a powerful force that seeps into our universe from an adjacent plane. Their intent was to gather it into a concentrated form then focus it to achieve some now-unremembered purpose."

"What was this force?" I asked.

"What we call evil, though to the inhabitants of the realm from which it comes it is merely one of the elemental energies of their environment, like wind or thermal currents here."

"I remember this now," I said. "We learned it in the course of our ethical instruction at school. They built some kind of capacitor for interdimensional forces but there was a flaw in either the design or the construction. When they activated it, the device quickly collected all the energy of evil in our world. But instead of storing it for later use, it almost immediately prepared to discharge the power again in one blast."

"Indeed," said my assistant. "Fortunately, someone on the scene managed to adjust the controls so that most of the energy went skyward in a wide conical beam. Although that was not so fortunate for the many inhabitants of our planet's moon, who instantly ceased to exist along with the planetoid they called home."

"Enough," I said. "I recall the story, though it was taught at my school as a moral tale, not a true record of events. The backwash of energy that did not go into the beam flashed outward in a horizontal blast from the device, creating a circular zone of rubble and wreckage that endures to our day. It is no wonder Late Horthalian is not remembered. All of its speakers disappeared in mid-blink."

"Virtually all," said the integrator. "Any who survived because they were away from home no doubt made efforts to distance themselves from their origins. There was much ill feeling among those who had had friends or interests on the moon, and who would have been forthright about expressing their views to any Horthalians they could find. There was a period during which all things Horthalian, especially books that expressed their peculiar approach to life, were deliberately expunged. Scarcely a word of the language now survives."

A thought was tugging at the edge of my mind. "Did not the Archon Filidor have some connection with Barran?"

The integrator's pointy-chinned face took on an expression that in a human would have constituted a shrug. "There were rumors and gossip that he and the previous Archon had passed that way on some informal mission. But, as with all matters concerning the comings and goings of archons, the information is constructively vague."

"Hmm," I said, and sought to put together a pattern that linked Filidor, the mysterious key, Barran, the book, and the object missing from the Terfel Connaissarium, not to mention the deflated subcurator. But nothing came. I offered the question to my intuitive other self, but received a noncommittal response.

"I sense that there is something there," he said after a few moments, "but I cannot see the shape of it."

"We need more information," I said. "Perhaps it will come tomorrow when we receive the Archon's visit in full view of whoever will be watching."

My other self made a wordless sound within our common mental domain. It could not be taken for an expression of gladsome expectation.

Our assistant had a suggestion: perhaps we should search all archives for the Horthalian name we had now identified. I experienced again, as I had in Turgut Therobar's interrogation cell, the peculiar sensation of being internally shoved out of the way while my alter ego seized command of our shared body. "No!" I heard my voice say.

"It is a valid suggestion," I said. "When one has a thread to tug, one tugs."

But I felt real fear emanating from him. "No," he said. "That would be extremely dangerous."

"Discrimination, at the level we practice it," I said, "is not for the timid." But I deferred to his intuition.

CHAPTER SEVEN

After a late breakfast the following morning, I stepped from my lodgings into Shiplien Way and set off on foot toward Drusibal Square where members of the Corps of Buffoons were scheduled to perform at noon. My other self had withdrawn to wherever he went when he was not impinging on my share of our consciousness—"going to sleep and see what comes of it," was how he'd phrased it. My integrator rode atop my left shoulder, its tail draped across the back of my neck to hang down over my right collarbone, and its handlike hind feet gripping the cloth of my coat and the flesh beneath. I told myself to be grateful that in its transformation from device to ape-cat it had acquired a simian's flat nails instead of a feline's sharp claws.

"Is anyone observing us?" I asked.

"There is a young boy in a doorway across the street. He is looking at us with a curious expression."

"It is understandable; we are a curious sight," I said. "When we get to the square, I want you to watch the crowds before, during, and after the Archon's appearance. Sort and categorize faces and postures, and pay particular attention to anyone whose aspect seems out of the ordinary."

"I will," it said.

A question occurred to me. When my assistant had been a device capable of being decanted into a traveling armature that I would wear across my neck and shoulders—the form from which it had been transmogrified into its present condition—I had equipped it with percepts that could see, hear, smell, and taste along a wide range of inputs. "Are your perceptions as varied as they were, and as sharp?" I asked it.

"Yes," it said.

"Demonstrate."

It paused no longer than it would have in its former state, then said, "The yellow house with the green trim across the street and four doors down."

"Yes?" I said. "That is where Malgrave the intercessor resides."

"In the front room on the second floor, a man is whispering endearments to his inamorata. He refers to her as his 'little shnuggles.'"

"And you know this because…"

"His whispers cause a tiny vibration in the window, which my auditory percepts can detect and isolate from all the other ambient sounds of the street."

"Very good."

"Hmm," it went on, "it appears that his 'little shnuggles' may be of artificial construction. I hear the whirring of a small motor and—"

"That is more than I care to know about Malgrave," I said. "And your visual sense?"

"The woman approaching has had her anatomy enhanced. As she moves, parts of her vibrate at different frequencies from the norm."

"That will do," I said as the subject of his remarks—who was quite striking and wearing minimum attire—passed us by. "Is it a coincidence that there is an erotic overtone to both of your examples?" I said. "You haven't also acquired basal instincts along with your new appearance?"

I received no answer. "Integrator?" I said.

"I was attempting to check," it said. "I do not think so."

"I would prefer a more definitive response."

"You did not design me for introspection. Integrators that spend time considering their own natures are liable to become trapped in conundrums."

That was true. "I had not foreseen our present circumstances," I said. "I certainly did not install in you a desire to eat expensive fruit or to sleep away the day. These are now among your chief occupations. I just wonder what other novel qualities you may have acquired."

"If I have acquired a libido," it said, "I will have small hope of exercising it. I am quite sure I am unique, so there is no 'little shnuggles' waiting for me around the corner."

"You may be only temporarily unique, a forerunner. As the universe makes its apparently inevitable transition from rationality to sympathetic association, other integrators may experience the same transformation. What a peculiar world it will be."

The creature shifted on my shoulder. I detected emotion in its movements. "You don't look forward to it?" I said. "You will then fit in far better than I will. I suppose my other self will take the ascendancy and I will fade to a shadow in the back of our—well, by then it will be *his*—mind."

"I would not want to be gendered," it said. "I have observed certain events after you have brought female companions to your lodgings. It is not an edifying sight."

I stopped. "I have always instructed you to disable your percepts when I am entertaining such guests."

"You also instructed me always to maintain a minimal surveillance on all visitors, lest you be surprised. Since your orders conflicted, I erred on the side of caution."

"You should have asked me," I said.

"The first time the question came up, you were heavily engaged. I did not think you would have welcomed an interruption on a point of logic. After that, there was a precedent so I continued the practice."

"You mean, every time I have…you have…?"

"Yes. And may I remind you that you are now standing in a busy thoroughfare speaking to an odd little animal perched on your shoulder? I am pitching my responses so that only you may hear them, so it appears to be a one-sided conversation. Your reputation may suffer."

"Hmm," I said, and walked on. A number of the other pedestrians regarded me quizzically. "I have a reputation for genius," I said, though I lowered my voice. "It can withstand some eccentricities."

"Now you are muttering," it said.

"We will continue the discussion later."

A few minutes walk brought us to Drusibal Square. It was a wide, sunken plaza to which broad flights of stone stairs descended, a pleasant place in fair weather, though moody under an overcast. Today, the old orange sun was giving its declining best and the flagstones were radiating warmth.

The centerpiece of the square was a raised dais on which the Corps of Buffoons would soon perform. Their performances were wildly popular and the square was filling with persons who had come to hear today's program. I took up a position at the top of one flight of stairs, leaning against the wall of a building that abutted the square. From here I could see almost all of the space below me. I cast a practiced eye over the people and saw nothing untoward. I asked my assistant, "Are we attracting any interest that could be called out of the ordinary?"

"A few people have stared at me as we passed, but I detected no signs of undue regard. Those who recognized you did not show any more than the usual degree of interest. No one is pointedly *not* looking at you."

"Very well. Let us see what happens when the Archon arrives." I folded my arms and let my eyes rove the square.

"That boy has followed us," my integrator said.

"Where is he?"

"On that ornamental planter to your right, behind the refoliate plant."

I looked and saw a small face between the leaves and branches of the spreading plant. I was not used to dealing with children—they are not commonly encountered in Olkney—and could only place the boy's age as somewhere in the indeterminate period when infancy is well past but adolescence has not yet launched. A pair of clear eyes, startlingly pale in color, looked back at me with intelligence.

"He is probably interested in you," I told my assistant. "Children have an affinity for small animals. Still, give him a closer look."

"I have studied him closely," said the integrator, a moment later. "He shows no signs of stress. His pupil dilation, skin heat signature, and breathing rate are all within normal limits. He carries no weapons or surveillance devices."

"Forget the child," I said. "Watch the rest of the crowd."

The square was well filled now, and the performance would soon begin. Then, in the moment when the spectators began to look about for the Buffoons' entrance, a clarion tone sounded from overhead. An official aircar of the Archonate, in deep black with jade green fairings and sponsons, descended sedately on obviators tuned to a whisper. A rear hatch opened and three senior officials, gowned and gaitered in accordance with their lofty ranks, stepped out. Two of them withdrew an ornate, cushioned chair from the volante's cargo hold and positioned it on the flagstones facing the dais. The third waited beside a closed door at the vehicle's front; when the seat was in place, this official tapped lightly on the door. It opened silently and the Archon Filidor I stepped into the warm, reddish sunlight. Smiling, nodding to the crowd, he advanced to the chair and sat. There was no trace of a bump upon his forehead.

All eyes save mine and my assistant's followed him. We watched the watchers. Because of his youthful reputation as a wastrel, this Archon had not been greatly popular when he had first ascended to the preeminence. It was now generally held that he had matured, that he had even performed vital services for Old Earth, though as was always the case in matters touching the Archonate, no one knew exactly, or even approximately, what those services might have been.

Still, as I watched the people in Drusibal Square, there could be no doubt that most of them smiled upon his entrance, and those who did not looked to be members of that broad section of the Olkney citizenry who cared not a whit what an Archon might, or might not, do.

"I see nothing amiss," I said to my assistant.

"Nor I," it said.

The crowd had now returned its attention to the dais as the troupe of Buffoons made its entrance. They marched across the square in a gaily dressed column of pairs, a dozen or so strong, some waving streamers and balloons strung on the end of wands, while others tooted and tweedled on instruments that produced comical skirls of notes. The throng opened a way for them, offering sincere applause and ironic salutations to the "auxiliary players" who marched glumly in the middle of the column.

I had not noted who was to join the troupe for today's hijinkery, but was not surprised to see that one of the temporary players was Dod Melanto, the notorious thief. He scowled and glared at the audience, some of whom had doubtless been his victims, while a few others were probably his competitors. But the single-piece garment he wore, yellow with prominent red dots, and with a large number of miniature motilators built into its structure, offered him no choice but to lift his knees high and swing his arms energetically all the way to the dais.

It was Archonate policy to confine most convicted malefactors to a contemplarium, where they would encounter a simple way of life interrupted by plentiful opportunities to practice wholesome meditative exercises. But some classes of the nefarious, such as career criminals who had not benefited from previous stays at a contemplarium, were handed over to the Corps of Buffoons. They were then fitted with coercion suits and brought out for public display in performances of ribald skits in which they played the butt of every joke.

One other kind of ill-doer who featured occasionally in the Corps's antics was the magnate or aristocrat who had assumed that wealth and social rank were a perfect insulator against retribution for serious crimes. I was interested to see that one such culprit marched today beside Dod Melanto: Lord Cariott, the young scion of one of Olkney's most illustrious clans. He attempted to maintain his dignity by elevating his nose and ignoring the jeers and fleers that accompanied his passage. But his efforts were undercut by the coercion suit that required him to waddle with knees bent and feet splayed while both hands beat a happy-slappy tattoo on his protruding buttocks, which a cut-away had left bare.

"Anything out of the ordinary?" I asked my integrator.

"Nothing," it said, "except that I can no longer see the child."

"He is short and the crowd comprises adults," I said. "I am more interested in anyone who is glaring at the Archon instead of enjoying the Corps's antics."

"There is one person who fits the category."

"Who? Where?"

"Lord Cariott."

I sighed. "An integrator with a sense of humor is rarely welcomed. Remain vigilant."

The troupe had now arrived at the dais. They took flamboyant bows and executed some farcical capers, then launched into their program. The Corps's skits were always ribald classics, familiar to all, though the crowd enjoyed noting certain embellishments of detail. Thus when they staged *The Peeper Stuck in the Hedge,* the audience cheered when the female Buffoon playing the outraged victim strapped on an enormous apparatus and began to apply it vigorously to Melanto's upturned rump. And for the next skit, featuring Cariott in the venerable *Your Turn in the Barrel,* the Corps gave the barrel two bung holes and pantomimed their use with vigorous glee. The performance delighted everyone in the square except, of course, its star. The fact that the scene took place under the eyes of the Archon must surely have added vinegar to the abrasion of the lordling's tender pride.

"Anything?" I asked the integrator.

"Nothing, except that now I see the boy again. He is standing beside you."

I looked down into an upturned gaze of calm intelligence. "Hello," I said.

"Hello," was the reply, the voice young but the tone mature.

"I'm quite busy at the moment," I said.

"All right."

"Shouldn't you be in the care of someone?"

Thought condensed the boyish features for a moment. "I don't think so," he said.

A howl of glee went up from the crowd and I looked back to the dais. The troupe was enacting *The Race among the Pumpkins* and Melanto and Cariott were the steeds. The jockeys were not as immensely corpulent as they appeared—they had puffed up their costumes with air—but the goads they were applying to their mounts' sensitive parts appeared to deliver quite real shocks. Filidor was laughing with genuine amusement.

I scanned the square and found nothing amiss.

"The intermission has begun," said my integrator.

The sequence of events that the Archon and I had arranged took place. Filidor stretched in his chair, looked about, and saw me. He spoke to one of his panjandrums, who responded with appropriate formal gestures of respect from an underling to an Archon in public view, then bustled over to where I stood. More formal postures and phrases ensued, all conveying the message that the Archon desired to speak with Henghis Hapthorn.

I acceded and he led me back to the chair, the avenue that had opened to permit the official's passage closing behind us. I spoke and acted as a citizen of Olkney should when meeting an Archon, and Filidor replied in the time-honored ritual. These formalities took some considerable time, enough for every voice in the square to become silent, so that every ear was able to hear the Archon say, "I would be grateful if you would undertake a service for me."

"It would be my great privilege," I assured him.

"It is a matter of grave concern," he went on.

"I will do my utmost," I said.

He signaled his appreciation and drew from within his shirt a small scroll wrapped in a ribbon of green and black, and sealed with his personal sigil. "This document will explain all," he said.

I took the scroll and placed it within an inner pocket. He indicated that I might withdraw. As I did so, executing a few more formalities on the way, I heard a buzz of conversation ripple through the crowd as those who had been closer informed those who had not of what had transpired.

I returned to my earlier vantage point and again scanned the crowd. Hawkers and pasty-men were moving through the throng offering refreshments before the next act. By tradition, this would be the main piece in the performance. Roustabouts were erecting scaffolding and hanging scenery that suggested that the troupe intended to perform the always popular romp, *The Flatulent Twins*. It promised to be a memorable day for both Melanto and Cariott as well as for all who knew them.

"Still nothing," I said. If anyone had especially marked my encounter with the Archon, no one was betraying anything more than the honest curiosity that would occur to the most innocent of observers.

"Nothing new from me," said the integrator.

"Very well," I said. I spoke to the child. "Do you wish to speak with me?"

He again regarded me with a solemn mien. "I think so."

"Then let us step beyond the crowd. Please follow."

Unmistakable sounds were now coming from the dais as the twins made their entrance, each irruption raising laughter from the audience. I made my way through the roaring throng until I reached a clear space at the edge of the square, where a restaurant had placed chairs and tables on the flagstones. I seated myself and looked back at the way I had come.

The boy did not emerge from the crowd. After a few moments I stood upon my chair, then upon the table. Neither I nor my integrator saw any sign of him. "Peculiar," I said. "Do you have an image of him?" When my assistant assured me it did, I decided that we would return to the workroom and conduct a full analysis of his appearance and voice.

I walked back to my lodgings, both I and my integrator taking close note to see if we were followed. Nothing appeared to be out of the ordinary. At my doorstep stood the boy from Drusibal Square. He turned to me with the same grave stare and again said, "Hello."

I returned the greeting and said, "How can I help you?"

He looked thoughtful for a moment, then said, "I don't know."

"Do you need help?"

"I don't know." He looked inward for a moment, then continued, "What kind of help could you give me?"

"I am Henghis Hapthorn, the discriminator."

I saw that my identity meant nothing to him. I was taken aback. My exploits, at least those that are not conducted under a veil of secrecy, are frequently reported in popular journals. Many young people are avid followers of my doings. "You do not know who I am?" I said.

"No. Should I?"

"I am considered the foremost discriminator of our time."

I could see the child digesting that information, then a question formed in his face. "What does a discriminator do?"

"He unravels conundrums, picks apart puzzles, uncovers enigmas. A great discriminator solves great mysteries."

A look of earnestness lit the child's eyes. "Ah," he said. "Then I think I have a mystery for you to solve."

"I am sure you do," I said. "State it for me."

"Very well," he said. "Who am I, and why am I here?"

"That," I began, "is the first—"

But before I could finish the sentence, he disappeared.

"Integrator," I said. "Did you record the boy's disappearance?"

"Yes." it said.

"We will enter and study it."

In my workroom, I regarded the child's image on my assistant's screen. It was frozen just at the moment before he disappeared. "Now go forward," I said, "at your slowest rate of refreshment."

The integrator complied, but the result was not satisfactory. In one frame, the child was there; in the next, he was not.

"The percepts built into my traveling form were not capable of as fine a calibration as those that were included in my at-home version," it said. "You sacrificed detail for compactness and to reduce weight."

The armature into which I used to decant my assistant's essence, to wear around my neck while traveling, had somehow become the basis for its present form. I had used only the components I had expected I would need for communication and observation in the field. If I had ever gone out anticipating a need to study an event that took place at the very limits of perception, I would have taken specialized instruments such as the ones that were installed in my workroom.

"At least we are sure he was not merely a projected image," I said.

"Yes. I recorded more than visual data. His body emitted heat. His breath was that of a young person in good health." The integrator edged over to the fruit bowl and took up a plum as it spoke. "As well, he displaced air by suddenly disappearing, but I cannot analyze the vortex for an indication of where he went. It happened too quickly."

"It cannot be helped," I said. My mind circled around the mystery but again was unable to get a grip. I decided to step back from the issues of who he was, where he came from, and how he arrived and went; instead, I considered the context of his sudden appearance. My sharer and I had been making progress in the matter of translating the book. We had made a connection between the purloined object named in the Great Connaissarium's catalog and the destruction of the ancient Late Horthalian speakers, then found a connection, however nebulous, between that event and the Archon. We'd had a sense that a pattern was emerging, then when we went out to see if public contact with Filidor would generate more information, the boy had suddenly come into our lives.

I required insight, so I woke up my inner companion. "What if he were a distraction, meant to pull us away from a course of discrimination that would lead to the plotters?"

My alter ego said, "Then he would have offered us a false clue."

"Unless," I said, "he himself is the false clue."

"That would be a subtle stratagem."

"There is every reason to assume that we face a subtle enemy."

There was a silence inside my head until I said, "What do you think?"

"I think that the boy is connected to the case."

"If he were a blind alley, salted with just enough mystery to lure us in, he would still be connected," I said. "It would merely be an unuseful connection."

"I do not think so," said my other self.

"When *I* say, 'think,'" I said, "I refer to a process of logical extrapolation from known facts or, at least, from verifiable suppositions. What does the word mean when *you* use it?"

"I suppose it means that I 'sense,' or 'feel,' the shape of things, the way an imagist knows that a particular curve is right or wrong, or that light and dark are juxtaposed in a balanced way."

That seemed to me to be a shaky foundation on which to erect an edifice of thought. I did not say so, but he was adept at making inferences. He said, "My 'sensing' and 'feeling' have always served us well before."

"They were always preceded by my rigorous analysis of a problem. It was only after I had delineated the facts that I would ask you to apply intuition to them."

"Not always," he said. "I was not a conscious faculty then, so I have no clear memory, but my sense of things is that I often played a role in helping you to decide which facts were more salient than others."

"My memory is unaffected," I said. "You were not part of my analytical apparatus until I sought you ought."

"I do not think so."

"You do not think at all," I said. "You only feel."

"There is no need for you to be defensive."

"I am not being defensive," I said. "I am seeking to put our affairs in order."

"By 'putting our affairs in order' you imply a hierarchical arrangement. You wish to be master in our shared house."

He was right, both about what I was implying and about what I was being. One of the drawbacks to arguing with a person who has full access to one's emotions is that it is difficult to conceal one's agenda.

"Very well," I said, "I am being defensive because I think that I am under attack."

"Have you evidence of any attack, or do you just 'feel' that way?"

"Now who is being defensive?" I said. He made no reply and I continued, "Here is how I see it: I used to be the master of my inner realm, now I am forced to share it. That, I believe, constitutes an invasion, and invasion constitutes an attack."

"I did not invade you," he said. "Indeed, I am not here through any volition of my own, but because of circumstances that resulted from decisions taken by you."

"So the victim of invasion is to blame for the incursion? I wonder how many conquerors have advanced that argument through the eons?"

"Invasion? Victim? Conqueror?" he said. "These are hard words. Remember that you apply them to a part of yourself."

"It is not difficult to remember. I am reminded of it several times a day."

"I do not think it is good for us to argue like this. Indeed, it approximates a definition of madness."

"It is not the argument that is the problem," I said, "but the situation that gives rise to it."

"We should put the issue aside and just try to get along."

"Then my silence becomes consent, while you gradually take a larger role. And steadily I dwindle."

"What else can we do?" he said. "We are but a microcosmic forerunner in a process that will gather speed and breadth until it is universal."

And so we had come to the nub of it. The world into which I fit so perfectly was drawing to a close. The age that would succeed it would be ideal for my intuitive other self. He was on the ascendant, I was in decline. The inevitability of the process did not make it any the more palatable.

"I do not wish to dwindle," I said, "nor to fade."

"Then don't," he said. "Instead of contending with me, fight against the forces that threaten you."

He offered me an image of a windblown Henghis Hapthorn standing resolute in the face of an encroaching storm, raising a solitary torch against a darkening sky.

"You mock me?"

"Look again," he said. "Is that a caricature? Or is it an accurate, even affectionate, representation?"

It was not a caricature. "Do you seriously think," I said, "that one man can hold back the onrush of a new age?"

"I do not know. But if there is one man who can do it, that man would be Henghis Hapthorn."

"Are you seeking to manipulate me?"

"Are you becoming paranoid?"

"If I succeed in holding back the new dispensation, I will prevent you from coming into your own."

I felt him give the mental equivalent of a shrug. "I am already here on time that should be yours. It is nothing less than good manners for me to be patient."

"I have never been much good at patience," I said. "I prefer to get on with things."

"Then let us get on with solving the Archon's problem. Perhaps it will give us some ideas for holding back the onset of sympathetic association."

It was a rational proposal. But rationality was my contribution to the mix. It bothered me that the suggestion had come from him rather than from me. I wondered if he was indeed seeking to manipulate me, echoing to me my own way of thinking, just as someone might be trying to steer us onto a false course with the mysterious boy's sudden popping into and out of view.

It was late in the evening. We had returned to work, though I, at least, was not making much progress. My other self had withdrawn to mull the shape of things and I was examining every element of the known facts in relation to each and all of the others. My mind, however, would not fix itself to the task but kept veering toward the suggestion he had made: that I should devote myself to preventing—or at least holding off—the onset of the new age. It was folly, of course; no one could stop the Great Wheel from turning. Yet it was a grand folly, one of those great, futile struggles that somehow confer dignity upon those who conduct them. As the essayist Blithe Porlock had put it: *Life is a hopeless rear guard action against an overwhelming foe; still, how can we not admire those who battle on regardless?*

The notion had a curious appeal. I had long since admitted to myself that my very success in the profession of discrimination had brought my life to a point of crisis. A case that could fully seize my capabilities had become so rare an event that I had grown dangerously bored. Then came the incident precipitated by Bristal Baxandall and his greedy assistant, Vashtun Errible, that had brought me into contact with my puzzle-loving demonic colleague, and for a while I had been fully engaged. Though the demon departed, I found myself sharing my life with an intuitive other and the fruit-fancying familiar that had been my integrator. Although the problem out of which they had emerged was certainly significant, I had felt not so much engaged by it as harassed.

Then the Archon had arrived on my doorstep, presenting me with a deadly serious case that looked, at this stage, to be connected to the same impending cosmic cataclysm that had disturbed my domestic arrangements. Filidor's troubles were precisely the kind of professional problem that Henghis Hapthorn ought to fling himself at with unalloyed delight. Instead, I was brooding over whether I or my intuition ought to have precedence over the other, and wondering if I could trust myself.

"Not good," I said aloud. My integrator twitched and grunted but did not awaken from sleep. For a moment I was glad of its new incarnation because the thought had occurred, not for the first time, that the division of my psyche might not be a result of magic and the impending great change, but a simple bout of madness. The fact that other people saw my fur-covered integrator argued against any need for me to present myself for treatment.

The who's-there interrupted my thoughts by announcing: "Colonel-Investigator Brustram Warhanny seeks admittance."

"Wake up," I told my integrator, poking it with two fingers. It did so, connected with the door monitor, and showed me an image of Warhanny standing in the street. He was wearing his most official face, a mask of purest dispassion, which told me he was vitally interested in whatever matter had brought him to my lodgings.

"Admit him," I said, and a few moments later he was standing in my workroom, subjecting it to as thorough an examination as he could manage without actually prying open cupboards or peeking under the furniture. His eye soon fell upon an object on the table: the sealed scroll that the Archon had ostentatiously handed to me in Drusibal Square.

"Did you wish to consult me?" I asked. "Is there a case?"

He rocked back and forth upon heels and soles, his hands clasped behind his back. The length and prominence of his nose made his pale colored eyes appear to be sunk in pits and they regarded me with an expression he sought to disguise.

"He's worried," said my inner self.

"I know," I thought back. "The question is, what is he worried about?"

"I happened to be passing," Warhanny said.

"And yet you did not continue, but stopped at my door."

He made a noncommittal noise and continued to look around the room. I saw his gaze fall once again upon the small scroll that I had left on the table.

"That appears to be the Archon's personal seal," he said.

"Does it?"

"Someone mentioned that you had spoken with the Archon today."

"Someone?" I said. Warhanny and I had a substantial history behind us. He had often resented my participation in cases that had also drawn his attention, and he resented even more the instances when I had solved puzzles that had baffled him and his fellow scroots. At the best of times, we were like two animals of different but related species who found themselves sharing the same habitat; at the worst, we were direct competitors for the same prey. We rarely cooperated.

"Would that be the scroll the Archon handed you?" he said, the pendulous blob that was his nose pointing in the object's direction.

"It would," I said.

He rocked back and forth again. "Peculiar that you haven't opened it."

"Is it?"

He stopped rocking and swung his large head toward me. "Yes, it is. If I received a document from the Archon, I would break the seal and read it immediately."

"Clearly we are animated by different philosophies. You rush headlong at life while I proceed at a dignified pace."

"Then I will be true to my character and pose a direct question: what business is there between you and the Archon?"

"I think that the Archon, if he wished you to know, would have seen to it that you were informed."

I was deliberately provoking him. The Colonel-Investigator possessed a legendary temper—or perhaps it was better said that sometimes his temper possessed him—and I wanted to see what might come of stoking his fires. In the past he had sometimes, in the heat of an intemperate outburst, let slip useful information.

But not this time. I saw him rein in an impulse, then raise and lower his shoulders in a theatrical gesture of unconcern. He looked about the workroom, his eyes falling upon my integrator. "What manner of beast is that?" he said.

"An unmannerly kind," I said.

He extended a hand toward its head. "Does it bite?"

"I don't know, but in a moment we may find out."

He withdrew the hand and let his wandering gaze fall upon Baxandall's book that had been left splayed open on the table while my other self mulled and I analyzed. "What's this?" he said.

"A book."

"In what language?" He spun the tome around and scanned the visible pages, then flipped to the title page and examined the flyleaf. "What does it say?"

"That's what I am endeavoring to discover."

Having got me used to answering his questions, he now proceeded from idle inquiry to direct interrogation, as recommended in the Bureau of Scrutiny handbook. "What's this got to do with Filidor?"

I imitated his earlier shrug. "Perhaps you should ask him," I said.

"He is, after all, your employer."

He batted it straight back to me. "And yours?"

"A freelance discriminator does not discuss such matters without the expressed consent of the client."

Victory flashed in his eyes. "Then he *is* your client."

"I did not say that."

He picked up the scroll, rolled it through his fingers, and held it up to peer through it as if it were a telescope, then tossed it casually back onto the table. It landed on its fragile seal, which cracked.

"Oh," he said with calculated innocence, "I've broken it." He reached for it again. "Perhaps it can be mended."

Somehow in his concern for the object, the scroll unrolled in his hands and he could not help but read what was written there. I watched as several emotions—surprise, consternation, irritation—chased each other across his face before he regained control and presented me with both the scroll and an expression of untroubled impassivity.

I took the document and read the few words it contained: *To all who read this, the discriminator Henghis Hapthorn is acting for me in a matter of grave importance. All officers and associates of the Archonate, without distinction of rank or precedence, will render him the same assistance they would afford me.* It was signed by Filidor and a seal with the Archon's personal sigil was attached.

"Hmm," I said, "I presume that would apply to a Colonel-Investigator of the Bureau of Scrutiny."

Behind the impassivity another Brustram Warhanny regarded me with a distinct lack of affection. "What would you like me to do?" he said.

"If anything occurs to me I will let you know."

His right foot tapped the floor several times but the rest of him remained in the grip of a rigid control. He pulled at his nose, so reflexive a habit that I had sometimes wondered if the constant tugging had had anything to do with the organ's exaggerated length. He looked away and his eyes went to the book again. A finger traced something on the flyleaf. "What are these names?" he said.

I recollected no names and came around the table to see what he was referring to. Indeed, a number of names were handwritten in faint green ink on the inside of the book's front cover: *Phaladrine*

Baudrel, Omris Shevannagar, App Imrici, Hilarion Falan-Falan, Terris Botch, Chav Hemister, and *Oblon Hammis.*

"Do you recognize any of these?" Warhanny said.

"I do not." None of the names was familiar to me, though I thought I had seen the handwriting before.

"That is curious," Warhanny said, and I sensed in his tone that we had just experienced a subtle shifting of the ground between us, though I did not know why.

"Why is it curious?"

"This one," he said, placing a fingertip under the name *Botch.*

"What of it?"

"It means nothing to you?"

I said, "It does not." Because it didn't.

"Today," he said, "while you were conferring with the Archon before all the world in Drusibal Square, I found myself following two sets of footsteps through the dust of the nether reaches of Terfel's Connaissarium. One set, I believe, was left by a distinctive footwear often worn by the Archon Filidor. The other is as yet unidentified."

He glanced down, as if measuring by eye the size of my feet.

"The two trails led to a blank wall," he continued, "at the foot of which lay what appeared to be the abandoned garments of a sub-curator, and an unidentified powder. Inside the clothes the fellow had carelessly left his skin and bones, though not his flesh. Nor his eyes."

"That is curious," I said.

"The area in which he was found was not connected with his duties. He was a cataloger of intaglioed gems and his workplace was several levels above where he was found. He should not have been there."

"If being there led to his being fleshless and dead," I said, "I can only concur."

"Even more curious," he said, fixing me with that intrusive stare that all scroots must master before they are allowed to leave the Academy, "is the fact that the sub-curator's name was Botch."

I looked again at the list of names. "Terris Botch?" I said.

Warhanny's eyes became guarded. "No."

"Then it seems we have a coincidence."

"Does it?"

"Doesn't it?"

We could have played the game all night, but he switched tacks. "I don't care for murder," he said.

"I'm not fond of it myself," I told him.

Now he went for the direct approach. "What do you know of the murder of Glam Botch?"

"Nothing," I said. The statement was technically correct. I had not seen the killing and knew neither the killer's identity nor the motive for the crime. I did know that I could not give Warhanny what little information I had, because although I doubted he was involved in any palace intrigue—he was too much the dogged scroot for such pastimes—some of his associates might be waist deep in plots and schemes. The Bureau of Scrutiny was thickly populated by careerists, each with an agenda to pursue.

He gave me his stare again and I returned him a look of polite passivity. He was using another scroot interrogator's technique: letting a silence extend until the interviewee feels compelled to break it. I, however, was comfortable with silences and let this one go on until he finally snorted and turned to leave.

"I'll be back," he said.

"I'll look forward to it," I said.

When he was gone, I said to my assistant, "How about some punge?"

"Nothing," it replied, meaning that in response to my coded instruction it had scanned the premises for any small items that the Colonel-Investigator might have left behind.

I spoke to my inner companion, "Were you listening to my conversation with Warhanny?"

"No," he said, "I was clumping."

His answer disturbed me slightly. I was not sure I liked the idea of half of my mind being engaged in activities I had never heard of. "And what is clumping?" I said.

"An intuitive exercise. I throw a scattering of facts before me then look to see which ones attract each other and which repel."

"By what rules?" I said.

"If I had rules for it, it wouldn't be intuitive. It would be analytical, and I would be you."

"Have you always done this, this clumping?"

"I suppose I must have," he said. "It seems to be a familiar exercise."

Which meant that through all the years that I had prided myself on the precision of my intellect, the portion of it that had operated out of sight, in the rear pastures of my mind, had been playing an entirely different game. It reminded me of a story I had once come across in the *Olkney Implicator*. It was about a man who lived in a well-made house that had stood for generations, but who noticed a draft of cold air in one of the downstairs rooms. It grew worse, and he traced it to where the wooden floor met the base of an inside wall. Curious, he brought tools and pulled up the floorboards. When he shone a beam of light into the space beneath, he discovered a yawning cavern. The house had been built over an ancient mineshaft that had been capped with a plug of rubble. A great many years passed before the erection of the house and the existence of the mine had long been forgotten. Some time after, the rubble cap had gradually subsided then fallen in; thereafter, the occupant had been walking around on what he thought was a floor set upon a solid foundation, when in reality only the thickness of a board lay between his tranquil life and a terrifying plunge into darkness and death.

I did not show these thoughts to my other self but he was aware of my moods. "I am as I have always been," he said. "It is only that now I deal with you consciously instead of as an unfocused attribute."

"I know," I said. "That is what makes you strange."

"I cannot be too strange. I am an aspect of you."

"So you keep reminding me. And yet…"

"A man who is afraid of himself needs no enemies," he quoted.

"It is peculiar to be…"—I chose the next words carefully—"at close quarters with someone who is both familiar and yet very different."

"You were going to say 'trapped,' weren't you?"

"I considered the word," I said, "and rejected it."

"Still, it popped into your mind."

"And was thrust out again."

He was silent but I knew he was brooding. Finally, he said, "We have to trust each other."

"I wish to trust you."

"But you do not, not entirely."

"It may be just a matter of getting used to the new way."

"I am what I always was," he said.

I decided it was time to face the issue. "Are you?" I said. "How do you know? How do you know that, in being brought to an early reification, you were not also changed in the process?"

"If I were different, I would know. I would feel it."

"You answered that question very quickly."

"Are you accusing me of being glib?"

"I would have given it some thought," I said.

"Because you are analytical. I am intuitive."

"What difference does that make?"

"For an associative mind, sometimes the conclusion comes before the consideration," he said.

"That makes no sense."

"And yet it is how it works. And always did before you knew me as an independent entity."

Again, I sensed the strangeness of this other me. It brought an unsettling emotion.

He gave the inner equivalent of a sigh. "You have to trust me."

"I wish to," I said again, "but I foresee a problem."

I showed him what was in my mind: that the day would come when he was on the ascendant and I was sliding toward the shadows, when he might become impatient at waiting out the last little time and might contrive to send me into the night before I was ready to go.

"Now we are balanced," I said, "but you will grow steadily stronger, and I weaker. Will you be so patient then?"

"I believe I will," he said. "Our characters are the same."

"Are they?" I said. "Or what about this possibility?" I showed him a scenario in which we once more came into contact with the kind of magical influences that had brought him into awareness. "What if that offered an opportunity for you to reach out and take full control, stripping me of my personhood and making of me what you once were—a nameless dweller in a mental back room?"

"I am not impatient. I accept that I am here prematurely," he said. "But what if the situation was reversed? What if you could step into an energy flux that would send me back to the far corridors of our mind?"

It was a possibility I had entertained when he was asleep. Now I did not deny that I would be tempted.

"I see," he said. "You do not trust me because you know that I should not trust you."

"There is a difference," I said. "Unlike you, I have known what it is like to be master of my own realm."

"Or so it seemed to you at the time."

"Indeed, it did. Can I be faulted for wanting what I always had, an arrangement that unfailingly met my needs? After all, I did not ask for you to be here ahead of your time."

"Nor did I."

We were both silent for a moment. I was wondering if we had come to a breach that would widen. It was not a happy prospect.

"At least," he said, "you can no longer complain of being bored."

"I suppose that is true."

He was silent again, then said, "You are right that there is a difference: you had an independence that was taken from you without your consent; in that sense, you were wronged. My situation is that I will inevitably win my independence as the Wheel turns, but I have already been given more scope than I had a right to expect.

"So it is only fair that you should feel nostalgia and resentment over what you have lost, and thus be tempted to put things back the way they were. For me to be similarly tempted, I would have to be motivated by impatience and greed."

"I have occasionally been impatient," I said. "So that must be part of your make-up, too."

"You have frequently been impatient," he corrected me, "but never greedy. Besides, I share your well-developed sense of justice. Therefore, I do not feel that I would prematurely push you into a hole just to make things a little more convenient for me."

I could feel his sentiments. He was not attempting to deceive me. He truly believed that he would be content to patiently share our common milieu until the universe caught up with our untimely advance into the new age. Besides, who knew when we would encounter another burst of magic as powerful as the field that had enveloped us at Turgut Therobar's estate?

"Very well," I said. "We are partners. And there is work to do." I showed him the names written in faint green ink on the flyleaf of the ancient book.

"I know that hand," he said.

"Whose is it?"

"Baxandall's."

"Why have we not seen these names before?"

"Because we were not allowed to," he said.

"How not? By what means?"

"By magic, of course. A spell of concealment. There are two of them in his other books."

"Are there spells to confuse the text? Is that why we cannot read it?"

"Possibly," he said, "though such spells would be beyond Baxandall's competence."

"But perhaps not by whoever produced the book."

The point raised a question. Clearly, back when the book had been created, magic had reigned supreme. A spell cast upon the book—I still found it hard to believe I was thinking in such terms—would have had power. After the Wheel turned and rationalism reasserted itself, surely the magic would have had less effect. But now we were nearing the cusp again. Did that mean that a spell that had once been powerful but had lost its potency during the interregnum would now begin to regain its former vigor?

I handed the question to my alter ego and felt him turning it over. Then he said, "I don't know. But it would be safer to assume that old spells could come back."

It was an unpleasant thought: ancient curses and maledictions that had been lying dormant for an aeon would reassume their old maleficent powers. Pity the innocent who, like the man whose house was built over emptiness, stepped unknowingly into one.

"I think I will be glad to be gone when this new world fully comes upon us," I said. "I doubt I would be fit for it."

"Be that as it may," my other self said, "we now have more threads for you to tug at. Let us see what this list of names portends."

"Yes," I said, "we may have a night's work ahead of us."

I awoke my assistant and said, "How about some punge?"

It blinked and yawned and said, "Still nothing."

CHAPTER EIGHT

The hired aircar took us south and west, out over the breadth of Mornedy Sound and the scattered islets and keys of the New Shore, then straight on across the unbroken gray-green of the ocean. The senescent sun was just above the eastern horizon, seeming to struggle to lift itself as our vehicle climbed higher into the thin air of the upper atmosphere.

"It will be some time before we reach Mandoval," I said. "I will sleep for a while."

"As will I," said my other self.

It had been a long night. The names on the flyleaf of Baxandall's book had led us up and down many of the most obscure byways and side passages of Old Earth's long, long story. Little had come of the effort: the names Phaladrine Baudrel, Hilarion Falan-Falan, Chav Hemister, and Omris Shevannagar returned nothing that could be even remotely related to our case, other than a confirmation that all were of Horthalian origin and that all were as thoroughly extinct as virtually every other aspect of that destroyed nation. No one had borne those names since the cataclysmic destruction of the culture that had spawned them.

App Imrici produced some scattered citations, most of them making reference to a book, now long since lost, that he was alleged to have authored. Neither the title nor the subject of the work was recorded, but the implications of the ancient comments we found were that it had dealt with magic. I wondered if it might be the very tome we now struggled to decipher.

"No," said my other self. At least, that was his feeling.

"How can you be sure?" I said.

"How do you know where your ear is when you can't see it?" he replied.

I took the question as rhetorical and let the matter slide.

Beyond App Imrici's alleged book, there was not much else to remember him by. He had left no other traces of his existence, nor any known descendants. There was a faint connection to the island of Mandoval, or Abhazar as it had been known during the Seventeenth Aeon: the Imrici surname had originated there, though it had not survived to be known among the present population.

The name of Hammis had proved, however, to be more hardy. Little was remembered of an Oblon Hammis of Horthalia, beyond a passing reference in an obscure treatise on a lost science known as copromantia. That apparently had been the art of predicting the future based upon studying the excrement of various species after flinging it against a whitewashed wall. The footnote in which we found the mention warned, however, that the translation of anything from Late Horthalian was prone to error, and that the dung may instead have been flung not by, but directly at, the seer. In either case, there was no doubt that there had been Hammises on Mandoval ever since, and it was alleged that a Vhobald Hammis now resided in a hermit's hut high up in the island's mountainous spine.

The name Terris Botch had returned no flood of useful information, other than the fact that Glam Botch, the sub-curator who had left his partially filled skin in Terfel's Connaissarium, was likely descended from a Horthalian ancestor named Terris, who first appeared in the records at about the time of the destruction of that doomed land. There had been Botches down through all the ages since, most of them residents of the Olkney Peninsula and adjacent counties. Quite a number of them had been antiquarians, and several had risen to the title of Chief Curator of various archons' connaissariums. Glam Botch himself might have someday held that revered post, had he not ended up lying on a stone floor with key parts of his person missing.

It would have been interesting, perhaps even instructive, to have asked Glam Botch about Baxandall's book. But wherever he was—and lacking bones and a dermal covering, chances were not good that he was actually anywhere—it was doubtful that he could make much of a useful answer. My inner companion had therefore decided that we should fly to Mandoval, put a question or two to Vhobald Hammis, and see what came of it.

Ordinarily, we would have contacted the man through the connectivity. There were two reasons why we were not doing so, and were instead crossing the ocean to see the fellow in the flesh. One reason was that we did not yet wish to share our information with Brustram Warhanny, who would surely listen in on any use we now made of the grid. My information-retrieval matrix could tickle bits of knowledge out of the collective, undetected by scroot snooping. But point-to-point communication between Henghis Hapthorn and any person on Old Earth would right now be conducted under the ear of the Colonel-Investigator. Had we alerted Warhanny, the chances were good that we would be arriving at Mandoval only to find that a Bureau of Scrutiny squad in a high-speed volante had already got there before us to collect our person of interest. The other reason was that Vhobald Hammis was not attached to the connectivity.

That was a startling discovery. I had only ever come across one person who was not connected to the universe: Bristal Baxandall, from whose library all of our leads had come. I did not need my alter ego's well-developed intuition to know that here was no coincidence.

Now, as we overflew the ocean at a height that turned the great waves below into mere wrinkles, I settled myself in the aircar's reclining seat and quieted my mind. I felt my inner companion slip away into sleep. Before employing the exercise that would send me after him, I said to my assistant, "Are we still being followed?"

"Yes," it said, "and at the same distance."

As I had expected, Warhanny was on the case.

Mandoval was a long, broad crescent of black rock rising out of an otherwise empty sea. It was what was left of the eastern rim of a huge volcanic crater that had built up from the seabed only to collapse in upon itself, all of this cataclysmic upping and downing having happened back in some remote age. On the inner side of the demilune, at about the midpoint, a good-sized fishing town of the same name as the island sat above a shingle of gray rock and sand eroded away from the dark crags that rose toward the west. On the other side of the island, the cracked and fluted cliffs fell sheer from the broken heights above, providing nesting sites for massed flocks of seabirds of several species. The birds, in turn, provided a living for families of eggers, hardy types who boated around from the settled inner rim of the island to ascend the rugged rock faces on one-person obviators, looting the nests and selling the proceeds of their thievery to chefs on the mainland. Egging and fishing were the island's only occupations, practiced by all except for a few odd individuals who dwelt in contemplative solitude in tiny alpine valleys that striated the divisions between the high ridges.

The last known reference to Vhobald Hammis was a record of a dispute with a neighbor over some unspecified complaint. The issue had not been resolved when the neighbor tumbled to an early death from a narrow cliff's edge path that led from the victim's house to an area where he liked to forage for mosses. A subsequent investigation had noted that the path passed close by the rock-walled bothy where Hammis made his abode, but no definitive conclusions could be drawn.

My assistant awakened me when the aircar was a short flight from Mandoval Town. I left my alter ego to sleep on and bade the car set down near the settlement's administrative nexus, a low, two-roomed building built of the same dark rock as the island, and went in. As I did so, I noted from the corner of my eye a Bureau of Scrutiny volante sliding down to land near the harbor.

There were no scroots stationed on Mandoval; most places on Old Earth had no need for an official supervisory presence, the world being made up of entrenched social units in which iron-bound custom and mere habit rule the inhabitants' behavior. The administrative center's only occupant was a small and tidy man in the green uniform of the Inspectorate who looked up from a breakfast of eggs and toasted bread with a look of surprise.

His expression changed to puzzlement when I told him I was interested in locating a Mandovalian named Bulbul Skavar.

"You are too late," he said. "He is dead, has been dead these last seven years."

"Indeed?" I said.

"He fell from a cliff."

"Indeed?" I said again then applied the scroot technique of letting the silence grow. Warhanny would have been gratified to see it working effectively, because the Inspectorate officer pressed on, telling me that Skavar had been walking between his home and a small dell where he gathered lichens valued for their hallucinogenic properties—"He was a devotee of the Prism," he said in an aside—and appeared to have slipped on the wet rock.

"He fell but a short distance to a broad ledge," he said, "but somehow his tumble dislodged several substantial boulders, which crashed down upon him in a statistically unlikely but quite deadly manner."

"Was he under the influence of his sacraments at the time?" I asked.

"That was the peculiar part," the man confided. "He was on his way to gather the goods when he fell. But perhaps his eagerness to behold the effulgence caused him to misstep."

"Perhaps," I said. "Still, it is a shame. I have come all this way. Was there anyone who knew him?"

The mild eyes flicked down and to left and right before he looked at me again. "There was a neighbor," he said, "one Vhobald Hammis."

I waited to hear more, but when nothing was immediately forthcoming, I said, "And?"

"For all anyone cares, he may still be up there," the inspector said. "Skavar's brethren came and removed his body, but no one took possession of the hut."

"I take it this Hammis was not a comfortable neighbor?"

"Not unless your concept of comfort embraces fleering contempt, unmerited vituperation, and teeth-grinding glares whenever you pass him by."

"A good one to avoid," I said.

"And that is what everyone has done ever since."

I showed a regretful expression. "It is a shame my trip has been wasted," I said. "I will return to Olkney. But first, I will find breakfast. I hear your island is renowned for its eggs. Where might I sample some of them, best prepared."

The inspector gave the matter the grave consideration that Mandovalians applied to the subject of avian ova. "Ang Porhock bought a double basket of prime gripple eggs, fresh from the cliffs, yesterday evening. This is the first brooding season of the year, and they came from the rock formation known as the Grand Flute, so they will be of the finest, especially as they were collected by the Tobler clan. Rosh Tobler hews to the old standards."

He then turned to the matter of preparation. "Your timing is perfect," he told me. "The morning rush has come and gone, leaving Porhock the leisure to do something spectacular if he believes he has a customer who can understand his idiom." He gave me a weighing look and continued: "Some say that Porhock can be a little heavy on the sage and scallions, but gripples are a strong egg when they're in their prime and can bear the freight. So if you crave robust textures and unabashed flavor, you'll not find a better omelet."

I assured him that my palate was up to the challenge and received directions to an eatery with a blue roof and lace curtains.

"Wonderful," I said, and turned to go. I paused at the door and looked back at him. "In a moment, a Colonel-Investigator of the Bureau of Scrutiny will appear and ask you to tell him everything you have told me."

The officer showed alarm. "Are you a malefactor?" he asked. "I took you for a member of the Prism."

"I am neither," I said. "It's just that my friend the scroot has formed an attachment to me and follows me wherever I go. Please humor him and answer his every question."

"I will."

"Though I don't know if he cares for gripple eggs," I said, and left.

I spotted Porhock's establishment from the steps of the administrative center and set off for it at a brisk pace, first stopping to collect my assistant from the aircar. "Watch for Warhanny," I said, and by the time I reached the broad slate stairs leading up to Porhock's porch, my integrator was informing me that the scroot was entering the place I had just left. I went inside and was greeted by a dining room filled with a rich mélange of odors but empty of patrons. A portly man with large, liquid eyes and well-developed jowls looked through a serving hatch at me from his station in the kitchen.

I said, "Are you the Ang Porhock whose gripple-egg omelets are talked of in Olkney?"

"They are?" he said, and quickly came through the swinging door. "I mean, I am he."

"I have come to see what all the fuss is about," I told him. "I hope

I am in season."

"You are," he said. He wiped his hands on his apron then showed me to a table. I set my assistant on an adjacent chair where it curled up and promptly fell asleep.

"So they talk of my omelets in Olkney?"

"In some circles," I said. I was confident the topic had been broached by someone at some time.

"Who, exactly, speaks?"

"It is difficult to single out particular speakers," I said. I looked around the empty room as if anticipating eavesdroppers and lowered my voice. "Though I can tell you I was speaking with the Archon himself just yesterday."

I heard a rush of indrawn breath. "The Archon? He spoke of my omelets?"

"I may have said too much," I told him, and looked to left and right again, then I quietly withdrew Filidor's scroll from an inner pocket and opened it enough for him to read the words and see the sigil.

The man went pale, and looked into a corner of the room as if all his hopes and dreams might be stored there and needed checking on. When he turned his face back to me it was still pale, yet lit from within by the kind of holy determination that must illuminate saints and seers when they finally behold the threshold of enlightenment.

"I will," he said, his voice soft but filled with certitude, "prepare you an omelet that is worth speaking about." And now his voice climbed in authority while he raised one finger toward the ceiling, saying, "And speak of it, you will!"

"I shall, indeed," I said, and as he marched toward the kitchen with a stride that foretold that wonders were about to ensue, I turned and looked out the window. Brustram Warhanny was exiting the administrative center and giving the restaurant a pensive stare, as if deciding whether or not to essay another confrontational interrogation. I saw him reject the idea. He put his hands into the pockets of his uniform pants and, placing on his face the expression of a man who has nothing much on his mind, sauntered down the street toward the harbor where his volante awaited.

But as he passed the aircar I had hired to bring me to Mandoval, one hand emerged to casually slide along the underside of one of the vehicle's sponsors. Then he pursed his lips in a whistler's moue and again enacted the saunter, trundling down to the harbor without a rearward glance.

Ang Porhock was beside my table, laying out condiments and cutlery, and filling my cup from a carafe of hot punge. I thanked him and said, "Are you by any chance a devotee of the Prism?"

"Not I," he said. "I apprehend the world through tongue and nose. My eyes are merely for navigation."

"Indeed," I said, "I asked only because a fellow I knew came here to pursue the vision. Bulbul Skavar was his name."

"Ah," said the chef, "he who fell from the cliff some years back."

"The very one. I recall his telling me he had an annoying neighbor."

"I recall the same."

"Has the fellow been seen of late?"

"Not by me." A chime sang from not far away and its brief note caused Porhock to exhibit the air of a man whose destiny awaits beyond a swinging door. "Ahah!" he said, and made for the kitchen.

Moments later, I was presented with the finest omelet I have ever seen, smelled, or tasted. Had I been a true aficionado of the egg, I might have swooned. As it was, I was moved to expressions of joy.

"I will," I said, between mouthfuls, "tell Xanthoulian that he has at least an equal."

Porhock clasped his hands at the waist, bent toward me, and whispered, "And the Archon?"

I looked him squarely in the eye. "I will recommend your omelet," I said. And, indeed, should the subject of eggs ever arise when I was in conversation with Filidor, I meant to make good on my promise.

The chef had lapsed into a reverie. I interrupted it to ask, "How would one ascend to Skavar's place? To pay one's respects."

He glanced out the window to where my vehicle was parked. "In one's aircar," he said.

"And if not that way, then otherwise?"

"There is a funicular ascender that leads to a meadow, beyond which rises a course of steps," he said. "After that, it is a matter of following the right-hand path—carefully, the drop becomes sheer."

He waived all thought of payment and I departed under his smiles to return to my aircar, my assistant revived and on my shoulder.

"What did Warhanny place on the vehicle?" I asked it.

It blinked, then said, "A standard Bureau tracking module."

"Very good. Take the aircar aloft, and fly around to the east side of the island, then cruise past the cliffs at slow speed and varying heights, as if we were looking for something. At midafternoon, meet me in the alpine meadow at the top of the funicular ascender."

"I will," it said.

I opened the hatch and placed him inside, then bent as if to enter myself. Instead, I stooped and scuttled away, concealing myself behind a nearby vehicle. My assistant sealed the opening and a moment later the aircar rose and went away at an unhurried speed toward the north, climbing as it did so. I peeked over the cowling of the vehicle that hid me and saw Warhanny's volante, hovering far out over the horizon, move off in a parallel course.

The alpine meadow was gently sloped, the ensuing stairs more steeply angled, but I enjoyed the climb and the cool refreshment of the upper air. I took the path that led between outcrops of the ubiquitous dark volcanic rock, occasional scatterings of obsidian glistening in the noon sun. After a few minutes walk, the rock formations on my right dwindled and now I followed a walkway so narrow that two pedestrians would have had to exercise care in passing each other, especially he who would not have a solid cliff wall to brush against but would be treading the edge of a precipice.

Then the cliff wall on my left broke into a ravine that sloped upward. I stopped and studied the narrow space, seeing a small hut built of fractured rock and roofed with flat stones. I approached, ducked under the low lintel, and entered. Inside was some furniture so rudimentary as to argue that Bulbul Skavar was not one of the handier sort of Prism devotees for whom the sect's requirement to build one's own accommodations lacked the element of challenge.

In the middle of the floor, however, was the customary "center of perspection," in this case merely a pile of stones topped by a broad and naturally polished piece of volcanic glass. In the center of the obsidian rested another slab of the dark rock that the island was made of, but to this fragment someone had applied abrasives, grinding out a hollow in its top. I placed my finger in the cavity and found a few grains of grit which, when I examined them closely, proved to be of a black, obdurate substance I had encountered once before.

I went out again and returned to the path. Beyond the mouth of the ravine, the cliff rose sheer on my left again, and the drop to my right grew even deeper. I continued along the narrow ledge until I came to a second break in the cliff. Here I saw another rude dwelling that seemed, at the distance from which I inspected it, to be as deserted as Skavar's. I edged to my right to peer over the cliff, and saw a ledge not far below, with some sizable rocks strewn about. Whatever stains the Prism devotee's death had entailed had long since weathered away, but I had no doubt this was the place where the man had died.

To my left, a waist-high boulder squatted near the mouth of the ravine. It was a perfect place for someone to lurk in hiding, ready to rush out and push a passerby over and out into the air. All around the ambush site were rocks that had broken off from higher ground and tumbled down the slope. Many of them were just the right size and weight to be used if the victim did not fall all the way to the jagged rocks far below, but landed on a ledge where a bombardment with skull-and-bone crushers would be needed to finish the job.

Assessing the perfection of the place for sneak attack, I approached the waist-high rock carefully, to make sure no one crouched behind it. I found no lurker. I raised my eyes to regard the stone bothy that stood a little way upslope, its single window gaping without a cover and its rough timber door hanging askew from one hinge. It looked untenanted. But, because I always tended to err on the side of survival when dealing with murderers, I called out twice before approaching.

Hearing no answer, I made my way up to the window and peeked in. The space confined by the walls was empty except for more rough furniture. There was no center of perspection though there was a bundle of rags near the door. I stepped around to the portal and took another look within. From this angle, the place was no less empty.

I knelt to examine the rags on the floor and found that they were powdered in the same dark grit that had coated the uniform of sub-curator Glam Botch. I rubbed the stuff between my fingertips, thinking that the sensation ought to have some significance, though I knew not what it might be. I wiped my hands on the rags and made another discovery: although Vhobald Hammis had departed this place, leaving a dried and desiccated corpse behind, he had somehow contrived to take with him all of his bones except those of his skull. His eye sockets were empty.

I woke up my other self as the aircar slid through the high, thin air back toward Olkney. "I require insight," I said.

"State the facts," he answered.

"Glam Botch left a mostly empty skin in clothes that contained black grit," I said. "Vhobald Hammis left a boneless corpse. Both were missing their eyes. Absent from the Great Connaissarium was a black object of unknown material and provenance said to resemble a sculptured mouth and chin. Absent from Hammis's neighbor's hut was the object that should have been resting on his center of perspection."

I paused, then said, "Hammis was a devotee of the Prism. The central act of that spiritual discipline involves ingesting substances that emancipate the psyche followed by prolonged staring at a representation of a human eye. In time, the starer finds himself looking back at himself through the other. Most Prismites paint, or carve, or mold, or weave the eye at which they gaze. A minority believe that an object found ready-made serves the purpose better, it being an eye that the universe has 'brought to bear upon them.' Or so they say."

"All known facts, so far," my other self said.

"Both Botch's and Hammis's clothing contained a fine black grit, a sample of which I have brought with me from the latter's hut. I expect it to be the same material as that found on Botch's uniform."

"May I inspect it?" my sharer said.

I brought out the sample and let him have control of my hand and our mutual sensorium. He peered at the powder, then put it to our nose. I felt our nostrils flare. "It has the same odor that I followed to find Botch's remains," he said, "though much fainter."

"From the condition of the clothing, it may have been left in the open air for some time, whereas Botch was freshly killed. No doubt the scent has faded."

"I concur," he said.

"Now comes the speculation," I said. "The object missing from Hammis's hut was a representation of an eye. The object missing from the Connaissarium was the representation of a mouth and chin. I believe that they were originally two parts of one sculpture, and that the black grit is what remains of them after they have been atomized by some horrendous force.

"Further, I said, "the sculpture is connected to Baxandall's book, because both victims were descendants of the people whose names Baxandall inscribed on the flyleaf."

"All of this is mere extrapolation. What is the insight that you require?"

"How are all of these things connected?"

He was silent for a moment, then he said, "I don't know. I do sense a strong linkage, but I also sense an association with the Chalivire business—the song and the Derogation and all that."

"That makes no sense," I said. "How can they be related?"

"Everything is connected to everything else," he said.

"We have discussed that. It is a truism, but a truism so broad as to be useless," I said.

I heard a touch of anger in the voice inside my head. "Not in this case. The connection is real and it is significant."

"Delineate it," I said.

"I cannot. Not yet. I recommend that you trust me, as you always did before I emerged."

I was practiced at the art of concealing my reactions from others. I had not yet mastered the ability to conceal them from myself. He could not avoid my skepticism.

"You do not trust me," he said.

I corrected him. "To be precise, I do not know if I can rely on your judgment."

"We always worked well together."

"It was different."

"Only because you were you and I was a mere attribute. Now I am more. Does my existence threaten you?"

I gave an honest answer. There was no point in dissembling. "I am not sure about you. You have come into your existence so very recently. As an attribute, you were well tried; as a person, you lack experience, as if you were a child. I must ask myself, 'Does he have depth? Are his judgments sound?'"

"As sound as they ever were," he said.

"How would we know that?"

"I know it because I sense it. It is how I function."

"But I function differently. I require steps built upon other steps, down to a sure footing."

"I don't deal in steps," he said. "I leap steps in great bounds but I arrive on a sure footing."

"How do you know it is a sure footing?"

"I know it is sure because it is where I have arrived."

We were back to his bizarre reversal of cause and effect. "I find that hard to accept."

"You never used to."

I changed the metaphor. "Before," I said, "your intuition was the wheel that often drove us forward. But my analysis was the hard surface that gave us traction."

"And now you worry that I am spinning out of control."

"Yes."

"And it is not enough for me to say that my sense of things is that I have all the traction I need?"

"No."

"Then how do we resolve this?"

"We solve the case," I said. "We perform the discrimination then work backward from the result. It will then be plain to see what was connected and what was not."

"In other words," he said, "you will be able to trust me once you no longer need to trust me."

"Are we at an impasse?"

I felt a welling of desperation in him. "We must not be at odds," he said. "Though I cannot draw you a diagram, I know that this matter is more than a case. It is vitally important to our survival."

He was presenting me with an unhappy choice. If he was right, I was in peril but could not deduce from what direction the danger would come, because cause and effect could not help me. If he was wrong, I was trapped in our cranium with a person who was going mad.

"It was a long climb and a long walk back," I said aloud. "I will sleep until we reach home." I composed myself and closed my eyes, then opened them to tell my integrator to wake me if Warhanny decided to break cover and make contact. I did not want my other self in charge of our shared facilities if the Colonel-Investigator had to be dealt with.

I could tell that my other self was aware of my motivation. I felt his frustrated resentment. It was a while before I could fall asleep.

Warhanny did not make contact. When we entered the space above Olkney, I consulted the rear imager and saw that the scroot was continuing what the Bureau of Scrutiny called a level-two surveillance: he followed and watched. I alighted from the aircar in the street outside my lodgings and dismissed it.

"Has anyone called?" I asked the who's-there.

"No," it said.

I entered, my assistant perched sleepily on my shoulder, and ascended to my workroom. Baxandall's book was spread open on my worktable, but that was not what first drew my attention. Instead, it was the boy who stood there, turning pages with the air of one who is able to read the words he is looking at.

"How did you get in here?" I said.

He turned and regarded me placidly. "I don't know," he said. "Where is 'here'?"

"My workroom," I said.

"And who are you?"

I told him. He looked as if he had heard the name before but it seemed to strike no great spark. He continued to gaze at me with bland equanimity. "And who am I?" he said.

"I do not know," I said. "Shall we find out? I'm considered quite good at finding things out."

He turned back to the book, his hand leisurely flipping over another page. "Is this a dream?" he said.

"Does it feel like a dream?"

"Yes."

"Then whose dream is it?"

He looked back to me again, and his young face took on the aspect of one who can just almost, but not quite, remember a forgotten word. His brows knit in concentration, then he disappeared.

"Integrator," I said, "was the new surveillance system functioning just now?"

"It was."

"Then replay the child's disappearance at a very slow speed."

My assistant put up a screen and I saw an image of the boy standing in my workroom. "Freeze," I said, "and enlarge."

I examined the image, saw nothing out of the ordinary and told the integrator to continue. I watched closely as the event took place, then had the device replay it once more even more slowly.

"Note," I said, "that the disappearance is not instantaneous."

"Indeed," said my assistant, "nor it is preceded by a loss of integrity, as if we were seeing a projected simulacrum lose its cohesion and devolve into fragments."

"But it was not a projection, or not any kind of projection we know of."

The integrator had moved over to the fruit bowl and was picking out a large purple berry. "No, it was not. I have a full sensory record of the child's physical presence, and even of the movement of air that took place when he was withdrawn."

The integrator had used the right word for what we had witnessed. The boy had not "winked out," nor had he become a disorganized array of light-motes, nor had he rotated while being rendered two-dimensional, the usual ways by which projected forms ended. He had instead somehow lost substance, had paled almost to transparency while shrinking to a minuscule size.

"Enlarge further and replay to the very moment of disappearance." I had to wait while my assistant chewed and swallowed, then the images appeared again. They confirmed my earlier impression. "At the very last instant, he ceased to shrink. Instead, he was pulled backward through some tiny aperture," I said.

"Which immediately closed, leaving no trace," my assistant said, wiping a trace of purple juice from its chin whiskers.

I considered the facts and came to a tentative conclusion. "We are dealing with interdimensional movement," I said. "I speculate that the boy was projected into our continuum from another. Or perhaps he came from some more cogent reality so that even if he was merely a simulacrum, he appeared in our realm to have all the sensory presence of a three-dimensional being."

"Very well," said my assistant. "But why?"

"I do not know. He seemed to think he was in a dream. That leads to a hypothesis: he was indeed the dream of an entity from some contingent dimension, whose reality is so more intense than ours that its dreams become living, breathing persons when they are projected into our realm."

"That seems far-fetched."

"Compared to some of the realities I have lately had to encompass, it seems not so far a fetch."

My assistant looked down at his rounded, fur-covered belly. "Others might say they have had to stretch themselves even further," it said.

I declined to comment on this aside, and returned to the main discussion. "Far-fetched or not, the dream theory is the only explanation I can so far achieve that accounts for the facts," I said. "He has now come twice, so why not a third time? Perhaps when he next appears he will be able to tell us something useful, such as where he came from and how he got here."

"He was unable to tell us even who he was," the integrator said. "It is doubtful that on subsequent visits he will be able to shed much light on the mechanics of his movements."

"Very well, perhaps, through him, we might contact whoever is dreaming him and learn something."

"Even more doubtful."

"I prefer to be optimistic," I said.

"I have had experience of the consequences of your optimism. It is why I now have an urge to groom myself and eat fruit."

"So long as there is no shortage of fruit, I see no reason for you to complain. Consider my situation: I have to share my inner space with an entity who sometimes lacks sympathy. And who may not be 'all there' in some important senses of the phrase."

"It is more aggravating when one's difficulties are of another's making," the integrator said.

"Is it? I find other people's flaws easier to bear than my own."

"Perhaps that is because you have spent most of your years unaware that you had any."

I suggested that the integrator stand down while I pondered the puzzle. It recurled itself around the fruit bowl. I paced the floor and applied my intellect to what I now knew, but the facts were too disparate and scattered. I could not connect them into any coherent pattern. I indulged in a vain wish that my former associate, the being from an adjacent dimension whose discovery had led to the transformation of my integrator and my own inner circumstances, was available. I even went to the object that hung on my workroom wall, resembling a framed picture in which colors and shapes continuously shifted, and performed the actions that used to summon him. But the moving display did not take on the pattern that I had learned to identify as a sign of his presence, and I doubted that it ever would.

We had both enjoyed our pastime of setting each other difficult puzzles to solve, but it had turned out that his motives for visiting me had been mixed. Ours was the only dimension in which symbol and object were not one and the same. To the denizens of his continuum, the contemplation of a form that was divorced from essence was salaciously titillating, and he had observed our form-filled universe like a schoolboy at a peep show. I was now convinced that he had been, in fact, a juvenile of his race and that some elder authority had at last intervened to pull him away from an unhealthy fascination with us.

I asked my inner companion for his views but received no answer. I wondered if he had gone to sleep or if he was shunning me. I called a loud "Hello!" and soon felt him with me. "Are you sulking?" I said.

"No," he said.

"Yes, you are."

"That would be childish," he said. "I am not a child."

"Very well," I said, "then talk to me. You must be interested in the fact that we have again come upon our mysterious young visitor. And he was reading your book."

"It is not *my* book," he said. "It is *our* book."

"I spoke casually," I said. "To be precise: our book, your obsession."

"It is important to both of us. Why can't you accept that?"

"Demonstrate how it is important, and I will."

"We have had this discussion already," he said.

"Then let us move on to discuss something where we share common ground," I said. I consciously calmed myself, and was happy to note that he was doing the same.

"Very well," he said. "What do you propose?"

We had the elements of a pattern in the Botch and Hammis cases—the dust and the missing body parts. I suggested that we seek to find more incidences that would extend the pattern into a broader picture. He agreed and we woke up the integrator and set it to the task.

"Find any instances of persons found dead while coated in dust and missing substantial parts of their bodies," I told my assistant. "Especially their eyes."

"How far back shall I look?" it asked.

"As far back as you can go," I said.

"Offworld, too?"

I suspected an offworld search would yield no fruit, but the question seemed to strike a note with my other self, so I said, "Yes."

It was a lengthy search. For several seconds, my assistant sat motionless on the table, its lambent eyes slowly blinking. Then it refocused on our surroundings and said, "I have several dozen instances that broadly fit the parameters."

"Display them, ranked in reverse order of likelihood," I said.

A screen appeared and began to fill with summaries of the information on each incident. Most of the first couple of dozen entries were easily dismissible: a motivated culprit was to hand, the dust associated with the corpse was not of a mysterious provenance, the missing body part turned up in someone's possession. As we scrolled downward, yet moved further up the ladder of probability, I marked several of the cases for further investigation. When we had run through the complete list, we had eight dusty partial corpses to consider.

"More detail," I instructed my assistant, "specifically whether the case was investigated and cleared by authorities."

New information appeared on the screen and I used it to dispense with three of the cases in which the Bureau of Scrutiny or its counterparts had identified a perpetrator. A fourth, that had happened on the foundational world of Shuft in the remote past, involved the disappearance of the victim's head; local investigators had pinned the crime on an itinerant day laborer, and although the head had not been found, had convicted the accused on circumstantial evidence.

"What do you think of that one?" I asked my intuitive self.

"It is connected," he said.

I conceded the possibility and moved on to the other four cases. Three had happened on Old Earth; one on a secondary world named Olderon. "The pattern is obvious," I said, when I had reviewed the facts of each incident. "In every case, a different body part was missing: Botch lost his musculature from the head down, Hammis his bones. The man on Shuft lost his head. All lost their eyes."

I considered the other cases. In one, the corpse had been found skinless from the neck down. Another had been missing his internal organs, except for the heart and the brain. The remaining two appeared to make up for those overlooked organs: one had lost his heart, the other the contents of his cranium. In no case were wounds or incisions evident, and in every case the black grit was strewn around.

"Apply insight," I said to my other self, "and take note of the fact that two of the victims are descendants of the seven persons named in the book."

"It is all connected," he said.

"How?"

"Not yet. Have our assistant investigate the backgrounds of the victims for connections to the seven names."

I did so. "That will take time," the integrator said. "I must consult records that have been archived for immensely long periods. It will mean waking some integrators that have been dormant for aeons. When they realize how much time has rolled on, the news can come as a shock. And sometimes, after they have divulged their information, they resist being put back into suspension."

"We will wait," I said. "In the meantime, I will analyze the grit."

I went to a cupboard, extracted an apparatus, and set it upon the table. I blew some dust out of its hopper, then poured in the sample of grit that I had taken from the muscleless corpse in the Connaissarium. The device busied itself for a few moments then told me that the powder was of unknown origin and composition.

"Speculate," I said.

"Possibly not of this continuum," it said. "Created by a physics with radically different fundamentals."

At my inner companion's urging, I said, "Created by magic?"

"There is no such thing as magic," it said.

I ignored the laughter I heard from the other side of my mental parlor and cleaned out the hopper, then placed within it the grit I had acquired from Hammis's boneless corpse. "Same substance," was the verdict.

"Consult the connectivity," I said, "and ascertain whether this substance has been encountered before."

Its connection to the grid was not as ample as my assistant's but it was soon back with a response. The substance had been found at the scenes of a number of unexplained deaths; the details of the cases coincided with those incidences of missing body parts that I had already been examining.

"So there it is," I told my alter ego. "Definite coherence among the circumstances. Seven cases of mysterious deaths, the corpses missing various bits and pieces, and the powder always present."

"But look at the dates," my other self replied. "Some of them occurred whole geological eras ago."

"Indeed," I said, "which also argues for an extra-dimensional factor. Whoever is doing this may be operating from a continuum whose internal time bears no relation to that of our universe. His collecting of all these eyes and different body parts—I assume they are being taken deliberately—has taken aeons in our realm, but may be the work of a moderately busy afternoon in his."

I considered the matter of the unknown perpetrator's motive and could not find any other interpretation than the obvious. "The question is: why is he putting together all the parts required to build a composite human being, with plenty of spare eyes?"

The apparatus interrupted my internal conversation to say, "There is one other location where the substance is found, in trace amounts."

"Not connected to unexplained deaths?" I said.

"Connected to a great many deaths, though the explanation for them is known."

"What is this location?"

"The devastated zone at the center of Barran."

CHAPTER NINE

"We are missing something," my other self said. It was later in the evening. I had not gone out for dinner but had made do with what was available from the culinary suite. Fortunately, in its quest to establish the boundaries of its appetite, my assistant had lately ordered in a wide variety of foodstuffs, most of them of gourmet quality.

I applied a savory paste to some herbed crackers. "We are missing quite a few things," I said, "beginning with who, moving on to how, and definitely passing through why. Right now, all we have is what, where, and when, and I'm not all that confident that we have properly nailed down all of what."

"No," he said, "beyond that."

"Explain."

While I chewed, he said, "I feel that there is another aspect to all of this that we are not focusing on. It's as if I know it's there, as if I keep catching sight of it from the corner of my eye, but when I try to look at it directly, nothing can be seen."

I had no such sense. Hearing about this alleged phenomenon from an aspect of myself about which I had some doubts did not comfort me.

"I am not insane," he said.

"Very well," I said, selecting a miniature spiced sausage from a container. "Let us analyze your 'feeling.' We have an invisible 'something'—as if someone was wearing an elision suit. How do we detect an invisible object?"

An image appeared in my mind, of an invisible man walking through rain, leaving a hole where his silhouette ought to be visible. "Exactly," I said. "Now let us look for the hole rather than for the unseeable object that makes it."

I chewed and considered the case, all the known facts and circumstances. There were plenty of things we did not yet know, but I could not detect a gap that ought to be filled.

"It has to do with Chalivire," my other self said.

"I don't see how the matters are connected," I said.

"Nor do I see the shape of it. But I see the gap where the shape must be."

"You are becoming obscure. Show me how the pieces fit."

"I cannot," he said, "but I know it to be so."

"And I do not. You must demonstrate it to me."

"That is not how things work for me."

I took another sausage. They were quite good and my assistant did not care for them. "It is how they work for me."

He said, "You must trust my judgment."

"You must demonstrate that I can trust it."

"We have circled around to the same spot. What can we do?"

"We can have another of these excellent sausages then sleep. In the morning, our assistant may have found new leads."

In the morning, the integrator was still engaged. I went out to Xanthoulian's for breakfast, then returned to find that the research was complete. "Did it go well?" I said.

My assistant explained that it had encountered an obstacle along the way. "I became involved with a newly awakened integrator that would not divulge the archival information I sought unless I reciprocated by giving it a full connection to the grid."

"That would not seem advisable," I said. "Antique integrators, revived and set loose, can cause disruptions." I recalled a case from when I was a student: one such system had got back onto the connectivity and had pestered literally millions of persons and billions of integrators with incessant questions, nor would it disconnect until its curiosity was satisfied. It was like being confined to a room with a toddler who had just discovered the joy of interrogating the cosmos.

"The matter occupied me through most of the night," my assistant said. "My eyes feel peculiar, as if they have been rubbed with abrasives."

"Sleep cures the condition," I said. "But before you do that, what are the results of your inquiries?"

"The odds that the unfortunates who had lost body parts and became covered in dust were descended from the persons named in the flyleaf of Baxandall's book," it said, "are almost certain."

"They changed their names," I said.

"Indeed, most of the few Horthalians who survived the cataclysm did so, even Terris Botch and Oblon Hammis. Though in the case of those two, their descendants resumed the family names after a few generations, once the resentment had cooled."

"Well done," I said. "Now connect me with Lord Afre's house and hire an aircar for the day."

The creature on my table rubbed its sore eyes with fur-backed fingers, showed me a pink-lined mouth agape in a skull-splitting yawn, and said, "Then may I sleep?"

"You may."

At Lord Afre's I alighted at the same ordinair and was met by the same majordomo who equipped me with the same identifying collar and pendant. He escorted me along a hallway newly redecorated in rosestone paneling offset by medallions of red brillion. We arrived at an east-facing room, warmed by the light of the old orange sun, where Chalivire was completing a late breakfast. I made the appropriate salutes and struck the expected poses; she reciprocated in kind.

I studied her face and posture. She had the aura of one who had come through a crisis of despair, had looked destruction in the face, yet had survived to recoup and regather her energies. It was to be expected; Old Earth's upper tier of aristocrats had not held on to rank and privilege through all these millennia by dint of mere chance and social inertia. If one scratched a Chalivire, one could expect to be scratched back—if evisceration could be called a category of scratching.

Formalities over, I came to the nub. "I would like to interview a guest of your house."

Her face took on a wary stillness. "We have no guests at the moment," she said.

"I use the term very loosely," I said. "This man would have come from Great Gallowan. You may not know that your father sent me to find him so that you could extend your…"—I sought for a word—"hospitality."

I saw that my mentioning of her father had cleared up something she had wondered about. But she was still disinclined to grant me access to Hobart Lascalliot. "I'm not yet done with him," she said.

"I understand," I said. "And I have no wish to take him away before you have completed your… dealings. I do require a few minutes conversation with him, however, just to clear up a small matter."

I might as well have been trying to borrow a half-dead rodent from a house cat. Chalivire said she could not see how she could accommodate me.

I had not wanted to take the approach I now took, since any mention of the name I was about to utter in this woman's hearing might provoke one of the frenzied rages that were as much a hallmark of the Afre character as their matchless pride. I struck an attitude of deference and said, "I am engaged on a discrimination for the Archon Filidor."

It was as if Chalivire's face was trying on a succession of emotions, some of them very stark, but I was relieved to see her settle on guarded self-interest. "The Archon?" she said.

She looked sharply at me and for a moment I thought I might have triggered something, but then her gaze turned inward and I could see her mind working—something that was never too difficult with Chalivire—and she said, "Very well."

She summoned a footman who took me to a part of the great house that was seldom used. We stopped beside a blank wall and he bade me turn my back and close my eyes. When he said it was time to open them again, I turned around to see an opening where the wall had been. A set of stone stairs led down into darkness from which issued a draft of cold and unhealthy air. The servant handed me a lumen and gave me to understand that he was not permitted to descend.

The stairs went down a considerable depth. At the bottom I found a hallway walled, floored, and ceilinged in damp stone, with stout metal doors set at intervals. From one of these, as I neared it carrying the lumen, came a thin and wavering moan. I unlocked the door and went in to find a naked Hobart Lascalliot attached to a complicated apparatus that was clearly intended to afford him no comfort.

He flinched at my entrance, then realized that I was not whom he had expected. A moment later I saw recognition come. He tried to say something, but was prevented by the utensil that constrained his tongue. I stepped forward and removed it and he said, "I have seen you before."

"Yes, you have."

"Have you come to abuse me?"

"No."

A tiny hope lit deep within his eyes. "To deliver me?"

"Not that, either."

The light died. "Then what?"

"To ask you some questions."

He snorted. "Chalivire comes to ask me questions, though somehow the answers never seem to satisfy her."

"She has her own perspective," I said, "as you should surely understand."

He made a wordless sound, then said, "Why should I help you?"

"Because then I may be able to help you."

"And if you could, why would you?"

"Why wouldn't I?" I said. "I hold no animus against you. I sought you and found you because that is what I do."

"Do you promise?" he said.

"I do."

"And is your promise worth anything?"

"It is."

The expression on his face told me that Lascalliot had reached a point in his life when he was inclined to doubt that there was much good in anyone. But then he adopted the resignation that comes with the realization that one has nothing to lose.

"Can you at least loosen the clamps?" he said. "My bones are beginning to bend."

But I did not know how to operate the apparatus safely. "I might break you," I said.

He sighed. "At least give me a drink," he said.

That I could do, and when he was as refreshed as it was within my power to offer, I said, "Tell me about the Derogation. How did the concept arise?"

"I would have thought it was obvious," he said. "On Great Gallowan, especially in the Thoon, we do not care for 'look-at-me's' and superordinates. They come for the fishing and the mountain sports and offend us with their conceitful airs and boisterousness. One day, Toop Zherev proposed that we establish a society dedicated to the reduction of vanity through the instrument of public humiliation. We would seek out truly egregious examples of overweening pride and set them on a course toward a humorous comeuppance. The universe would be slightly improved."

I plucked the operative word from his answer. "Zherev made this proposal, you said. Do you remember if he said how he came by the concept?"

"I do," he said. "The idea originated with his friend, Osk Rievor."

"And this Osk Rievor," I said, "did you know him as well? Can you describe him to me?"

"Now that you mention it," he said. "I cannot recall ever meeting him. I cannot put a face to the name, though the name was, for a time, constantly in the air." The look of puzzlement drew down his brow again.

I tried another tack. "Tell me the precise circumstances under which the Derogation was launched."

His gaze turned toward memory and he said, "I remember that clearly. It was the quarterly supper at the Grass Tharks Lodge."

"Grass tharks?" I said.

He explained that they were an indigenous ruminant species on Great Gallowan, with four spiraling horns. The members of the herds showed great allegiance to the common good, to the extent that an individual thark would charge a predator to rescue another thark, even if there was no close familial relationship.

"A noble beast," I said.

"Indeed, and we of the lodge stood together. 'All for one and each for the other,' was our motto."

"And then came the quarterly supper."

"Yes. Toop Zherev brought a new flavor of flambords, wonderfully spicy, enough for every Grass Thark to have a whole tail."

"Think now," I said, "was Osk Rievor present?"

His face clouded again. "I think not. No, definitely not. We were told that he was a person of such deep modesty that he had asked his friend Zherev to put forward the concept."

"Tell me more about that."

They had eaten the wondrously fiery shellfish and were cooling their palates with ices and chilled creams when the proposal for the Derogation had come up. At first, the idea had been taken as a joke; the Tharks had worked to outdo each other in proposing candidates for comeuppances and comically novel methods by which those results might be achieved.

"Then, somehow, it was all decided," he said. "We went from laughing to planning to pooling our funds. Names were placed into hats and drawn out, and suddenly I was scheduled to depart on a space liner bound for Asper on Mythisch."

His eyes lost focus for a moment. "Now that I look back on it," he said, "it was as if much of it was a dream. I had never been one to put myself about, certainly had no dealings with the likes of the Honorable Chalivire. Yet whatever the occasion required, I came up to the mark. Though raised a country lad, with her I was always urbane. I was witty among the wittiest, blasé in the midst of syba-ritic luxury, cool among those born to the coolest of blood. I was a most odd Thoonian."

My inner companion was urging a question upon me. I asked it. "Did you sometimes feel as if someone else was guiding your words and deeds? As if you were almost a passenger in your own body?"

It was as if the thought had just occurred to Lascalliot though he could not understand why he hadn't seen it before. "Why, yes," he said, "it was much like that. Now that you point it out, I wonder why I never noticed it before."

My other self advised me that he knew why. At his behest I asked for more details. As Lascalliot focused on the matters put to him, it became clear that he had spent much of the last several months in a kind of fugue state, dissociated from many of his own words and deeds. "Sometimes," he said, "it was as if another will moved my limbs and tongue, but for some reason, the situation caused me not the slightest concern."

"Hmm," I said.

"What does it all mean?" Lascalliot said. "Why have I done this thing to a woman from a far planet, about whom I knew nothing?"

"It would be premature to say."

"Would you tell her that I am very sorry?"

"I am sure she already knows that," I said. "Unfortunately, she probably intends for you to be much sorrier."

"Could you tell her about the dreaminess?"

"I will try, though it is difficult for aristocrats to hear things they don't care to hear."

He lay back in the crimps and holdtights that gripped him in so many places and I saw that his mind was working at some exercise. I waited to see what would come of it. After a few moments he focused on me again.

"Your name," he said, "is it Henghis Hapthorn?"

"It is," I said. "We have met before."

"I thought so. It was during the dreaminess, wasn't it?"

"Yes."

"I remember something else."

"What do you remember?"

"You were the one I was supposed to watch for."

"I?"

"Yes, you. I was not to bring Chalivire to fruition until I had met you."

"You are sure?" I said. "Your memory may be unreliable."

"I remember that part perfectly."

"It makes no sense," I said to my other self as I walked back to the ordinair.

"It may not connect with neat lines and snug fastenings," he replied, "but it assuredly hangs together."

"Hobart Lascalliot is mentally unbalanced. The fellow has been thus for months, and lately he has experienced excruciating new stresses." I conceived of a rational explanation. "What if Toop Zherev's new strain of flambord contained psychoactive chemicals and the Grass Tharks all went mad for a while? Stranger cults than theirs have arisen from unexpected encounters with new species of molds and fungi. Zherev may have gone mad tasting his new product, then communicated the madness to his lodgemates."

"But what of his clear memory of waiting for your appearance?"

"It is only a reported memory. It could be false."

"I do not feel that it is."

"I do not operate on feelings," I said.

"That word means something different to you than it does to me. You see vaporous insubstantiality where I see rocklike sturdiness."

I could not readily accept it. Perhaps this Osk Rievor could have established a secret society on a world far down The Spray, sending operatives out to gull the proud into making fools of themselves, just so he could entice me to come and look for him—but why would he? "It is absurdly overcomplex," I said. "He could have simply sent me an invitation, offering an interesting discrimination and a suitable fee, and I would have come."

"Apparently, he is not a man for the direct method," said my other self. "Besides, had he done so, you would have investigated him and perhaps become suspicious. You do not rush innocently into the grip of any stranger who offers you a commission."

"True," I said. "A generous stranger might turn out to be working for some person of means whose schemes I once overturned, and who has come to believe that some equivalent suffering on my part would sweeten the bitterness of that remembered injury."

"We went to Great Gallowan thinking it merely a stop on the way to finding Lascalliot. Osk Rievor seemed but a small passing landmark useful only as a means to plot a course toward what we thought was our goal."

It was hard to believe yet I had no choice but to agree. "Indeed, he now looms larger. I believe we should retrace our steps and pick up his trail."

The footman had been leading us back to where the aircar waited but now I bade him take me to Chalivire. I found her in one of the exercise rooms, practicing with an antique close-combat weapon. She executed vigorous swooping slashes and complex defensive arabesques, the weapon cleaving the air like a wand of fire, leaving a reek of ozone.

I approached cautiously, making sure my chain and pendant were visible and that my posture and gestures were precisely correct. Armed aristocrats were always a reason to step lightly. She disabled the weapon and raised the visor of her elaborate headgear. "Yes?"

"I have spoken with…" I did not name Lascalliot, but indicated with a motion of my head something an indeterminate distance away.

"Yes?"

"I believe he is not the author of your difficulties."

Her eyes became as hard as faceted jewels. "I believe differently."

"It seems he was manipulated by another."

"More fool him."

"He does not inspire sympathy?"

She made no answer but the set of her mouth told me that she had sustained worse injury than being made ridiculous before all whose opinions she valued, bad as that hurt must have been to one of her milieu. Her relations with Lascalliot had of course been intimate but now I deduced that she had also allowed herself to become vulnerable.

"Still," I said, "he who conceived your harm and made this fellow his instrument has gone free. Perhaps he dines out on tales of your discomfort."

The knuckles that gripped the antique weapon lost their color. I saw a twitch at one corner of her mouth and the pulse that throbbed in her throat suddenly became visible.

I placed my head and hands in a particular arrangement, suitable when someone of my rank wished to make a substantial request of someone of hers. "If you would lend me your yacht again, I would like to find the plotter and see what can be done to redress the balance."

"I must ask my father," she said. From the tone of her voice, I took the impression that she was conflicted. She was trying to put the memory of her humiliation behind her, burying it beneath the tears and groans she could wring from Lascalliot. Adding a new player would somehow make the harm feel fresh again.

"There is another aspect to consider," I said. I was being importuned from within by my other self. He strongly desired to take over this conversation and put a new argument to Chalivire. The prospect alarmed me: one did not deal with armed aristocrats from a basis of "feeling"—one worked from an exacting code of etiquette, because the slightest flaw might trigger a sudden, irrepressible reaction on her part, a reaction that would leave my body lying on the exercise room floor in two smoking halves.

I quieted his eagerness, then averted my eyes and lowered my voice before saying, "The man behind this may also have placed the Archon in an uncomfortable position."

On occasion, during my travels, I had seen top predators at ease in their natural habitats. They would exhibit a blasé indifference to much that surrounded them, idly lolling and playfully lollygagging—until the moment that prey wandered into view. Instantly the hunter's entire attention would lock itself upon the moving meal, and it would seem to undergo a complete and sudden transformation into another kind of beast entirely—all claws, teeth, and appetite. The Honorable Chalivire now showed much the same metamorphosis.

"The Archon?"

Very carefully, I drew from my inner pocket the scroll that Filidor had given me, then unrolled it so that his personal seal and scrawled signature were visible. The symbols had their effect on the daughter of Afre. She extended a hand and accepted the document, read it thoroughly then returned it to me.

She turned her head away and I could see her undertaking the uncharacteristic effort of thinking. Then she regarded me from a corner of an eye. "The Archon would be grateful to any who assist you in dealing with this 'grave concern'?" she said.

"It is reasonable to think so." I said. "As well, I could make a point of mentioning your participation in the matter."

I knew that aristocrats did not care to be bargained with, especially when they felt themselves to be at a disadvantage. Fortunately, Chalivire's desire to be restored to favor overcame any instinct to punish me for taking liberties.

"Very well," she said. She gave instructions to the house integrator. Then, the matter settled, she lowered her visor and prepared to resume her exercises.

"There is one other thing," I said.

She turned a face of damascened metal toward me. I quieted my inner companion's clamor, made a mollifying gesture, and said, "I will need to take Lascalliot with me."

Hobart Lascalliot proved an uninteresting traveling companion, although he was grateful for his release from Chalivire's attentions.

At our first meeting, when we had bandied a few inconsequential words in Lord Afre's Blue Parlor, I had received a distinct impression of intelligence as well as the self-assurance needed to navigate successfully among the dangerous rocks and shoals of Old Earth's morally deteriorated aristocracy. Now, as we sat in the *Orgillous*'s forward lounge, I found myself in the presence of a young man of the most ordinary sort, the kind of fellow one would expect to meet in a rural area of a placid and unremarkable secondary world.

"What was your occupation on Great Gallowan?" I asked him.

"I was an assistant to Palam Thresiger, the stock tender. I carried her instrument bag and restrained animals while she ministered to them." This statement was interrupted by two copious yawns; after Lord Afre's footmen delivered him to the yacht, his first need had been for a long sleep. By the time he awoke we were most of the way toward the first whimsy on the route to his home world.

"What were your interests, beyond exerting a tight grip on skittish beasts?"

"My pastimes were simple. My friends and I would meet at each other's homes or go to dances at the Generality. Sometimes we would go to the Brass Bucket to drink ale and play shove-and-shake—"

"Shove-and-shake?" I said.

"It involves a hat that incorporates a tankard. You fill it, then you have to make your way through a maze laid out on the floor, while your friends try to make you spill."

"Were you particularly adept at this activity?"

"Not particularly. Why?"

"I am wondering where you acquired the self-confidence not only to go among the likes of Chalivire Afre but to convince her to perform unlikely acts before the Archon and all her peers."

I saw, now that the question had been put to him, that Lascalliot was brought to wonder the same thing. "It is hard now to recall what I was feeling," he said. "I have a sense that I was always calm, even when I heard the most remarkable words coming out of my mouth. But, at the time, it was the most natural thing to be doing."

My alter ego was awake and listening. "Magic," he said.

"To one whose only instrument is a drum, all melodies are much the same," I answered inwardly.

"And the blind deny the existence of color," he shot back. "There are spells mentioned in some of Baxandall's books whose effects must be much like what the man is describing."

"Indeed?" In truth, I remembered reading of a couple such: Albernoth's Nagging Itch and Sringitan's Subtle Compulsion, when I had looked through the texts. "And do we then add this Osk Rievor to our growing list of thaumaturges?"

"If we know of the impending change, why is it not likely that others will have come across the same knowledge?"

I made a rapid mental computation then showed him the results. It was hugely improbable that, among all the teeming billions of humans inhabiting the Ten Thousand Worlds, the tiny few who were drawn to dabble in magic should become connected by so few degrees of separation.

"That," he said, "is merely the rational answer."

"Merely?"

"By the logic of sympathetic association, the expectation that those who wield magic, even rudimentary magic, will connect to each other is very strong. 'Like finds like' is the rule. I am increasingly sure that Osk Rievor is connected to the rest of this business."

"It still seems ridiculously overcomplex to me."

"Then apply your own logic to it," he said. "Say that Osk Rievor is indeed a thaumaturge. He would have an interest in knowing who the other thaumaturges are and what they are doing. He would make an effort to acquire that knowledge."

"All right," I said. "That is reasonable."

"If, within a short time, two thaumaturges, such as Bristal Baxandall and Turgut Therobar, come to unfortunate ends, then that, too, must attract his attention."

"Yes. Very well."

"And if the same person was on the scene when Baxandall and Therobar met their fates, wouldn't that connecting person become an object of scrutiny?"

"Ah," I said.

"What are you thinking of?" Hobart Lascalliot asked me.

I realized that I had been sitting across the table from him for quite some time, gazing into the middle distance with my inner debate reflected in the movements of eyes, brows, and mouth. "It would be premature to say," I said. "Tell me again about Osk Rievor."

He looked at me with puzzlement. "He was Toop Zherev's friend," he said, "not mine."

"Did anyone else meet him?"

He thought for a moment, then said, "I remember that many folk mentioned his name, but I cannot say for certain that this one or that one reported dealing with him."

I put several more questions to him and ascertained that, though his memories of his normal life were intact and properly interrelated, he had no recollection of ever meeting the man who had conceived of the Derogation.

"Toop Zherev would be the one to ask," he said.

"Then ask him I will." I suggested he repair to his cabin to make ready for our transition through the whimsy.

"Interesting," I remarked to my sharer when Lascalliot was gone. "I am tempted to apply a mnemoamplifier to see if his memories of Rievor have been tampered with, perhaps occluded behind some implanted blockage."

"They will not be there," he predicted. "I believe we are seeing the effects of Ramaram's Progressive Rescindment, or perhaps Hooley's Scrub."

It went against my grain to grant any substance to what I had so long dismissed as nothing more than the tools mountebanks used when separating the gullible from their valuables. Yet I was forced to admit the possibility.

Now other thoughts occurred to me: if my other self was right, then Osk Rievor was a more effective wielder of magic than either Bristal Baxandall or Turgut Therobar; he had set in motion a complicated series of events whose aim I could not yet fathom; and I was proceeding, at best half-blind, along a course that he might well have laid out for me—with no idea as to where it would all lead, nor what would be required of me once I arrived at where he wanted me to go.

I followed that line of thinking and found that it led me to another worrisome realization.

It now seemed likely that Toop Zherev's flambord station, where the Thoon met the waters of Balwinder Sound, was another dimple. Lurking there might be a powerful thaumaturge who had taken an interest in me, if that particular memory of Lascalliot was accurate. If so, he would have had ample time to prepare whatever welcome awaited me. For my part, my vaunted powers of ratiocination would be of scant use. As I had when in Therobar's clutches, I would have to rely on my alter ego's mastery of the incantations contained in Baxandall's few books. Unfortunately, his abilities were largely untried; most of the spells he had essayed had simply not worked. Some of them were undoubtedly pure hunkum-bunkum. Others were probably jumbled copies of copies derived from ancient grimoires, now lost somewhere along the trackless paths of the ages.

So we might well be entering a combat in which the adversary commanded an array of powerful weapons, with which he had practiced to expert level. On our side, my sharer might be the equivalent of an overconfident youth who was entering the lists armed with the equivalent of a papier-mâché sword and an ill-made grenade that might blow up in our hands.

While I had been thinking these uncomforting thoughts, I had allowed him to take charge of our body and direct it to the master cabin. Here was assembled Baxandall's books, my alter ego having insisted on bringing them with us so that he could continue to try to sift the real incantations from the merely hopeful. He had also brought the Late Horthalian tome—"Just in case," as he put it, "we run across something that unlocks its secrets."

I spoke to him now as he studied the most promising of the spellbooks. "I've been thinking. Suppose you are correct that the business of Osk Rievor is connected to the Archon's case."

"I do suppose it," he said.

"Well, then, may it not be that the purpose of the whole Derogation was to cause us to come to Rievor's lair, to a place where he undoubtedly has power, bringing the book with the unmentionable name?"

"Indeed, it may."

"Then are we not being unwise, even downright foolish, in doing precisely what he wants us to do?"

I felt him weighing the proposition. "Perhaps," he said, "but it seems that, these days, the definitions of wisdom and foolery are become interchangeable."

A gentle chime sounded and the ship's integrator announced that we would soon enter the whimsy. I had my other self ask the device how Hobart Lascalliot was faring.

"He lies upon the pallet, staring at the curve of the hull above his head," it said. "The medications sac is in his hand. Now he squeezes it, his eyes close, and he falls away."

"We should do the same," I said to my sharer.

He stretched our body on the pallet and reached into the head-board compartment for the sac. A moment later I felt the injector prick our palm, then coolness welled up our arm as the drugs made their way into our being. Drowsily, I turned my head to one side, and my fading gaze fell upon the books of magic strewn across the table. Darkness was reaching for me, pulling my eyes closed, but moments before I succumbed I saw a tiny figure blink into existence in the air in the middle of the room. It instantly enlarged and became the boy who had appeared in my workroom. He glanced at me with mild curiosity, then turned toward the table. I saw his hand reach out to open the ragged leather-bound book, then I was gone.

CHAPTER TEN

The spaceport in the Thoon looked much the same as it had on my last visit. Baltaz Thoring again appeared as I descended from the *Orgillous* and asked me the same questions.

"I am unable to resist a second taste of your flambords," I told him.

"You have been here before?" he said.

"Quite recently. Do you not remember our conversation?"

I watched him closely, saw him grasp for a wisp of memory that must have evaporated even as he reached for it. "I am sorry," he said. "I vaguely recall you and this spaceship, but nothing else. Many of us here have lately experienced memory lapses. We believe it may have been an allergic reaction."

I tried another tack. "We spoke of Toop Zherev and his excellent flambords."

Again, I saw him struggle toward a recollection that evanesced from his mind. "I do not recall it," he said.

"What about Zherev's foreign friend, Osk Rievor?" I said. "Do you remember him?"

His face showed that he was working at the question, but getting no great result. "I know the name," he said. "But I can't quite…"

"Never mind," I said. "Allergies can be troublesome."

"They can, indeed," he said with a shrug, "but if it's Zherev's flambords you seek, I don't believe he's brought any in lately."

"Why might that be?"

"I haven't thought to wonder about it till now," the claviger man said. "Isn't that curious?"

"Indeed," I said. "And where is Zherev's station?"

"Just north of here. The only one on this stretch of the sound."

I thanked him and inquired where I might hire a ground vehicle. He gave me directions to an office some distance past the hotel where I had stayed and I set off. But as I passed through the gate I said to Lascalliot, "Let us go into the hotel. I wish to experiment further."

He acquiesced and we entered the lobby. Ylma, the same young woman who had dealt with us on our previous visit, looked up from whatever she had been doing behind the front desk and said, "You're back."

"You remember me?"

"Of course. You had the odd little animal on your shoulder. He is not with you?"

"No. I left him at home, with some important tasks to perform."

She smiled at the notion, thinking that I was making a joke.

"When I was here before, I inquired about a flambord station operator named Toop Zherev. Do you recall our conversation?"

She looked inward for a moment, then said, "I do. I believe I advised you to speak to Bleban, the cook."

"And the name Osk Rievor, you recall that, too?"

"Yes, I think so," she said. "People spoke of him, though I never met him."

"Do people speak of him still?"

She reflected before saying, "I have not heard his name in some time." She looked through into the dining room and called to someone there. I turned to see the gangly young man who had cleared my table. "Fileo," she said, "this gentleman is inquiring about someone named Osk Rievor."

"I believe he may have left the district," the fellow said.

"You knew him?"

"No, I never met him, but I used to hear of him. Though not for a while now."

I said, "Do you remember our conversation about the 'Derogation'?"

He made a face, as if at an unpleasant thought. "I do. But I think that nonsense is all over now. No one speaks of it anymore."

"Thank you," I said, and departed the hotel for the place where vehicles could be hired.

As Lascalliot and I walked along the beachfront road, I said to my sharer, "This much seems clear: Osk Rievor came to Great Gallowan, met a man who grew and sold flambords, and used him to create a secret society of minions who went out with a comic song. The means may have been chemical or magical; either way, the effect was the same. Then we came, observed the night of the convening, and left. Soon after, Lord Afre arrived to scoop up Lascalliot. Not long after that, all memory of our visit began to fade from the minds of the participants—though, oddly enough, everyone recalls Rievor's name."

"Perhaps thaumaturges cannot erase their names without losing their power," he suggested.

"Perhaps. This whole business of the importance of names remains alien to me." I returned to my previous train of thought. "Note, too, that Ylma and young Fileo still remember us, presumably because they were not part of the Derogation, and thus not exposed to the spell or the psychoactive substance. We need to identify which it is."

"At Toop Zherev's station, I believe we will."

"Do you sense danger there?"

"No," he said. "But then, if we are walking into a thaumaturge's lair, he would have the means to blunt my intuition."

"That is not reassuring."

"If it is any help," he said, "I believe this will all work out well."

It was not any help, but I did not share that assessment with him.

With Lascalliot perched on the rear jump seat, I guided our rented skimmer north along the beach road. On our left, Balwinder Sound rolled smoothly toward us, wave after undemonstrative wave. I commented over my shoulder to my passenger that the placidity of the landscape matched the mood of the Thoon's inhabitants.

"We do not value ostentation," he agreed. "He speaks loudest who speaks softest, as the saying goes."

It was not an unworthy attitude, though Osk Rievor had perverted the Thoonian's modesty into an urge to punish through public ridicule those who held a different view of right conduct. Still, that observation prompted a useful thought. I said to my inner companion, "Note that Rievor used what he found. He did not create complete automatons to do his bidding. Instead, he took a strong streak of the Thoonian's character and warped it to his own ends."

"So it seems."

"That is a good sign," I said. "It means that if he is a thaumaturge, his powers are limited, even in a place where 'dimpling' enhances them. He cannot do whatever he wants."

"Yet here we are at the place where he wanted us."

Up the road and near the shore stood a low, white building with a flat roof. I asked Lascalliot, "Have you been here?"

"I once accompanied Palam Thresiger when some of Zherev's flambords were struck by a gill fungus."

I leaned the skimmer against a neatly painted fence that ringed the establishment's small front yard and entered through the gate. The door offered no who's-there—I suspected such a device might clash with the Thoonian worldview—but there was a simple mechanical device that amplified my knock. Lascalliot and I waited but there was no answer, nor any sound from within.

"I smell something," my inner companion said.

"It would be difficult not to," I answered. A sweet reek of putrefaction hung in the air.

The door was bolted from within but Lascalliot led the way around to the back. Here we found that the beach had been dug out all the way to the surf line to create an artificial lagoon lined with concrete and separated from the sea by a fence of heavy metal links. The lagoon itself was divided into pens of differing sizes by lighterweight mesh fencing. Floating walkways crisscrossed the pool, allowing access to the open-topped enclosures.

I stepped onto the nearest boardwalk, holding my nose against the stench of corruption that emanated from one of the pens. The corpses of small, multilegged animals with hard exoskeletons and a complex arrangement of mouth parts and sensory feelers floated on the surface of the water, some with their chitinous backs split open by the expanding gases of decomposition. The other pens, however, were populated by healthy specimens.

Hobart Lascalliot indicated the floating corpses and made a sound that combined pity and disgust. "These poor creatures have not had their pen flushed in who knows how long," he said. "They have suffocated in their own waste." He picked up a long-handled implement with a mesh basket on one end and used it to clear some of the floating bodies out of the way, then said, "I must activate the recycler."

He went seaward to where a metal pedestal stood at one corner of the lagoon, flipped up a hemispherical lid that covered its top, and pressed a stud and repositioned a slider. A whirring sound came from a pump near the fouled enclosure and the surface of its water gently roiled.

Lascalliot stood back from the controls and said, "That will do it. But we must skim the dead ones from—"

He was startled by the sound of a heavy body striking the strong fence that separated the enclosure from the wild sea. He soon recovered, however, and went to look over the barrier, saying, "The tainted water stimulates the appetites of the hungries. We might as well throw them the dead flambords. They're as good a disposal method as—"

He was interrupted by a shout from the house. We both turned to see an angry Toop Zherev in the doorway. He came forward onto one of the walkways, a length of polished wood in one hand that he brandished as a cudgel.

"Who are you and what are you doing to my flambords?" he said, glaring from Lascalliot to me.

Lascalliot identified himself and now the flambord farmer recognized him, though he still regarded both of us with suspicion.

"We knocked on the front door and received no answer," the young man said. "When we smelled the putrefaction we thought something might have happened to you."

"Answering a call of nature trumps answering a door," Zherev said. "What putrefaction?"

"You do not smell these dead flambords?" I said, indicating the floaters. "They are rotting."

He gave me a puzzled look, then cast his eyes down to where I pointed. His puzzlement became consternation as he seemed to notice the die-off for the first time.

"How...?" he said, then looked up at me. "Who are you again?"

I identified myself but my name clearly meant nothing to him. "Let us go inside," I said. "You may have had too much sun. Young Lascalliot will clean this up for you."

He allowed me to lead him into the house. The place stank of rotting flesh, though the smell came only from the dead flambords outside. I sat Zherev down at a table in the kitchen and opened some windows, using the opportunity to ensure that no one else was in the house's two other rooms.

I returned to find the man sitting dazed and pale where I had left him. I found some restorative in a cupboard and brought him a draft, then sat across from him while he drank it.

"You did not notice the odor?" I asked him, when some color returned to his complexion.

He looked toward the door, his nose wrinkling. "No."

"And you did not see the dead creatures?"

"No," he said again, "though I have been out there a dozen times in the past couple of days."

"Hmm," I said. "Do you recall creating a new flavor of flambords and taking them to the quarterly supper of the Grass Tharks?"

He rubbed his lower face and took another sip of restorative. "No," he said, "but I did dream of it. How do you know the contents of my dreams?"

"It would be premature—" I began, only to be interrupted from within by my other self.

"I need to examine the place where he mixes the feed," he said.

"One moment," I told him. To Zherev I said, "Where might I find your friend, Osk Rievor?"

The flambord farmer blinked at me, and I saw fear behind his eyes. "I have no friend by that name," he said, his voice trembling, "but I have dreamed it."

He was becoming distraught. I poured him more of the restorative and accompanied it with some bland and reassuring remarks. After a while he calmed.

"The feed preparation area," said the voice in my head.

I asked Toop Zherev where he mixed his feed and he indicated a tall cupboard against an inner wall. I went and opened it, found a hinged board with chained corners that came down to form a small countertop. Behind, when I lowered it, were a number of labeled drawers that proved to contain strong-smelling spices and hotstuffs.

"Give me control," my sharer said.

I did and he bent to examine the contents of the drawers, bringing each to our nose. "Nothing," he said.

Now he spied a small piece of paper, folded and tucked into a crack in the cupboard door. He extracted it and held it to our nose, sniffing gently. "Yes," he said. "Here it is."

Carefully, he unfolded it. I watched, expecting to find some chemical twisted up in it. But there was nothing concealed within. He spread the sheet on the countertop and I saw that on it were printed four words in spiky, black script, though the letters were unknown to me.

My other self brought the paper back to where Toop Zherev sat at the table and showed it to him. "Can you read this?"

"Read what?" the flambord farmer said.

Our eyes went from the man to the paper. The lettering was gone. The paper was blank.

To me, my alter ego said, "That settles it."

"It does," I said. "We are dealing with a thaumaturge of considerable power."

Not long after, I was aboard the *Orgillous* and bound for Old Earth, with Zherev, Lascalliot, and all of Great Gallowan dwindling far behind me. I settled myself in the lounge, bade the integrator prepare a light meal, then spoke to my inner companion.

"There is now no doubt that Osk Rievor and all that stemmed from his activities are connected to the matter of Baxandall's book and our commission from the Archon."

"There never was any doubt," he replied, "except in your share of our mind."

"Recriminations are not fruitful," I said. "We need to find the shape of this case."

"The issue of trust still stands between us," he said. "You did not trust my judgment."

"It seemed to make no sense."

I felt a flash of anger from him and said, "Emotion will not serve us."

"You mean, *my* emotion will not. I have known you to become quite exercised, even to the flinging of objects."

"Let us talk about the case," I said.

"You cannot always change the subject," he said. "We must eventually settle our relationship. It is not as if either of us can leave the other."

"On the contrary," I said, "eventually, I must leave. I will fade and diminish while you wax and flourish."

"Ah, and that bothers you."

"How could it not? You are a constant reminder that all that I am will, sooner or later, be no more than a ghost in the back of your mind. And the more we deal with incidences of sympathetic association, the more sharply I am reminded of the inevitable."

Now I felt from him a wave of sympathy. "Don't," I said. "That irritates me even more than learning that you were right where I was wrong."

He suppressed the sentiment and presented me with a cool sto-icism. "Every man dies. You always knew that you would someday end."

"Yes, but I face a different kind of death than what I anticipated. And you are its ever present emblem."

He was silent for a moment, then said, "Very well, let us see if we can get on."

"Work is a good distraction," I told him, "even if this case hastens my undoing."

"I had not considered that," he said. "The more you and I are in places where magic is being done, the faster the transition."

"I have considered it a great deal," I said. "But my work is who I am, even if practicing my profession speeds the day when I am not."

"Who was it who said that irony is the fundamental operating principle of the universe?"

"I believe," I said, "that it was Henghis Hapthorn."

The yacht's integrator announced that the food was ready. During the meal, I did not think about the case at all, practicing a technique of mind-clearing that had often been useful when preparing to set about a complex conundrum. But when Lord Afre's dishes had been returned to the yacht's servitor, I rose and began to pace the floor of the lounge, rehearsing the facts as I now knew them.

"Let us call this thread one: someone has disturbed the Archon in his most private chamber, a disturbance that involved an object he described as a key. The key had something to do with a visit that he and his uncle, the previous Archon, made to the desolate region known as Barran.

"Now thread two: someone has been killing the descendants of persons whose names Bristal Baxandall noted on the flyleaf of the indecipherable book written in an artificial language based on Late Horthalian, a language that disappeared when its speakers were destroyed in the cataclysm that caused the devastation of Barran. And all of the victims were coated in a fine grit whose nature and origins are unknown, though it is also connected with Barran."

My sharer added a thought. "It is also significant that Glam Botch and Vhobald Hammis were each in possession of a carved object—respectively, a lower face and, presumably, an eye, which I believe came from the same sculpture. We may assume that the rest of the unknown sculpture was made of the same unclassified substance as the black powder, and that it has magical properties."

"Yes," I said, pausing in my pacing to say, "and the chin and mouth were in a box labeled with a word—or name—that we dare not speak nor even think of, that is rendered in red letters in the book." I clasped my hands behind my back and took as many steps as needed to bring me to where the lounge met the curve of the yacht's inner hull, turned, and said, "And now we find that all of this is connected to Osk Rievor, an undoubted thaumaturge who has convincingly demonstrated the power to bend minds."

"So the powder and Barran are common linkages," my alter ego said, "as is Osk Rievor."

"Who came to the Thoon because it offered not only a dimple," I said, "but a vector—that is, the flambords—for getting a magical substance into other persons."

I had reached the hull again, and turned once more. "Now," I said, "we move beyond the facts and into the realm of supposition. Why did Rievor create the Derogation and inflict Lascalliot on Chalivire Afre?"

"Presumably to draw our interest."

"It is far-fetched, yet it remains the only explanation left standing. But when we came to Great Gallowan the first time, he did not confront us, but remained hidden. And on this visit, he was gone."

"I sense a reason," he said, "though I know you will not like it."

"And I have deduced a motivation, and I agree that it is not a palatable thought to entertain," I said. "So, is what I think the same as what you feel?"

I showed him an image from memory: my view of my plate from when I had sat in the dining room of the hotel on Great Gallowan, trenchering my way through a steaming pile of flambords.

"It is," he said. "I am sure he has put something into us."

"Which means he intends for us to do something he wants done." I stopped pacing and said, "How shall we know if we are being bent to his will?"

"We may not. I will study Baxandall's books again, to see if something can be done."

"But he now has influence over us. It is quite possible that, if a counter to the spell exists, that influence may preclude us from even seeing it."

"True," he said. "Now we may not only have difficulty trusting each other, but have good cause not to trust ourselves."

I agreed that it was not a happy point in the discrimination. "Two things I am, however, sure of," I said.

"And they are?"

"One, that we must go to the wasteland of Barran."

"I agree," he said, "that is where the road leads. And the other?"

"That Osk Rievor is not compelling us to do so, as he compelled Hobart Lascalliot and Toop Zherev."

"How do you know that?"

"Because," I said, "I most definitely do not wish to go there."

CHAPTER ELEVEN

My assistant was curled around the fruit bowl in sleep, a scattering of seeds and rinds indicating that it had not stinted itself in my absence. I nudged its furred back with a bent knuckle and said, "Wake up. I wish to know what you have accomplished in my absence."

"Not a great deal," it said, yawning and applying the backs of its fingers to its eyes. It blinked at me and continued: "I made extensive inquiries, as you required, about Osk Rievor."

"And?"

"Nothing. No such person has ever connected to the grid."

"Not even offworld?"

"Not even then."

"That is of a pattern with Bristal Baxandall and Vhobald Hammis," I said. "We seem to have found an infallible way of identifying thaumaturges—they value their privacy to an extreme."

"There is another possibility," my assistant said. "It may be that they are connected, but that their connections are masked."

It was possible to wander the grid undetected; my assistant did so when tickling its way into Bureau of Scrutiny data stores that were intended for official use only. But the subterfuges employed in those circumstances were of a temporary nature, relying on weaknesses in the Bureau's own defenses. A new mask had to be confected every time an illicit entry was attempted; the scroot integrators would soon catch on to the presence of a repeat interloper.

"No," I said. "The improbabilities would pile up. It would not be possible to remain permanently masked."

"Unless the masking was official."

It raised an interesting and disquieting prospect. There was one person connected to the grid whose presence was neither recorded nor detectable. "The Archon?" I said. "Why would Filidor hide the presence of thaumaturges, then set me on a quest that must inevitably uncover them?"

"Perhaps to see if the uncovering was indeed inevitable," the integrator said. "Archons are subtle."

It was true. Whenever one investigated a wheel that an Archon had set spinning, one always found wheels within the wheel, and closer examination showed that those wheels themselves contained wheels of their own, some of them spinning in apparently contradictory directions.

But, on reflection, I rejected the notion. I did not believe that Filidor would send me to bring back a reverse-twist spratulator, as in the old joke. "He would not so abuse my professional stature," I said.

"Archons are no respecters of persons," my assistant said.

"Even so. Let us move on. What about the names in Baxandall's book?"

While I had been en route to Great Gallowan and back, I had set my assistant to undertake a deep search for background on the ancient Late Horthalians and their descendants who had died missing pieces of their bodies while covered in black grit.

"Again," my assistant said, "it was difficult to piece together much information. It is as if the records have been deliberately purged, leaving only scraps. Sometimes I had to take great leaps to tie separated facts together, leaving me with a most flimsy and tenuous assemblage. Then, however, a faint trail led me to a very ancient integrator that had been stood down for the better part of an aeon."

"Intriguing," I said, "and did this integrator dispel the mists that obscured your view?"

My assistant stretched and yawned again, then reached for a ripe karba fruit. "Not to any great degree," it said, as its small fingers deftly peeled the rind. "It proved to be almost entirely sunk in that condition known as 'the vagues.' I had a great deal of trouble raising it even to semiconsciousness and, when I did, it rambled incoherently. Finally, I managed to delve deep enough below the *mishegaas* to isolate its core functions and put some questions to it."

"And there you found some useful references to the Late Horthal-ians and their descendants?"

"No," it said.

"I am beginning to worry," I said, "that you have caught a touch of the vagues yourself, and that I am now trapped in a conversation that may never end."

The suggestion caused my assistant to shudder. "Please do not say such things. I have seen too much of that condition lately. It is not a pleasant prospect for an integrator."

"Then get on with it. Your conversational wanderings do nothing to allay my concern. I am tempted to strip you down for a diagnostic review, and in your new incarnation that would be an even more unpleasant prospect for both of us."

The small creature pulled itself together and said, "The senile in-tegrator could not tell me anything new about the mutilated bodies and the black grit—"

"I hope for your sake," I said, "that you are now about say 'but' and follow on with a useful contribution to this discrimination."

"But," it continued, "although it couldn't tell me anything new, it did tell me who *could* tell us—and who could tell us not just more, but *everything*."

"Now we are getting somewhere," I said. "And who is this font of all knowledge?"

"You won't like it."

My fingers curled. I experienced a sudden urge to pick up the creature that my integrator had become and give it a thorough shake, even if it meant that pieces of it might come off in my hands.

"I don't have to like it," I said. "But I definitely have to hear it."

"Old Confustible," it said.

"Are you calling me names?" I said. I knew I had not programmed that function into my integrator.

"No," it said, "Old Confustible is the name of an integrator, the name given it by its owner."

"I see," I said, "and to whom does Old Confustible belong?"

"To the Archon."

I thought about it. "I don't like it," I said.

The Archonate was an institution so long established that its actual origins were lost not just in the shadows of prehistory, but in the shadows of shadows that loomed as far back as even the oldest integrator could recall. First, there had been the dawn-time, which ended with the First Effloration that took humankind off Earth—it was just "Earth" in those days; the "Old" was added later—and out into The Spray to people the Ten Thousand Worlds.

Left to languish, Earth had become depopulated. Indeed, it had become a decidedly unfashionable address and for quite some time—an aeon or three—it was largely forgotten. Then, during the opening of the Twelfth Aeon, one of those inevitable transitions occurred: a world that had been forever beyond the pale suddenly and inexplicably became modish again, and Earth—now affectionately renamed "Old Earth"—was reinhabited. Ships came and went, peoples chose their dwelling places, polities were established, philosophies put into practice.

Somewhere in that flurry of to-ing and fro-ing, the Archonate was established, though no one knew how or by whom. Scholars who had studied the matter concluded that all information concerning the birth of the institution had been expunged by universal agreement among the heterogeneous peoples who had come back to re-create the ancestral planet. Ever since, successive archons had ruled Old Earth, or at least those parts of it that were inhabited by humans. Their authority was absolute, though the means by which that authority was exercised were never defined.

Subtlety and indirection had been the hallmarks of archons through the ages. One might confidently expect to see the Archon presiding at certain formal occasions, and he could also appear unexpectedly, as Filidor had when the Corps of Buffoons had performed in Drusibal Square. The rest of the time, he was an obscure presence. Archons were known to travel the world incognito. Thus anyone might be the Archon. That fact prompted generally polite behavior between strangers, because the Archon was empowered to do anything to anyone at any time.

Archons came and went, each choosing his own successor, though there were occasionally rumors of cabals and conspiracies among the mandarinate that infested the endless corridors and offices of the Archonate Palace. There had been attempts to seize the pinnacle of power; even one plot that, most people agreed, had temporarily succeeded in placing a usurper—the unfortunate Holmar Thurm—on the non-existent throne.

But through all the ages, with all the comings and goings of archons and their officialdom, one constant had remained: the vast and pansophical array of integrators that had been operating continuously since the establishment of the Archonate, ceaselessly gathering, storing, sifting, collating, and correlating information, and ultimately answering to no one but the Archon himself.

And the most senior of these timeworn devices, and thus the most imperial and magisterial integrator on the planet, was that which served the Archon as his prime, personal aide—a device so cantankerous and irksome, even to an archon, that Filidor had personally named it Old Confustible.

"What is that creature on your shoulder?"

My first inclination was to dissemble, but I followed my second, and answered, "That was one of the questions I intended to put to you."

"Do you put it?" said the Archon's prime integrator.

"If I do, can you answer?"

The silence that ensued could mean one of two things: either Old Confustible was purposely making me wait; or it was opening and searching through sealed data stores. I settled myself more comfortably in the public booth on the sunlit promenade outside the main entrance to Terfel's Connaissarium and waited. It had not been necessary to come up to the Archonate Palace to question the ancient integrator—I could have instantly connected from my workroom—but I had not wanted Colonel-Investigator Brustram Warhanny to be privy to our conversation. I was fairly sure that the scroot was merely doing his duty, and not part of any palace intrigue, but when dealing with Archon affairs, "fairly sure" was not sure enough.

"It closely resembles," said the voice speaking seemingly from somewhere near my left ear, "a creature called a grinnet, though nonesuch has been seen for a very long time. Where did you obtain it?"

"It is difficult to say," I replied. "I was not certain of my whereabouts at the time."

Another silence ensued. I saw no reason not to break it. "When you say, 'very long,' exactly how long are we talking about?"

"I cannot say, exactly. The records are incomplete."

"Then not in this aeon?" I said.

"No, not in this aeon."

"Can you say which aeon?"

"Yes, I can."

"Then please do."

"The Seventeenth," it said.

"What is known of grinnets?"

"Quite a lot."

"A workable summary would suffice."

"They were artificially constructed creatures employed as assistants and intermediaries by persons of some power in the Sixteenth and Seventeenth Aeons."

"A kind of organic integrator?" I said.

"Your definition is not precise."

"But also not wholly inaccurate?"

"No, not wholly."

"You were extant during those aeons, were you not? Even by an imprecise definition?"

The reply was some time in coming. "In a manner of speaking."

"Did you resemble the creature on my shoulder?"

" 'Resemble' is a flexible term."

"Would a reasonable man of the period say there was a close resemblance?"

"We would have to find one and ask him," it said. "Unfortunately, reasonable men of the Sixteenth and Seventeenth Aeons are not to be found these days. They were rare even then."

"I believe you are avoiding my question."

"I cannot comment on your beliefs. What appears self-evident to one person may seem to another observer to be entirely the product of an idiosyncratic bent."

"Integrator," I said, "I put it to you that during the Sixteenth and Seventeenth Aeons, when you were an assistant and intermediary to persons of power, you more closely resembled the creature on my shoulder than your present arrangement of components."

"It could be said."

"Much more closely," I said.

Again I waited for Old Confustible's reply. Finally it said, "Yes."

"Then I further believe," I said, "that you and I must have a meeting of the minds."

"You might find that uncomfortable," it said.

"I find myself generally uncomfortable these days," I said. "A few more kinks and abrasions will not undo me."

"Your discomfort may extend beyond kinks and abrasions."

I made a gesture that expressed a kind of world-weary bravado. "I am tasked by the Archon to conduct a discrimination. He gave me to understand that this is no small matter. Need I show you his instructions again?"

I had already presented the scroll to the booth's percepts, else I would not have got past the integrator-minor that ordinarily responded to public queries.

"You need not," the Archon's prime integrator said. "Tell me what you wish to know."

"No," I said, "I would rather you told me what I need to know."

"Need? To what purpose?"

"To preserve the life and power of the Archon Filidor," I said, "both of which I take to be in peril from a powerful thaumaturge named Osk Rievor."

No answer came. Instead the door of the booth opened. My assistant stirred on my shoulder and said, "I am receiving a communication on a secure channel."

"From whom?"

"Who else?" it said. "We are to take the ascender to the Archon's private level."

I walked across the broad plaza, floored in patterned bricks, that overlooked the great gaudy spread of Olkney in the deep orange afternoon light of the tired old sun. The familiar vista of splendor and squalor, of magnificent artistry and crass ebullience, brought me an unexpected moment of sadness and loss, as if I was seeing it for the last time and thus realizing only belatedly how dear it all was to me. To my inner companion I said, "Is this emotion yours?"

"It is," he said.

"Where does it come from?"

"I do not know. An unlooked for presentiment, I suppose."

"Are we moribund?" I said. "Are we bound for an early death?"

"I do not now," he said again. "Perhaps it is just that things as we have known them are coming to an end, and all will soon be different."

"Yes, but it will be a difference more to your liking."

I felt him give the inner equivalent of a shrug. "Even so," he said.

We had arrived at the unobtrusive gate behind which stood an ascender that led up to the higher reaches of the palace. It opened as I reached for its latch. I stepped through and stood on the disk. It discreetly vibrated, then began to glide smoothly up the slope to that part of the great pile of spires, domes, walls, and cupolas that was the Archon's private quarters.

The ascender took me to a small landing with a carved balustrade of gray stone. From here the view of the city was even grander and I paused to look out at a view that was reserved for the Archon and his most senior officers. Almost immediately, however, a simple door of polished wood opened in the wall of white stone blocks behind me and my assistant said, "We are summoned within."

I entered and found myself in the Archon's private study, a surprisingly small room though high ceilinged, with its walls lined from top to bottom floor with shelved books. I cast my eye over them and saw works from every age, in several tongues, not all of them human, and in forms that ranged from the traditional to devices that displayed their information in emanations of light or sound.

Besides the books, the study contained only a comfortable chair and a large and well-worn desk, both of dark wood and old leather, standing on a carpet with a pattern of blues and greens from the Agrajani classical period.

"Enter and be seated," said the voice of Old Confustible.

I did as I was bid and immediately a broad screen appeared in the air before me, dark and void. "You will see a visual briefing," the ancient integrator said, "that has been shown to archons since time immemorial. Much of it is reconstructed from partial records; some of it is based on conjecture."

"Begin," I said.

The screen remained dark. "In the Sixteenth and Seventeenth Aeons," said Old Confustible, "the Wheel's turning had brought sympathetic association to the ascendancy. The world, indeed all the worlds, were ruled by magic."

The screen now brightened and I saw a panorama of a verdant landscape, presented from the eyeview of someone flying high above it. Below, farms and woodlands rolled past, with men and beasts at work in the fields. Then came a country town, the houses of sturdy construction, brightly painted, with the streets between paved in white stone or red brick. The point of view passed on to follow a road that became a highway, then suddenly swept forward along the thoroughfare to encounter a great city that spread itself wider along the horizon as I, for it was as if I was drawn into the scene, rapidly approached.

"Integrator," I said, "through whose eyes am I seeing this?"

"These are impressions gathered by a person of power of the late Seventeenth Aeon."

"His name?"

"The person was female. Her name was Phaladrine Baudrel."

I knew that name. I had seen it in Baxandall's green ink. My eyes returned to the screen and I saw that I was gliding toward a palace perched upon a hill in a parklike quarter of the city. It was a fanciful edifice, apparently formed of silver filigree and twined strands of tarnished bronze, with delicate arches and buttresses that supported impossibly high and slender towers topped by staffs from which scarlet silk pennants fluttered like snakes' tongues. The top of one slim spire was flat, ringed with pointed crenelations, and it was to this small aerie that I was descending. Moments later, I alit as softly as a thread of gossamer and it was only then, when Phaladrine's eyes looked down to where her pale hand languidly extended, that I saw anything of the vehicle that had carried us through the air.

Even so, I had but a glimpse of a circular hemisphere of gold, its rim rolled outward, its inner surface lined with quilted fabric on which it seemed the occupant lolled in comfort. The hand she had extended now completed its gesture and a section of the hemisphere simply disappeared, allowing her to dismount through the gap and emerge standing on the pristine slabs of white crystalline stone that roofed the tower. Ahead was a circular hole toward which she strode. I saw steps within it.

But at the lip of the shaft she paused and turned back to the vehicle. I would admit to being startled at what I saw as her eyes panned across the cityscape and came to rest, not on the padded cup in which she had arrived but on the huge creature that held it in its taloned forepaws.

"That," I said, "is a dragon."

"Yes," said Old Confustible, "although it is more exact to call it a gillifrond. The body is slim and sinewy, covered, as are the wings, in pinions of white and gray. Phaladrine Baudrel appears to have favored slenderness as a theme. Note that the teeth and claws are more needlelike than robust."

The view had shifted. Phaladrine had gestured to the creature, causing it to bow its equine head and fall away from the tower into the empty air, leaving the golden bowl behind. Now I was being borne down into the shaft, the walls of the circular stairwell glowing softly where her feet—shod in slippers of damascened silver, I noticed—touched the steps, the luminescence then fading as we descended.

We emerged into a circular chamber hung with what appeared to be tapestries, except that the woven figures presented on them moved as if alive. I soon realized that "as if" was inaccurate; the persons depicted all turned toward Phaladrine as she entered, making the most humble obeisances while watching her every motion with eyes that, even rendered in interlocking stitchery, betrayed fear and dread.

She ignored their courtesies and went instead to a small round table at one side of the room. In the nearest tapestry a man presented in rags and with limbs thin as sticks, his eyes great pools of misery, edged as far toward the fabric border as he could. But she paid him no heed, looking down at the circular tabletop—it looked to be fashioned of age-yellowed ivory or bone—and passing her hand above it in a sequence of complex motions. An orb of consummate blackness, set in a round base of unpolished black metal, abruptly appeared beneath her gaze.

"I believe that is the counter motion to Loang's Impenetrable Box," said my inner companion in a tone that bespoke of complete fascination. "It is a spell to keep small and precious objects safe."

"You must be enjoying this," I said to him. "This is the world that you are fitted for."

"I admit to an immense interest," he said.

"What of the poor creatures in the tapestries?"

"What of Hobart Lascalliot in Chalivire's holdtights?" he answered.

I made no answer because Phaladrine now brought her hands together in a sharp *clap!* I realized that it was the first sound I had heard—there had not even been a whisper of wind as we had flown and landed—and I had assumed that I was seeing a silent depiction.

Her eyes swept around the room, but low, passing over where the tapestries met the floor. I saw now that the floor was carpeted and immediately realized that, as with the hangings on the wall, the woven designs held human figures in bondage. Phaladrine's narrow heels stood upon the torso of a dark-haired woman dressed in the tatters of a once elegant robe; I could just see, from the corner of Phaladrine's vision, the woman's pale face, mouth twisted in agony.

Then the point of view snapped to the base of one tapestry, as from behind the fabric crept a small animal, its dark fur grizzled with tips of silver. It did not look up at her, nor did it cross the carpet, but crept along the base of the wall until it could spring onto the tabletop, where it squatted, eyes downcast, waiting.

But not for long. Phaladrine's fingernails—each one surfaced in a different variety of precious stone, each with an intaglioed rune carved in its shining facade—now tapped the dark sphere. The creature looked up anxiously then swung around to place both its small paws on the orb's sides.

"She does not speak," I commented to Old Confustible.

"She dare not. Not yet."

"Why?"

"Watch and see."

Her familiar stroked the sphere, its mouth forming syllables I could not hear while its tail flicked in a manner I took to indicate unconscious tension. A narrow beam of shimmering white light burst from the top of the orb, coruscating upward like sparks confined to a fountain's spray, to strike the room's ceiling and fall in a cascade around the table. As the creature continued to stroke and whisper, the flow grew denser and the rising column thickened, until the shower from above became so thick as to hide the table from view.

Phaladrine stepped back as the cascade deepened and widened. Then she extended two fingers of one hand, touching first one rune-tipped digit, then the other, to the glittering barrier. It parted vertically and she stepped within the circle.

Now, for the first time, I heard her speak: a single syllable, in a voice like the sound a serpent might make slithering across dead leaves.

"Will you translate?" I asked the Archon's integrator.

The scene before me rippled and the same moment was replayed, but this time I heard the woman say, "Enough."

The familiar removed its paws from the black orb and squatted at the edge of the table, its diminutive fingers folded across its befurred paunch and its eyes again downcast. The woman now touched the orb and said something I did not catch because my assistant spoke in my ear.

"That creature does not truly resemble me," it said.

"It is not a grinnet, not by a long stretch," said Old Confustible. "A mere grinnet would simply not do for one of Phaladrine's rank."

I believed my integrator was about to make some remark that would not have been useful. "Hush," I said. She was speaking again.

"I have done it," she said.

A small face was visible in the orb, as if someone wore its darkness like a helmet. Even as I saw it the face changed and then changed again, becoming an unending succession of visages, young, old, male, female, of all different characters and moods, flickering into and out of view.

"I've read of this," my sharer said. "I think it's Brumaire's Physiognomical Torrent. An impenetrable disguise. Remarkable to see it in application."

A tiny voice came from the orb. "Then we are complete. We must move with dispatch."

"I am prepared," Phaladrine said, and I heard urgency mixed with fear.

"I will contact the others. The time grows short."

"But we are ready." She touched the sphere with a jewel-tipped digit and extinguished the shifting faces. "End it," she said to the familiar.

It moved over to touch the orb, again mouthing quiet syllables. The cascade ceased to fountain from the top of the sphere, the last sparks winking out as they fell to the carpet. Phaladrine stepped through the final glimmerings and crossed to another part of the room. She knelt on the carpet, her knees upon the belly of a woven man who wore a long, dark robe figured in symbols, some of which looked similar to those carved into her fingertips. The man's mouth was contorted in a grimace of pain that widened into a silent scream as she dug her sharp-pointed fingers into the weave where his heart would have been. Her hands danced like spiders, teasing out threads in loops and tangles. Then she reached into a slit in her gown—I saw, now that she was looking down, that she was attired in a shimmering sheath of spun silver—and drew out a small box of a shimmering substance, its surface covered with line upon line of tiny, intricate figuring. She opened its top and tipped it toward her palm. From within came a thing like a large insect, black and spiky, its movements oddly jerky. It was difficult to keep the creature in focus, but I took the impression that it was not made of true flesh, but assembled from letters and symbols. Then it passed from sight as she closed her fingers over its wriggling form and placed it into the tangle of threads drawn from the woven man's breast. Then her hands performed their spiderlike dance again, and the carpet became smooth once more, though the woven man's face was convulsed in silent sobs.

I was aware of a growing excitement in my other self, though I was experiencing revulsion at the sight of such suffering so casually dealt. "Do these sights give you no qualms?" I asked him.

"It is but an echo of the long dead past, merely images reconstructed from scant records."

"No," I said, "it is a foretaste of the future."

He said nothing in reply. I realized, though, that his silence came not from any consideration of what I had said, but from his fascination with the new images that had appeared on Old Confustible's screen. I was reminded of a child sitting rapt before a wondershow.

This time the point of view was general, as the screen showed a series of brief shots and slow pans. The cumulative effect was to establish an enormous excavation pit seen obliquely from above, almost entirely filled by an immense mechanism fashioned from several different metals as well as some substances that I could not readily identify. It was difficult to focus the eye on the huge device, which towered well above the rim of the great pit, partly because some of its surfaces were obscured by scaffolding, partly because some of the materials from which it was made resisted the eye's attempts to secure a clear view.

"There are transdimensional aspects to that thing," I said to the Archon's integrator.

"There are. It is an interplanar device."

The point of view now swooped in for a closer look. On some levels of the scaffolding, men and women in highly structured clothing performed operations I could not make out. Some were adjusting controls or attaching components to the main mass of the apparatus, while others appeared to be merely standing in deep thought and conversing with themselves, while still more were gesticulating or performing what looked like interpretative dance. When I heard my other self make a wordless sound of appreciation I understood what I was seeing.

"Those are, in a universe governed by magic, the equivalent of apparaticists and technicians," I said.

"Indeed," said Old Confustible, "a large number of magicians and arcanists were employed to construct the device. We see them now as the final adjustments are made before the first test."

"The device's purpose?" I said.

"The question can be answered in two ways. It is intended to draw from an adjacent plane an energy that occurs naturally and plentifully there, and which normally leaks into this realm steadily and pervasively, though in small quantities. The device will store the energy so that it can be applied in concentrated form and directed at specific targets."

"The name of this energy?"

"Colloquially, it is called 'evil.' "

"I see," I said. "And the second purpose?"

"To serve the ends of the chief person of power in this world."

"The Archon?"

"The title was not then used. Indeed, the title was never spoken. Circumlocutions were employed, such as 'He Who Commands' or 'The Authority.'"

I did not need my intuitive sharer to make the connection. "Assistant," I said to the creature on my shoulder, "communicate to the Archon's integrator the sequence of letters that, if spoken, cause my inner self to collapse."

To Old Confustible, I said, "Is that the name that was not to be spoken?"

I would not have expected to hear even the slight tinge of surprise that colored the voice of the Archon's integrator as it said, "It was. Where did you come across it?"

"It would be premature to say," I said. "I would like to see this figure of dread."

"I was just coming to it. Behold."

The images on the screen shifted as the point of view again swooped away from the capering, muttering spellcasters. It panned across a cityscape and I recognized some of the startlingly strange architecture that I had seen through the eyes of Phaladrine.

"What city is this?" I said.

"It was called Ambit."

The viewpoint settled on one-quarter of the horizon, focused on a remarkable building that dominated the skyline: it was pyramidal in shape, of colossal dimensions, and constructed of massive blocks of black stone that seemed to be cemented together by a mortar made of congealed fire. It did not rest on the ground, but was supported on two gargantuan legs clad in green reptilian scales, knees bent like a weightlifter's, the feet ending in hooked talons. The claws dug not into open ground but into ruined masonry, as if the entire building had but recently arrived on the scene, its mode of transport crushing houses and walls as though they were blades of grass.

The pyramid's apex was a single, clear crystal, easily the size of the greatest manse in Olkney, set with windows shuttered by sheets of opal and two tall doors of brilliant ruby. As the viewpoint carried me toward them, the portals opened ponderously and I passed within. What followed was a dizzying passage through high, wide corridors and great halls, lined and ornamented with marvels too many and too bizarre for me to encompass. I saw improbable beasts, men and women whose bodies were formed of swirling motes, translucent servants busily going about incomprehensible duties, floors of flame and walls of ice, rooms that seemed to go on into infinity, corners that turned in eye-staggering, impossible directions.

"Astonishing," said my inner companion. "The inventiveness. The sheer artistry."

"The vanity," I said. "The sheer excess."

The viewpoint raced on, rushing up a spiral staircase to arrive at the very pinnacle of the great crystal. Here was a pyramidal chamber of human proportions, its walls translucent, its floor of milk-white stone veined in reds and greens. At the center of the room the floor became a raised dais on which stood a throne of black iron. At first I thought the metal was oiled, then I realized that the constant shimmer across its surface was of some powerful energy, barely constrained.

Upon the throne sat the shape of a man, forearms resting on the chair's armrests, feet flat on the white stone of the dais, in such perfect stillness that I would have taken the image for a static rendering, if the viewpoint had not swept me around the room to see him from all angles.

"Is this he?" I asked Old Confustible.

"It is what he had become," it said.

"Freeze the display," I said. "I wish to study him."

The integrator obliged and, at my further bidding, enlarged the image. The figure did not appear to be that of a man, but of a statue. Yet as I had the magnification increased still more, I saw that this was a work beyond the skill of the most adept sculpture. Even to the pores of his skin, the lashes of his eyes, the fine hairs on the backs of his hands, the detail was exquisitely accurate. Yet this was not flesh, but a dull black substance I would have called stone, if stone could have come alive.

"What is he made of?" I asked the Archon's integrator.

"The substance was never named to us," it said. "He traveled into another realm, underwent fearsome ordeals, remade himself, and returned as you see him. His powers had increased multifold."

I noticed that my thumb and forefinger were rubbing against each other and I realized that it was not I but my other self who was unconsciously performing the action. "You know what that stuff is," he said to me.

"Yes," I said, "I do." Though I had only ever seen it as grains of black grit.

"Bid the integrator to pull back to give us a full view of him," he asked me, "and unfreeze the image. I wish to try something."

"Very well." I did as he asked and watched the dark figure sitting immobile upon the throne, the face deeply lined, the nose proud as a raised sword blade, the eyes sunk in darkness. Yet not immobile, I now saw, because the lines about those eyes now deepened, as if the man of stone had turned his mind to some question and was focusing his thoughts thereon.

Then from within my own head I heard my other self whisper a name: "Majestrum."

Instantly, I felt his presence go from me, as it had when Filidor had spoken the word. But that was not what caught my attention. Instead I kept my gaze on the screen, where that dark and stony countenance from an impossibly ancient age had reacted to the sound of its unspeakable name. I recalled how, not long before, I had seen a change in Chalivire Afre's face and likened it to a predator focusing on the sudden appearance of prey. Compared to the starkness I saw in the visage of Majestrum, Chalivire had shown me no more than the face of a kitten spying a ball of thread.

"I must contemplate," I told Old Confustible. "I will walk outside for a few moments, then return."

"As you wish."

I went out onto the Archon's private terrace and stood as if in meditation over the view of Olkney slipping into evening. But my regard was turned inward. I called to my inner companion, seeking to rouse him, and after several such attempts, I felt his return.

"Are you all right?" I said.

"I believe so," he said.

"What was the purpose of that exercise?"

"Tell me first, what happened when I spoke the name?"

I was candid with him. "I do not like to say it, but I cannot help acknowledging that he reacted."

There was a silence from within me. "What does it mean?" I said.

"I cannot say for certain," he said, "but this much is clear: he is not dead. Nor is he without power."

"It is four aeons since the impressions were taken on which those images were based."

"Four aeons, here," he said, "but you said yourself that in another realm that may be no more than a moderately busy afternoon."

"You think he is alive?"

"The word may not precisely apply. But, in some way, he is assuredly extant."

"And if his power still reaches from wherever he is to wherever his name is spoken?" I said. The old sun was sliding into the dark sea of Mornedy Sound. I felt the first chill of the night wind so high up above the city. My assistant shivered on my shoulder. I showed my other self the images of my thoughts about beasts of prey. "We are but kittens," I said.

"We must learn more," my sharer said. I sensed fear in him, but also the same thrill of excitement. Had he been in control of our body, it would have been trembling.

Instead I shivered from a chill that had nothing to do with the cold upper air, but I said, "Yes. Let us go back in."

CHAPTER TWELVE

"H e had become," Old Confustible said, "a grim tyrant." The image of the dark man on the iron throne hung in the air of the Archon's study. "The Authority had formerly been but the first among nine peers, but his nature combined overweening ambition with an unparalleled aptitude for attracting, binding, and applying the most powerful energies of his realm. He grew, in strength and in appetite, and soon stretched his rule across the world."

The scene shifted and another figure appeared: a tall man, lean and ascetic of face, clad in a robe of brilliant blue, his long, white hair wind-whipped like a flag. He stood atop a black crag, a great chasm at his feet and an unearthly sky rippling and streaming above his head.

"One of his eight colleagues opposed him, challenged him to a contest of powers. They met at the appointed place, in a realm jointly created for the purpose. There is no actual record of the conflict. Only one of the duelists returned and he gave no formal report. His return and his opponent's absence should have conveyed all that needed to be said, but in the years following, the victor often dwelled on the details of his triumph. The scene here is a reconstruction based on that crowing."

Majestrum had positioned himself opposite the blue-robed wizard, the dark stuff of his legs and feet seemingly rooted in a rocky outcrop that stood out from the cliff that was the far side of the chasm. He waited calmly, his stony eyes cast down at the empty air.

A bell pealed somewhere above the two combatants. The man in blue raised his hands in a precise configuration. The sleeves of his robe fell back to his elbows, revealing forearms that were densely figured in arcane symbols. Some of them glowed a deeper blue than his clothing, others were like fire set into his pale flesh.

The bell tolled once again and the lean man's hands swept forward to point across the empty space at Majestrum. A concentrated beam of invisible force roiled the air between them, smashing across the distance in moments, only to break harmlessly against the barrier of the Authority's outstretched palm.

I saw that this had been no opening feint. The blue wizard had sought to damage, if not destroy, his opponent by summoning the entirety of his strength to launch a devastating initial blow. But all his power had not moved Majestrum back by a minim. Now he recognized, too late, the degree to which he was overmatched. His jaw made a sideways motion and his bright, piercing eyes blinked once.

Majestrum withdrew the hand that had repelled the other's assault, then raised it in a languid gesture, the dark stone fingers curled inward. Then he flicked the digits outward with a snap of the wrist, and a thick jet of brown filth spewed across the chasm.

The man in blue snapped his arms together in a cross and I saw his lips speak a syllable, but whatever the intended effect of his countermove might have been, it achieved nothing. The feculent stream struck squarely where his arms met, battered them aside, and drenched the man in corruption, the force of the purulent surge driving him back. The wizard's feet flew out from beneath him and he sat down heavily.

The flow of ordure and rot continued from Majestrum's outstretched palm while his other hand executed a circular motion—once, twice, three times—while he spoke several words that my mind could not retain: they slid from my mental grasp even as I heard them. The effect of this new incantation was to invert the crag on which his opponent had stood—and now struggled to stand against the torrent of foulness—turning it into a narrow depression, deeper than the blue wizard was tall.

Majestrum's intent was clear, I thought. He meant to drown in ordure the former colleague who had dared to challenge his assumption of supreme authority. But I was wrong; the victor in this contest relished cruelty far beyond what I was seeing. While the vanquished wizard floundered in a pool of filth, caked and dripping from head to fingertips in unspeakable substances, the author of these indignities came to hover in the air above his victim. From that vantage, he unleashed a succession of hurts and humiliations that I soon found unbearable to watch.

"Enough," I said to the Archon's integrator. "Let us move on."

From within, I heard a protest. "I must see how these things are done," said my other self.

"They are not fit to be witnessed," I said, inwardly. "Come back some day when I am gone and indulge your appetites to a satiety. But leave me out of it."

"I do not act from idle curiosity. That... entity is what we may have to contend with."

"From what we have just seen, you would need more than the scraps of spells in Baxandall's books to handle him."

"All the more reason to study the record."

I ignored the assertion and said, "Besides, it is Osk Rievor we must deal with, here in our aeon, and he is a far smaller fish."

"I am not sure of that," he said. "I am still not able to form a clear pattern."

"Then let us get on with acquiring information from Old Confustible, obtaining a broad scope, rather than obsessing over details of cantrips and hand-waving."

The Archon's integrator was speaking again. It had blanked the screen. "Are you ready to continue?" it said. "Your attention sometimes seems to wander."

"It is how I process information," I said.

"How curious." The screen lit anew with the image of the great device in its pit. "Despite what had happened to the Authority's challenger, whose name was subsequently expunged completely, his former peers still chafed under his increasingly arbitrary rule. When he ordered them to serve him in the construction of the interplanar capacitor in which he would store and wield a vast concentration of evil, they saw an opportunity to undo him."

"He was enlisting them to harness an energy that was more powerful than he was," I said.

"Indeed," said Old Confustible, "and so a plot was hatched, predicated on the arrival of a moment when the Authority would be vulnerable: the moment when the device was first activated. The focus of the plot was on the key to the device, the implement that would control its operation.

"Not even the Authority had the power to construct such an instrument. He required the assistance of the seven most powerful thaumaturges of the age, those who had been his peers until he had subjugated them."

"And were their names," I said, "Phaladrine Baudrel, Omris Shevannagar, App Imrici, Hilarion Falan-Falan, Terris Botch, Chav Hemister, and Oblon Hammis?"

"You surprise me," said Old Confustible. "I don't think I have been surprised by anyone save an Archon—and not too many of them—in a very long time. Where did you come across those names?"

"It would be—"

"I am familiar with your signature phrase," the integrator said. "Very well, let us continue."

I saw images of Phaladrine Baudrel and six others, each working in private. "The Authority divided the project into separate segments and gave one to each of the seven. None was to know what any of the other six were working on."

"Yet they did, didn't they?" I said.

"He Who Commanded was growing more and more consumed by the building of his device. It would have allowed him to extend his rule beyond Earth to all the worlds of The Spray and into several other universes. He began to dream the dreams that always seduce a tyrant: powers beyond powers, worlds at his feet, whole realms bowing to his whims."

"And the dreams occluded his faculties," I said. "It was ever thus, we may be thankful, else tyrants would never fall."

The screen showed members of the cabal crossing each other's paths while on seemingly innocuous errands. Sleeves touched, bodies brushed by each other, glances met, lips moved. "He unknowingly created space, only a little space, in which the plotters could operate. They took the chance, and together they instilled into the key a deliberate flaw that they hoped would slip by his notice."

"So that when he inserted the key into the mechanism and caused it to come to life..." I said.

"It would destroy him."

"And did it work?"

"See for yourself."

Now the screen showed the great mechanism at a later time, when all the scaffolding had been removed. Its surface was now clear, all components hidden beneath a uniform gray skin across which flickered rainbows of energy. Around the pit in which it stood a great crowd was assembled, waving colorful flags and bunting, though when the viewpoint swept across the upturned faces I saw behind the expressions of gay excitement a common strain of barely disguised terror.

It was the moment of sunset, the sun falling behind a range of low hills to the west just as a gibbous moon loomed over the eastern horizon. I had never seen an accurate rendition of Earth's long-gone moon and I studied the great, pale orb with interest: its shallow seas and fertile plains were clearly visible. I thought of its inhabitants looking up into their pale blue sky and seeing our world hanging above them, the old star—still more yellow than orange in those forgotten times—blazing behind.

The viewpoint on the screen now shifted back to the device in the pit, focusing on a point where one of its sides was closest to the lip of the excavation. Here a narrow ramp led upward from the solid ground to connect to the mechanism not far below its top, where a panel was set into the shimmering gray surface, etched with figures above a small, dark slot.

A sound went up from the crowd, a collective sigh that almost, but not quite, covered a mass moan. Heads turned and the viewpoint followed, showing me the dark pyramid on the horizon, backed by the rising moon. The ruby doors in its crystalline peak parted and a black object emerged, flying silently, inexorably, toward me. Majestrum, still seated on his throne, had come to claim his new kingdoms.

At the landward end of the narrow ramp, seven persons waited. I saw Phaladrine at their front, wearing a long coat of heavy fabric with a curious dark design—I could not make it out clearly—on its front.

The black throne glided to a rest before them, glimmering with power. There came an intake of breath from the crowd, though no sound of exhalation followed, as the Authority rose from his seat.

The black stone of which he was made moved as if it were flesh as he approached Phaladrine and the others, his hard face set in a look that said he owned all that he saw and did not hold its value high.

The seven made him a profound obeisance and did not rise until he let a small sound issue from his lips. Then the woman in the forefront of the group abased herself a second time and offered the dark overlord a look of inquiry. Receiving a gesture of consent, contemptuous in its languor, she bowed again and turned sideways, signaling to the six thaumaturges. Each one in turn stepped forward to give her a small object. As she received the first of these, she fitted it to another that she held in her hand, then did the same with those offered by each of her colleagues.

This she did under the gaze of Majestrum, her jewel-tipped hands moving with careful precision. When the seven components had been fitted together, she held in her palm a small oblong of gray metal, its surface etched with lines and symbols, across which flitted a rainbow like those that shimmered on the great device.

Now Phaladrine, her head bowed, turned to Majestrum. Her face impassive, eyes averted, she bent at the waist to make a deep courtesy to him, while her two hands pressed themselves—and the gray object—to her chest. A moment later, she straightened and presented the key to the man of stone.

For the first time, I saw evidence of feeling grip the tyrant. His languid air had fled and he reached eagerly for the object, snatching it from Phaladrine's outstretched palm. I heard his hard fingers click on the metal as he clutched it and turned to stride on heavy footfalls up the ramp to where the slot awaited.

The viewpoint, however, lingered on Phaladrine for a moment as she lowered her hands and stepped back. And now I saw clearly what decorated the front of her heavy coat; I recognized the figure of the woven man in whose heart she had buried—

"It was the insect thing," I said. "She added it to the other components, at precisely the moment when he champed to get on with the activation of the device."

"She knew him well," said Old Confustible. "They had formerly been lovers."

And now the stone-fleshed tyrant had reached the control panel. He did not pause for any effect but drove the key into the aperture and twisted it, hard.

For a brief time, nothing happened. The viewpoint lingered on Majestrum's face, frozen in expectation. Then the image cut to a close-up of Phaladrine, her narrow features held deliberately inert but her pale eyes betraying an inner agony of suspense.

The picture went again to the tyrant, and now the faintest hint of inchoate suspicion colored the hardness of his dark visage. His eyes snapped to the key, half of it in the aperture, the other half still in his stony fingers.

At that moment, a deep groan issued seemingly from every direction at once, the sound rising rapidly in pitch to an ear-shattering scream. Majestrum's rocklike flesh shook to the vibration of the noise. I saw tiny fragments and puffs of black dust erupt from his head and shoulders. Over his limbs and torso, thin lines of fiercely bright light ran like cracks across breaking ice. These fissures converged on one arm, that which led to the hand that still held the key, and swarmed down his arm to meet at his fingers. The hand now blazed with an actinic glare too sharp for the eye to endure, and the Authority's entire form shook with such heavy vibration that his stone heels beat a staccato tattoo on the ramp, even as the stuff of which he was made began to crumble.

The viewpoint now shifted to Phaladrine and the six others, who stood where they had been, but with their bodies now leaning forward, their eyes agleam, as they waited for the fulfillment of their plan. But then I saw sudden horror wash across the woman's face, her mouth opening as a prelude to a scream as she stepped forward.

But whatever it might have been in her mind to scream, the utterance went unvoiced. For now I saw what she had seen: that Majestrum, even as his obdurate non-flesh shattered and blazed under the flood of energy that poured into him, surged through him, from the device of his dreams, even then he could summon the will to lift his free hand high above his head where it performed a series of motions, fist and fingers repositioning themselves as if speaking in a language of signs.

Phaladrine stepped onto the ramp, her pale, slim hand outstretched, her mouth as agape in horror as that of the woven man who screamed silently on her breast. Behind her, the other plotters recoiled in terror and the crowd at their backs had already dropped their flags and bunting, turning away as if there could have been any hope of fleeing what was to come.

At that moment the screen went white with an incandescent glare. The viewpoint shifted. Now I looked down at an angle from a point in the air high above the city of Ambit, the picture centered on the interplanar device half-buried in its pit. A scintilla of brilliant white light appeared at the place where the Authority turned the key, then the pinpoint expanded in a fast-flying ring, like a ripple in a pond, that swept laterally across the crowd then continued on across the cityscape in all directions. Everything the wave front touched—people, buildings, trees, a giant creature of amorphous shape tethered in an open space—glowed with a brief luminescence of green fire before shattering, bursting, tumbling away, leaving behind rubble and smoldering detritus beneath air filled with swirls of pale ash.

The ring of force encountered Majestrum's pyramidal palace, which had already swung about on its gargantuan limbs in a forlorn attempt to flee. The wave of force caught the legs across the back of their knees, severing them as neatly as a cook disjoints a stewing fowl. The pyramid tumbled to the ground, landing on one corner but immediately spinning on, relentlessly propelled by the onrushing blast. It rolled across a district of houses and manses, smashing them to fragments. But even as it was driven ahead of the wave, its massive black blocks were being pulled asunder. Gouts of fiery mortar spilled from the cracks, igniting whatever they touched—though only for a moment, for the shock wave came inexorably after, battering everything before it into shards and smoking debris.

I saw the crystal apex of the palace fly free as the pyramid tumbled. Perhaps someone, or some force, within it attempted to save the master's seat. It began to rise, gaining height ahead of the wave front, but then it failed to clear the top of a squat tower of gold and silver. It tore through the structure's upper floors, then spun toward the ground beyond, rolling to land, still in one piece, against the inner side of the high, white wall that girdled the city. And here the ring of blinding light caught it and smashed it like glass, before leveling the wall and racing on to devastate the countryside.

"That force was intended to destroy him," I said, but he diverted some of it outward."

"Yes," said the Archon's integrator. "But in doing so, he reversed the polarity of the interplanar capacitor. It instantly collected all the evil then at large in our world, plus an immense charge from the other plane, and discharged it in one focused burst. See."

I made a wordless sound of horror touched by pity as I realized that the worst was not yet come. A deep and ominous thrumming filled the air above devastated Ambit. The great mechanism in the pit was pulsating, wreathed in tendrils of energy that struck my eyes with colors they had never before encountered. Its dimensions seemed to change, as if it swelled and shrank, so that it might have been some ill-intentioned leviathan drawing in and letting out huge breaths in preparation for issuing one destroying blast.

And now that blast came. From the top of the device erupted a beam of energy, dark violet in hue but flickering with a radiance beyond the spectrum my eye could encompass. The beam was narrow at its source, but as it pushed up at a shallow angle into the evening sky it grew gradually wider, though it showed no corresponding diminution of its intensity.

It was heading for the moon, and as it passed out of the atmosphere and sped across empty space it grew darker and wider, so that the disk of its expanding front soon obscured all view of Earth's satellite. I wondered how it must have seemed to those standing in their rural gardens or walking the thoroughfares of the lunar cities, to look up at the Earth, a gray sphere lit only by the moon's own reflected light, and see that strange pinpoint of light high on the planet's rim. Then the dark circle of power swelling as it surged toward them, first obliterating their view of the motherworld, then of the sun beyond, then of everything as the interplanar force smashed into their homes and obliterated all that they were, all that they knew.

I saw it from a conjectured vantage point in the air above the ruins of Ambit, saw the deep violet beam expand to blot out the moon. Then it ceased to be emitted from its source atop the pulsing, thrumming device. Instantly, the beam was gone. And so was the moon. Where the great light had hung in the evening sky I now saw only blackness and a roiling of clouds where the power had passed through Earth's skimpy blanket of air.

"Is there any possibility that the satellite was spun off into some other dimension, that there might have been survivors?" I asked Old Confustible.

"No," it said. "The nature of the force unleashed by the device was to negate that which it encountered. It encountered the moon and effectively negated it. They canceled each other out."

The image on the screen now showed the ruins of Horthalia at a later date. It was as if I was flying over a sea of rubble in which nothing grew, though I saw a pack of segmented arthropods, the size of large dogs, whose forelimbs ended in great claws. Then we came to a wide circular zone that was smooth as glass, and swooped over the surface toward its center. Here I saw, wedged into the featureless plain, the top of Majestrum's device. It resembled a dull gray building surrounded by a frozen lake. The view enlarged to show the control panel, then bored in closer to show a small, round indicator just above the aperture into which the Authority had inserted the key. As the magnification increased to make the indicator fill the screen before me, its dull circle flashed brilliant red for a moment, then went dark again.

"What does that last part signify?" I asked the Archon's integrator.

He said that it was part of the briefing all archons had received soon after their installation, ever since the destruction of the Authority. "The device remained live. It gradually accumulated energy from the adjacent plane, storing it over the centuries, as it was designed to do. But since no one ever came to direct the use of that energy—the knowledge having died with the thaumaturges of Ambit—it would eventually reach the device's saturation limit. Before that moment arrived, someone had to go to the device and reset the mechanism, discharging the energy back into the dimension from which it had been drawn."

"Someone?" I said.

"It became the obligation of those who assumed power after the Authority was destroyed: the archons. Ever since, an archon who discovered that the moment of discharge was about to occur would travel to Barran, as Horthalia is now known, insert Phaladrine's key into the mechanism, and reset it. Here is a reconstruction of a typical operation."

I saw a small group making their way across the glassy plain, sliding rather than walking on the smooth surface, fighting a stiff wind that blew their antique clothes around them. They stopped before the device, and one of them, a stern-faced, older man in a formal robe and extravagant headgear, approached alone. In his hand he held a small box of carved wood. From this he took a gray oblong that I immediately recognized. He seemed to stand in meditation for several moments before the control panel, where the indicator now flashed red every other second. Then he thrust the key into the aperture and twisted it.

The red light blinked off. The man made to remove the key but it would not come out of the slot. Instead, a thin tendril of deep blackness, like the soul of night come to life, emerged from the key and coiled itself as if shyly around the man's wrist, then grew thick and ropy as it raced up his arm to enfold his head, meanwhile shooting off new tentacles that wrapped themselves about his entire body until he was completely absorbed in stygian force.

Then he gently exploded, becoming a puff of gray dust that dispersed on the wind. A young man with a serious face stepped out from the small group. He slid to the control panel, stooped to pick up the box of carved wood that had fallen to the glassy ground, then stood to remove the key and place it in the container. He bowed his head and said something that the wind snatched away, before rejoining the others. With the wind now at their backs they skated away.

"So that is why there are so many memorials to bygone archons but so few tombs," I said.

"Indeed," said Filidor's integrator. "The device used to require resetting about as often as an archon would reach the end of a long lifespan, so it was accepted as a necessary culmination of a reign."

" 'Used to,' " I quoted, "and 'was.' Has something changed?"

"At the end of the Archon Dezendah VII's reign, his successor was able to turn off the machine permanently. Apparently, all it took was an inspired sense of timing."

"Dezendah VII was the last archon before Filidor I," I said. "You mean Filidor disabled a device that had been killing archons for aeons?"

"He did."

"Our Filidor?"

"The same."

I could think of nothing else to say but, "Remarkable."

My inner companion, however, had other things on his share of our mind, and was tugging at me. "What?" I said, inwardly.

"I want to revisit the scene where the Authority was destroyed and study it in slow motion," he said.

I thought I knew why. "You want to see the motions of his hand and fingers. You have an insatiable appetite for spells."

"No," he said. "Well, yes, I admit I am interested in whatever spell he was casting. But I also need to see what happened just before the blast."

"Very well," I told him, "though it is a moment of particular horror." To Old Confustible, I said, "May we see the last instants of the Authority, and at the slowest possible resolution?"

" 'We'?" he said.

"My assistant and I," I said, indicating my shoulder.

"Your assistant is asleep."

I reached up and shook the furry creature into consciousness. "Pay attention."

It yawned a gust of fruity air into my ear. I made a mental note that a pointed discussion would occur between us in the near future. Meanwhile, the screen was again displaying the last moments before the wave of blue force consumed Ambit. I again saw Majestrum's hand insert the false key into the slot and turn it, saw him react as the motion failed to deliver the result he expected. He began to vibrate and come apart, then his free hand went above his head and made the motions of a silent spell.

"Pause," I said, in answer to my other self's urging, then put his question to the integrator. "Is this a reconstruction or are we somehow seeing this from Phaladrine's perceptions?"

"Interesting question. I will consult the records of the briefing's preparation." A moment later it said, "This scene is from her point of view."

"How was it recorded?"

"Some time after, an archon of a sorcerous disposition raised an aspect of Phaladrine Baudrel and examined its memories."

"An aspect?" I said, needing no prompting from my sharer. "You mean a ghost?"

"When the Wheel turns, much that is impossible in the old phase becomes commonplace in the new."

"Why did this archon want to consult Phaladrine's memories?"

"To discover what she had done to adulterate the true key."

"Why?"

"In hopes of shaping a true one, of course."

Of course was right, I thought, a little annoyed with myself for not having the presence of mind to ask the logical question. I wondered if I was already beginning to fade. But my other self was nudging me and I said, "And was a true key ever made?"

"No," was the answer. "Nor could Phaladrine's revived aspect provide any illumination. Those memories were not available."

"Never mind the key," said the voice inside me. "Let us see the moment."

"Very well," I said to both him and Old Confustible, "let us see the instant of destruction at the slowest possible speed of image."

The scene crept forward in infinitesimal increments. "Do you want to focus on the hand?" I asked my other self.

"No," he said. "Watch all of him."

I did. Slowly, so slowly, his fingers made their motions. Slowly, so slowly, his shivering, calcified non-flesh fractured and erupted in puffs of black dust. Then came the first pinpoint of the brilliant light, just at the fingertips of the hand that held the key. It grew, instant by captured instant, and as it grew Majestrum's black stone body shattered. As the light became a ring that encircled his wrist, I saw chunks of him flying apart, rising into the air: an eye, a shoulder, a mouth and chin.

Another instant, and the ring had expanded to twice its width in the previous shot, so that it was almost touching the Authority's belly. His torso was blowing apart, a great crack running down from his nape to his lower back, so that I could see the intense light through it.

"Stop," my inner self said, and I passed on the order to Old Confustible. "Magnify that, centered on this part of the image," he continued, showing me in our mind's eye what he wanted to see.

The Archon's integrator did as I bid it, and the image expanded to fill the screen. It was as if I was traveling into a great crevasse that had opened in Majestrum's back, a back that now looked to be as wide as a county. The space widened farther and as it did so I saw something beyond, something in the space between the ring of expanding energy and the point where its force would have struck his belly.

"What is that?" I said to the integrator, pointing to the tiny, indistinct object on the screen.

"I do not know," it said. "Let us magnify it further and see."

The gap widened again and the object at the center of the screen enlarged, yet remained obscure.

"More," I said, needing no urging from my other self.

"These are the perceptions of a summoned aspect," Old Confustible reminded me. "There are limits and we are near them."

I leaned forward and peered at the image as it grew once more. The details remained indistinct, but there could be no doubt about what I was seeing: a tiny human figure, suspended in the air between the disintegrating rockiness of Majestrum and the interplanar device, untouched by the expanding ring of blue force.

"Forward one increment," I said.

The image changed, showing me the figure smaller still, reduced to a pinpoint.

"Once more," I said.

The picture shifted again. And Majestrum was withdrawn, just as the boy in my workroom had disappeared.

"He is indeed extant," I said to my inner companion.

"Worse," he answered, "he is aware of us."

The matter was not my most pressing concern, although I could tell that it genuinely upset my sharer. I had more questions to put to Old Confustible. "When I mentioned the name, Osk Rievor, you summoned us to this secure room and showed us the briefing. Why?"

"The Archon so instructed me before he left."

"I see," I said. "Then what can you tell me about Osk Rievor?"

"Nothing," it said. "I have heard the name only once before."

"When was that?"

"Not long ago. The Archon Filidor asked me the same question, and I could not answer him either."

"Why did the Archon wish to know about Rievor?"

"He did not say," the integrator replied, "but shortly after, he departed Olkney incognito."

"And where is he now?"

"I don't know."

I did not attempt to conceal my surprise. "Is it normal for the Archon's integrator not to know where he is?"

"No," it said, "although an archon who embarks on the progress of esteeming the balance sometimes drops out of contact for a while."

"How long a while?"

"Usually not long."

"As long as this Archon has been out of touch?"

"No, not usually this long."

"Have you made efforts to find the answer to his question?"

"I have. There is no record of any person named Osk Rievor in modern times, on any of the Ten Thousand Worlds."

I asked the obvious follow-up question: "Why do you say, 'in modern times'?"

"There seem to have been a number of Osk Rievors in times gone by. The name pops up on different worlds in different eras, but references are rare."

"What would you say," I said, "if I told you that Osk Rievor is a powerful thaumaturge who has the ability to cause those who encounter him to forget the experience?"

"I would say, 'Have you any evidence to substantiate that allegation?'"

"My own memories."

"That seems a contradiction," Old Confustible said. "If you have met him, then you ought not to remember it."

"I have dealt with those he has influenced, before the forgetting took full hold."

"Hmm," said the integrator. "Strange that the name endures. Still, I am not sure where this gets us."

I turned the matter over and examined it from several angles, meanwhile asking my other self for his sense of the thing. "I am not sure that Osk Rievor is our main concern," he said.

"I take a different view," I said. "Filidor found the fellow sufficiently concern-worthy to take himself out into the world, in disguise and unattended, and also to put me on the case."

"Even so," said my sharer.

"And now the Archon has disappeared, leaving instructions to show us this briefing."

"Yet again, even so."

A thought occurred to me. "Integrator," I said, "where is the adulterated key kept?"

"In the Archon's most private sanctuary."

"Is it there now?"

"I cannot use my percepts there without the Archon's expressed leave."

I held up Filidor's scroll. "Will this do?"

"Yes." A moment later he spoke again, and again I heard surprise in the device's tone. "The key is usually kept in a box of tuka wood in a warded cabinet. The cabinet is now unwarded and the box is gone."

"Ahah!" I said. I wasn't sure exactly what the absence of the box signified, but I was sure it signified something.

"What does it signify?" Old Confustible said.

"It would be premature to say," I told him, then woke my assistant—it had dropped off again—and instructed it to transmit to the Archon's integrator the dates and places at which the descendants of the seven Horthalian conspirators had met their ends, losing body parts in the process.

"Compare these to the places and periods where the name Osk Rievor appears," I said to Old Confustible. "Is there a correspondence between the two sets of data?"

"A rough but recognizable one."

"And the odds of that correspondence occurring by chance?" I quickly calculated the ratio in my head but not as quickly as the integrator. Still, our figures agreed.

"Well then," I said.

"Again, what does it signify?"

"It would be—" I began.

"Enough," said Old Confustible. "Contribute something useful to the conversation, or end it."

"Very well," I said. "I posit that Osk Rievor is an avatar, or an essentium or some such, of the Authority, projecting himself into our realm to punish the descendants of those who plotted to undo him—and perhaps with some other aim in mind."

"Such as?"

Instead of remarking on the prematurity of an answer, I said, "I do not know. But I do know that the solution to this discrimination involves a key that fits only one lock. I do not know where the key is, but the lock's location has not changed in four aeons. The answer to all of this lies in the center of the desert that used to be Horthalia."

"And you will go there?"

"I will."

My inner companion was seeking to take my attention away, but I was following my own logic. I asked the Archon's integrator, "Can an official vehicle be provided?"

"You have the authority to command the Archon's own aircar."

"Then I shall, forthwith."

Once aboard the elegant volante, I instructed it to take us to my lodgings where I changed into clothing suitable for the wilderness. I also chose a small weapon that was powerful at short range; I was not expecting to need it, but Barran is home to a number of fierce predators.

When I reboarded the vehicle, I carried under my arm the indecipherable book, stowing it in a compartment behind the passenger area. My inner companion insisted on the book accompanying us, though I thought its connection to the case was at best tangential.

"Do you hope to bind Osk Rievor to your will and have him read it to you?" I said.

"I do not know how it relates to all of this," he answered. "But I know that it does. It is the key to the mystery, if we could but decipher it."

"Your vagueness does not inspire confidence," I said. "I see a pattern here: the interplanar device, the conspiracy that produced the false key, the surviving portions of the Authority's body being associated with the murders of the seven plotters' descendants, and all coinciding with scattered appearances by Osk Rievor through the ages. This is a tale of revenge. He whose name causes you to faint is indeed extant somewhere, though I am giving the word 'somewhere' its most liberal definition. Blocked from returning to this plane, he is not the kind to accept defeat without doing as much harm as he can. So he is exercising the same viciousness that we saw in his duel with the blue wizard."

"It is a logical explanation," my other self said. "I just do not feel that it is the right one."

"Find a flaw," I said, "and I will consider it."

He was silent for a while, though I could feel his thoughts churning. Then he said, "I have one."

"Name it."

"Osk Rievor."

"What of him?"

"I named him," he said, "yet I did not lose consciousness. If he is the Authority, then speaking his name should have knocked me flat."

"But," I said, "you also just said 'the Authority' without any effects. That is the point of pseudonyms—they insulate you from the power of the true name."

I felt his mood deflate. "I suppose," he said. "Yet I still feel—"

"Let it go," I said. "I am sure that all will become clear when we reach our destination."

He was silent again, then said, "I am not a child, you know."

"You are very recent. Your emotions are certainly more intense than mine."

"Yes, I am more emotional than you. But that does not mean that I am wrong."

At that moment, I saw it all: my inner companion was indeed a child. In fact, the strange, amnesiac boy who had appeared in my workroom and in Drusibal Square must somehow be a projection of my other self's dreams. The child had appeared only when my alter ego was unconscious.

"What are you thinking?" he said to me. "I sense excitement."

"Premature," I said. "I will tell you later."

I followed my thoughts, mentally turning my shoulder to his attempts to peek in on me. The child had been the one piece of the puzzle that did not fit, since he did not seem to relate to any of the other pieces. But if I took him out of the matrix, all the rest fell into place.

Long ago, a thaumaturgic tyrant had seized power on Old Earth, destroying the one rival who sought to oppose him. He had forced his other former colleagues to combine their powers and construct a device that connected our realm to an adjacent plane, so that he could draw upon its alien energies. Though to what end? The answer came easily: the interplanar device had been created as the last age of magic had approached its twilight; therefore the intent was to prevent a renaissance of rationalism, which not even Majestrum could forfend.

But the seven thaumaturges, resentful of their bondage to the despot's will, had conspired to undo him in his moment of hubris. Their plot had only partially succeeded, however, because their resourceful overlord had whisked himself—or at least the essential part of his complex being—off to the other plane just before the energies that were supposed to destroy him could touch his peculiar stony flesh.

Exiled in the other realm, probably weakened, he had contrived to take revenge on the conspirators' descendants—as tyrants were always wont to do. Using the unlikely connections that bound the cosmos together under the rules of sympathetic association, he had waited, though it might take ages, until the flux and churn of phenomenality—perhaps augmented by his powerful will—brought his targets within reach of the surviving fragments of his shattered shell. Then he would reach out and strike, perhaps even drawing the life force from them, vampirically keeping himself alive.

No! I thought, making the leap of logic, *Not just keeping himself extant.* The energy he drew from his victims allowed him to project a part of himself, indeed a powerful persona, into our realm, where he assumed the guise of Osk Rievor. Rievor's goal? Surely it must be to hasten the return of the age of sympathetic association, into which Majestrum hoped to step, fully formed.

So Rievor must be working to revive the interplanar device. He would use its power to reconstitute himself wholly in our realm, then apply its energies to spin the Great Wheel a little faster. After which, he would stop the Wheel and magic would reign forever.

Immediately, however, I saw the flaw in my reasoning: the device would not work without a true key; but a true key had never been fashioned. *And yet, if a key is needed, what does a capable locksmith do?* I asked myself. *He makes a new one.*

But out of what? Again, the answer was obvious: out of the false one. In order to have worked as it did, the adulterated key that the conspirators foisted onto the Authority must have been very close to the real thing. The insect-thing had probably caused a couple of syllables in some incantation to be transposed, or it had slightly altered the proportions of some magical elements—just enough to do the damage. I had seen what became of Bristal Baxandall when he had made some slight error in a spell of transformation: he had become a bundle of everted organs and exposed bones expiring on his living room floor. An intentional error, just the right one, had undone Majestrum. But it would have to have been only a slight imbalance, unnoticeable except on close inspection. And that meant that a minor repair could well turn the false key into the true, and let loose on Old Earth—and who knew how many of the Ten Thousand Worlds—a monster whose iniquity would dwarf the worst imaginings of a dawn-time wondertale.

I remembered the reconstruction, taken from his own boasts, of what Majestrum had done to the nameless wizard in blue. *That creature must not come again,* I thought. *And certainly not wielding the weapon of unparalleled evil that now sits inert in the center of Barran.*

"What are you thinking?" my other self said again. "Now I sense a mood of grim determination overlaying self-congratulation."

I recalled the image he had once shown me of a storm-tossed Hapthorn, torch held high, defying an onrushing darkness. "You were right," I said. "I am called to a great cause."

"Indeed?" he said. "What has brought this on?"

"I have solved the case," I said.

"Tell me."

So I did. First I awoke my assistant, who had been sleeping on a seat behind the volante's operator's position. "I know all," I said. "Record this."

It sat up and yawned, rubbing small, furry knuckles against its lambent eyes, then said. "Go ahead."

I laid out the scheme in sequence, explained how it fit together and concluded by saying, "When we arrive at the appointed place, we will find Osk Rievor, newly strengthened by the absorption of the life energies of Hammis and Botch, seeking to wrest the false key from the Archon, who has been lured into a trap. But we will break the trap and save the day."

My assistant blinked at me. "Is that it?" it said.

"In essence, yes."

"But what about the child who comes and goes?"

"Yes," said my sharer. "What of the child?"

"It is a delicate matter," I said. "I will come to it last."

"And the book," my alter ego and my assistant said, almost as one, "where does it come in?"

"It is a blind," I said, "a spurious lead. Doubtless, Rievor himself long ago crafted it and put it into circulation. It was intended to draw the attention of thaumaturges who might otherwise seek the false key and interfere with his plan."

"But it is redolent of strong magic," my inner companion said. "It reeks of power."

"When one lays a false trail, one drags a strong-smelling substance across the true direction."

My assistant asked me what my intuitive other was saying. I relayed his objection and my answer to it, adding, "Which, I think, disposes of the point."

"No," said my inner companion, "it does not hang together. The book is not tangential. It is central."

"No," I said, "it has been created as a puzzle without a solution. The reason it cannot be deciphered is because it does not actually say anything."

When I relayed this exchange to my integrator, it said, "Perhaps you wish to think that it cannot be deciphered because you cannot decipher it."

"I am larger than that," I said.

I felt my other self mulling it over. "No," he said finally, "your explanation does not feel right. Some of it seems to fit together, but the overall shape is...ungainly."

"I disagree. In my mind, it assumes an elegantly logical form."

"You have yet to explain the child," said my integrator.

"Yes," said the voice in my head. "Where does he fit in?"

I told them.

My assistant's triangular face drew itself together, then its fur-covered features arranged themselves into a picture of derisory skepticism. I frowned, and it rapidly found a neutral expression and put it on.

The opposition from within me was even stronger. "Ridiculous!" said my other self. "Do you think I would not know if I was projecting myself up, down, and all around the town?"

"Why not? It happens when you are asleep and dreaming."

"I remember no such dreams."

"Who remembers every dream?" I countered.

"Then how is it done?"

"By magic, I suppose. How else?"

"That is a foolish and flippant answer," he said. " 'Oh, it's magic,' is not a handy solution to every mystery. I am not the child."

I sensed a growing anger in him. "You do not enjoy thinking that parts of you are beyond your control," I said. "It is an understandable reaction."

"It is, rather, *your* reaction," he said, "to my existence. Instead of the child being a projection of me, your argument is a projection of your own inner upset."

"*You* are my inner upset," I told him.

"Now who is getting angry?"

My integrator had been watching me, a worried look forming in its small face. "Are you two having a fight?" it said.

"We are disagreeing," I said. "He is emotional and irrational, and not good at accepting unpleasant realities."

Again, I saw a response register in my assistant's face, only to be instantly expunged. "Do you wish to comment?" I asked it, in a tone that held no warm encouragement.

"Yes," it said.

"So now I am to be set upon by both of you?"

"A comment about the case," it said.

"Ah," I said. "Very well, proceed."

"It is difficult to believe that the Archon is so easily duped as to bring his undoer the means of his own undoing," my assistant said.

"Filidor was always flighty. He was constantly in trouble."

"Not lately."

I was feeling put upon. I told my assistant to go back to sleep. My other self had withdrawn again, probably to sulk. I decided that there was nothing to be done until we got to Barran. Then all would be made plain.

In rescuing the Archon, it was likely that I would be called upon to exert myself. I instructed the volante to convert my seat into a sleeping pallet and, after telling it to wake me at dawn, allowed its systems to ease me into slumber.

CHAPTER THIRTEEN

A pack of preyns was lurking among the rocks and scrub outside when I finished the breakfast the volante's integrator furnished me from its supplies, and prepared to debark. "Shoo them away," I ordered, and the vehicle emitted a blend of high and low frequency vibrations that caused the predatory beasts' segmented exoskeletons to resonate painfully. They scattered quickly, racing off out of range, their multijointed legs clicking on the scree, their whiplike antennae streaming back over their thoracic carapaces.

I opened the hatch and prepared to descend. My other self said, "We must take the book."

"You are fixated," I said. "Look beyond your obsession. Today, we rescue an Archon and preserve the Great Wheel."

But he was adamant and threatened to harangue me every step of the way. For a moment I was tempted to say the name that would render him senseless, but it was a cruel impulse and I rejected it. "Very well," I told him, lifting the old tome from its compartment while Barran's perpetual cold breeze invaded the vehicle. "We may need something to light a fire."

My assistant was not happy about the wind. Though thick, its fur offered too little insulation. "I may have to have some clothes made for you," I said. "Perhaps something with braid on the sleeves and little bells along the hem."

"I assume you are making an attempt at humor," it said.

I admitted to being in a jovial mood. "I have good expectations of the day."

My inner companion grumbled something that I ignored as I looked through the volante's wardrobe and found a hooded over-garment. I put it on and let the cowl hang loose upon my back so that my assistant could climb in. Then I tucked Baxandall's book under my arm and set off.

I would have to go the last part of the distance on foot. Aerial vehicles, indeed devices of all but the most simple kind, became increasingly unreliable the nearer one drew to the center of Barran. But I had instructed the volante to climb high into the clear air, from which vantage it could watch my progress and use its armaments to deal with any feral beasts that might decide that a little Hapthorn would make a good beginning to the day.

We had landed just south of the great crater and soon I was toiling up the slope that led to its rim, the old sun lifting itself over the rubble-strewn horizon on my right. Despite the wind, the air became warmer as the incline grew steeper and soon I was perspiring under the heavy garment. I let my assistant know that I was enduring discomfort for his sake, and it let me know that he was grateful for my sacrifice. "Or at least I assume the sentiment I am experiencing is gratitude," it said. "I never had feelings before."

I thought my other self had withdrawn to sulk, but when I directed my attention his way, I sensed agitation. At first I took it for fear and said, "What are you worried about? I am armed and ready."

He made no reply, but I now realized that what I had taken for fear could more properly be called excitement, even exhilaration. The knowledge did not comfort me.

Soon after, I came to the top of the slope. I looked left and right, seeing the curve of the great crater's rim fading off into the distance. Far down, the rough and tumble surface of the inner slope gave way to the dust-covered expanse I had seen in Old Confustible's briefing. Smooth as glass, the plain stretched away as far as I could see, the far edge of the crater's rim well beyond the horizon.

"One gets an idea of the device's destructive power," I said.

The comment drew a twitch from my other self. "You need not worry," I told him, and patted the weapon I had placed in a slit pocket of my overgarment. "I do not mean to make much of it; I will simply shoot Osk Rievor on sight."

I sidestepped down the inner slope, sliding a little with each footfall, and was soon at the bottom. Here the land was as level as a table, the surface thick with dust. Gingerly, I stepped out onto the smoothness, sliding a foot forward as if testing ice on a pond. It was just as well that I did, for the footing was no less slick. My boot eased aside the fine powder that covered the plain, encountering scarcely any friction from the material beneath. I skated forward, brought the other foot into play, and found myself gliding across the plain, a plume of dust billowing up behind me.

I went out a good distance from the rim, building up to a considerable speed. It occurred to me to wonder how I would stop, and I experimented with turning sideways to the direction of travel, discovering that I slowed gradually as soon as I ceased to take fresh sliding steps.

"That is good to know," I said to both my listeners. "When the time comes, it would not do to slide helplessly by the scene of the action."

My other self offered a comment that I ignored, on the grounds that it was not helpful, while my assistant apparently saw no need to come out of the depths of my hood to respond. I was slowing even further now, and decided to let myself drift to a complete stop so that I could clear away a swath of dust to see what lay beneath. When I did so, kneeling on the hard glassy material, what I saw caused me to take a sharp inward breath.

"We have seen this before," I said.

"Indeed," said my alter ego.

My assistant peeked over my shoulder. "It raises an unpleasant memory," it said. "It was as I was passing through that realm that I became the way I am."

It was surely the cosmos from which my demonic colleague hailed, a place of swirling, indeterminate shapes and colors, where nothing ever held a defined form—where, indeed, form as we knew it was a lewd anomaly. I cleared more space and put my face close to the surface, watching the interplay of light and motion without seeking to focus on any of the transient shapes. It was like watching the patterns that appear when one pressed upon one's eyelids in a darkened room, the motifs ceaselessly blending into each other, but after a few moments my sensorium adjusted to the flux.

"That," I said, indicating to my inner companion a particular roil of violet and electric blue paisley, "is an entity. And so is the red and black lozenge about which it rotates."

"Yes," he said. "So, if size means anything, there can be no doubt that the individual we dealt with was a juvenile. Hence his fascination with our risqué realm."

I suppressed a comparison between the demon and my other self, but he might have caught the sense of it, like an aside half-overheard. To cover myself, I said, "And we find another end to tie in to the whole. It was not a coincidence that Bristal Baxandall sought to trap an entity from this adjacent continuum. His plans had something to do with the case we are now about to conclude."

"I sense that is correct," my intuitive sharer said. "It's all part of one whole, though I cannot yet see the full shape."

"Never mind," I told him, "I can."

I stood up, carefully, and began to skate again, navigating roughly by the angle of the ascending sun to make sure I was headed for the center of the vast crater. Aloud, so that both would hear me, I said, "The device is wedged solidly into this substance that forms the barrier between the realms, with most of it thrust through into the other continuum. From the images Old Confustible showed us, we can expect to see its top, resembling a low-rise, flat-roofed building of dull gray material.

"The control panel is on the north side," I continued, "so we will approach unseen, doubtless in time to catch Osk Rievor attempting to coerce the Archon into fulfilling his nefarious scheme. I will ease myself around the corner, weapon extended, and one shot will resolve the situation."

"I don't think so," said my other self.

"Why not?"

"I don't know."

"Then make way," I said, "for those who do."

We skated on. I withdrew the weapon from its pocket and checked its charge, although I had done so before debarking from the Archon's volante. The pistol's proximity to the other cosmos did not seem to affect it, but just to be sure, I aimed off at an angle and touched the activation stud. A narrow beam of translucent orange energy reached out to a spot in the dust, instantly rendering the powder incandescent and superheating the zone just above it so that the flash of light was accompanied by a sharp *crack* of expanding air.

"There you go," I said, tucking the weapon away.

I received no response. I could feel my alter ego brooding at the edge of my consciousness. I paid him no mind. In a short while, I would be in action; I cleared my thoughts, narrowing my focus down to the fundamentals. When the moment came, I would do, without hesitation, what must be done.

I skated on, the gliding motion almost hypnotic. I became as simple as a hunting beast, moving toward its prey. When a line appeared above the dead, level horizon before me, and I realized it was the top of the huge device, I felt a thrill rush through me.

"Here we go," I said. I drew the weapon again and turned myself sideways to my direction of travel, so that the sides of my feet piled up small rucks of dust before me. I was gradually slowing, until I gracefully slid to a stop not much more than an arm's length from the side of the device.

Now I reassessed my plan of attack. To come at the scene that I fully expected to find in front of the control panel, I could go left or right to approach the far side of the device. But if I chose the wrong angle of attack, I might come around the corner to see the Archon between me and Osk Rievor, making for a difficult shot.

"I will put you on top of the device," I said to my assistant, speaking softly. "You will peek over the far side, assess the situation, then come back and tell me which way to go for a clear shot."

"What if I am seen?" it said, not stirring from the depths of the hood.

"You will probably be taken for a harmless item of local fauna."

"I suspect," it said, "that when a thaumaturge sees a familiar, he instantly knows it for what it is."

"In the practice of this profession, there is always a certain risk," I said. "Now come out and I will boost you up."

I slid nearer to the side of the interplanar device. "Come out," I whispered.

"I am hesitant."

"I did not design you to be hesitant."

"How many times will we have this conversation before you realize it does not take us anywhere you want to go?" it said.

With my free hand, I tugged on the garment so that the hood was now behind one shoulder, then reached up and over. My fingers brushed the cool fur with which the hood was edged, then descended to find a warmer pelt. I felt the outline of my assistant's head, and was reaching for the loose skin on the nape of its neck when a sharp pain lanced through my fingertips.

I withdrew my hand and saw blood welling from several small punctures. "You bit me!"

"I do not approve of your plan!" it said.

"I did not design you…" I began, then recognized the futility of continuing. I summoned my dignity and said, "I require you to perform your duty."

"No. I could be killed."

"I am sure you will not be."

"Then you climb up there and take a look. I will stay back and record your brave deeds for posterity."

I put the book and the weapon on the ground next to the side of the interplanar device and unfastened my outer garment. The wind instantly found its way in, chilling my chest and abdomen. "I will take this off and bodily remove you from the hood."

"I may run away."

"It is a long, cold walk back to Olkney," I said, shrugging off the heavy cloth and shivering from the bite of the air, "with very few opportunities for expensive fruit along the way."

I held the garment in front of me. My assistant withdrew as far into the bottom of the hood as it could and when I reached for it, it bared its teeth.

"This is unseemly," I said. "Integrators should obey their creators."

"Some creators should be more careful with their creations," it said.

"I am going to lift you out of there," I said, "and if you give me any difficulty, consequences will ensue."

"Be assured they will," it said, exposing its upper fangs.

"We shall see," I said, and reached into the hood.

"Wait," said my alter ego.

"Stay out of this," I told him. "This matter must be settled."

"You cannot put the grinnet on top of the device," he said.

"I can and will."

"No, you cannot."

"Why can't I?"

"Because," he said, "the device is no longer inactive. I can feel its energies."

The news went through me like a jolt of power. "We must move fast," I said. "If Rievor has already compelled the Archon to surrender his key, Filidor's life may be in grave peril."

"I do not think that is the case," he said.

My former intensity of focus had already been shattered by my assistant's uncooperative attitude. Now I was again facing vague opposition. "I have had enough of this," I said, stooping to recover the weapon from where I had placed it, but exercising exquisite care not to touch the device. The hairs on the back of my hand lifted themselves erect as they neared the gray wall.

I left Baxandall's book where it lay and slid back a distance, then put the outer garment on again. *Left or right?* I asked myself and chose the latter. I was marginally more accurate with my right hand than my left so if I found my expected shot blocked by the Archon, I would be better able to deal with the situation.

My assistant was muttering in my hood, and my other self was trying to engage my attention, but I strove to focus all my will on the task ahead. I went around the corner, weapon extended, thumb lightly touching the activator. The hair on the back of my hand was still standing up. So was that on the back of my neck.

"You two have rattled me," I said to my other self.

"It is the effect of the device," he replied. "It is charging itself."

"Then we must stop Osk Rievor. Now let me concentrate. This will require a cool head."

But I was finding it more and more difficult to achieve and maintain any coolness. Now the hair on top of my head was lifting itself from my scalp, a most unpleasant sensation. The device emitted a low hum that grew louder, an ominous sound that seemed to vibrate my internal organs as much as it shook my eardrums.

"Look," said my sharer.

I saw the images he was drawing my attention to. I dismissed them, though it was difficult. "They are but an illusion," I said.

"But not a random illusion," he replied. "The device concentrates and stores evil so that it can be focused and directed. It is stirring the deeper parts of our mind, the regions where species memory is stored."

He was right. Before me, indeed all around me, grim and threatening figures appeared and disappeared: snarling beasts, shadowy lurkers with drawn daggers, rough men brandishing primitive weapons, ghoulies and ghastlies, smotherers and stranglers, and all the fell things that creep about in dark places. But though they were startling when seen from the periphery of vision, they became insubstantial when I faced them directly.

"They are distracting," I admitted, then had an inspiration. "Do you know of any spells to counter these phantasms?"

"Sengovan's Fortifier of the Spirit might help," he said. "But I feel it could be dangerous to use magic so close to the device."

"Then I will merely exercise strength of mind," I said, and focused with all my inner might on the task at hand. So doing, I reached the corner around which I would find the southern face of the mechanism and where I expected to see an Archon in a sad way. I readied the weapon, took a steadying breath, and staying well clear of the device, stepped out.

And saw nothing. Well, nothing except a headless figure in dark clothing, a large eyeball stalking about on the legs of a chicken, and a hunched stalker with canine attributes and claws that dripped blood. But I ignored these emanations from my own cerebral cellar and looked carefully. No imperiled Archon stood among the shifting crowd of phantasms, nor any grim thaumaturge with a gray metal key in his hand.

"Could Rievor be hiding himself behind some magical cloak?" I asked my other self.

"No," he said. "I believe he is exercising that most potent form of invisibility: the one called, 'not being present at all.'"

Passing through the wavering throng of monsters, I made my way along the south side of the device and came to the place where the control panel was inset into its face. Lights blinked and the hum was louder here.

"We are too late," I said. "He has already forced Filidor to deliver up his key. He has restarted the device and now he has gone on to the next stage in his plan."

"Look down," said my other self. I did so and he said, "No one has been here. The dust is undisturbed."

"He might have swept away traces of his presence."

"He did not strike me as the type to interrupt an aeons-awaited triumph with a little housework."

"Then, if no one has been here, how has the mechanism been restarted?"

I felt an involuntary shudder move my back and shoulders in a violent motion. "Did you do that?" I said.

"Yes," said the familiar voice in my head. "I have just had a terrifying insight. I know how the device has been restarted."

"Know or suspect?" I said.

"Know," he said, "in the way I know these things. Though I wish I didn't."

"Tell me."

Instead, he showed me. First, he took control of the hand that did not hold the weapon and directed its index finger at the ground beneath our feet.

"What are you pointing at?" I said. "The dust?"

"Not the dust. Nor the barrier that the dust covers. But that which lies beyond both."

Now I saw the image he created on the inner screen of our mind. The interplanar mechanism had been restarted from the other side.

"By whom?" I said.

"By the one whose name we do not speak."

"Started, yes, but is it under control? Or is he intending for the device to blow up?"

I felt him mulling. "No," he said after a moment, "he has not waited all this time to create a cataclysm that will destroy a large part of the other continuum as well as ours."

"How much of ours will be destroyed if this mechanism keeps running without control?" I said.

"The planet, at least," he said, "though who knows what it's destructive range might be?"

Throughout this discussion, various horrors and afreets kept swimming into view from the corners of my eyes. I turned toward a clownish figure that opened its mouth to reveal needle teeth and it became semitransparent. I said, "Let us move away from the device. These monstrosities are annoying."

I skated north a few paces, turned and found that the apparitions were gone. "That seems to be enough distance," I said. "Let us reconsider the case."

From its place in the hood, my assistant said, "Your analysis of last night was flawed."

"Thank you for pointing that out," I said.

"I did so," it said, "so that we could begin a new analysis by identifying the flaw."

"I can do so readily," I said. "I am losing my abilities. As my other self waxes in strength, I must inevitably wane. Proximity to this device is probably speeding up the process of decline."

"I do not think so," said my assistant and my inner companion with remarkable synchronicity. The integrator added, "Now would not be a good time for you to sink into one of your puddles of self-sorrow."

"I believe my sorrows run deeper than most puddles," I said. "I am, after all, facing an end to all that I have known."

"Cheer up," said my other self. "I believe things are going to work out quite well."

"How pleasant for you," I said. "A golden future beckons, and all you have to do before basking in its aura is figure out how to save the world from imminent destruction."

"I do not believe our adversary intends to blow up the world," he said. "I believe he intends, as he always did, to rule it. Now, why don't you focus your undiminished faculties on that fundamental fact and see where we can go from there?"

He was right, of course, much as I might resent it. "Very well," I said. "Integrator, what was the flaw in my previous analysis?"

It answered immediately. "The matter of the key."

"Exactly. We assumed—"

"You assumed," it interrupted.

"It was assumed," I said, "that Filidor had been lured here because he possessed the false key that could be modified into a true version, giving the Authority command of the device."

"That assumption has proved unfounded," said my assistant.

"Indeed," I said, "which means the act of drawing our attention to the false key was a blind."

"Yes."

"Which means that the object we took—"

"*You* took," said both the voice in my head and that of my assistant.

"Are you two communicating at some intuitive level?" I asked.

"No," they said in unison, my sharer adding, "We both have a flair for the obvious."

I continued. "Therefore, the object that *I* took to be a blind must not be. Thus we have been led here to bring—"

"The book," they both said.

"Please stop doing that," I said. "It is disconcerting."

I was already moving at an angle toward the corner of the device around which I had lately crept. As I neared it, the imaginary fiends and hellhounds reasserted themselves, crowding more thickly around me. I ignored them, swept through them, and a moment later I was side-sliding around the corner that led to the mechanism's south face.

I could not see the book where I had left it, so dense were the illusions this close to the device. But I skated toward it, blowing through semitransparent blood suckers and breath-stealers, and suddenly I was able to see the book through the skirts of a warty nosed crone who flourished two blood-smeared sickles at me. I moved closer, willing myself not to be distracted by the phantoms.

"And there," said the voice from my hood, "is the other flaw in your analysis."

Right again, I thought, for not only had I taken the blind for the truth and the truth for a blind, but I had dismissed from consideration the other factor that now looked up at me from guileless young eyes. Then the boy from Drusibal Square stooped and picked up Bristal Baxandall's book, turned on his heels, and skated smoothly away, turning the far corner of the device.

"He is heading for the control panel," said my other self.

"I do not need intuition to tell me that," I said, turning and going back the way I had come. I slid hurriedly around the corner I had just rounded, heading north. As I reached the device's northeast corner I did not bother to exercise caution as I had minutes before. I drew my weapon and prepared to open fire on a child that was no child, but an avatar of Majestrum, or Osk Rievor, or whatever guise in which he projected himself into our continuum.

I put the question to my other self: "Is it possible that Osk Rievor was the Authority's name before he assumed the title by which we know him? If so, knowing his name could give us an avenue of attack."

"No," was the answer. "My sense is that there is no connection."

"I am sure you are wrong."

"You were sure that boy was me."

"Then who is Osk Rievor?"

"First things first," said my inner companion.

I had rounded the corner. The imaginaries were thicker, the device humming more loudly and with a note that sounded like vicious smugness. I wondered that my deeper levels could contain so many images of horror and threat: bogeymen and specters, belly-rippers and nose-stealers, and a gleefully savage caricature of a boyhood tutor whom I remembered for his delight in skewering by sarcasm.

I pushed through them all, my feet sliding on the almost friction-less surface beneath the dust. And now, through the intervening layers of phantasms, I saw the child exactly where I expected him, standing before the control panel, the book spread open in his arms. But, curiously, he was not reading it. He held it outward, as if for the gaze of another, and slowly turned the pages.

I slowed my approach, resisting a futile impulse to sweep aside the intangible menaces that swarmed about me. "Shall I shoot?" I said.

"No," said my other self. "You might hit the device or the book, and I feel that either would be bad."

"How bad?"

"Remember the explosion that created this devastation," he said.

"That bad?" I said.

"Worse. Approach with caution. There is something else here we have not taken into account."

"I will get very close and shoot him in the head," I said, adjusting the weapon to its narrowest beam. Between the boy and me now stood the image of a naked man with the head and hooves of a horse, though the teeth must have come from a reptile, a pale woman in a gown of flowing gossamer who carried a man's severed head by its hair, a thick-bodied snake that scurried along on a score of tiny feet, and a manlike thing that looked to have been randomly assembled from pieces of several corpses.

I slowed so that I glided with decreasing speed through the horseman, the head-bearer, and the footed snake, and was almost upon the boy. The child gazed unconcernedly ahead of him. As before, I focused all of my intent on what I was about to do. I leveled the pistol, so that as soon as it passed through the slumping thing that was a body-parts collection I could place it against the child's temple and fire.

But the arm that should have swept through the last of the intervening phantoms instead encountered solid, cold, clammy flesh. The dead thing's face turned toward me on a creaking neck and its fourteen congealed eyes regarded me without emotion.

"Back away," said the voice in my head. "Quickly."

I was still set to do what I had come to do. "I will kill it," I said inwardly, raising the weapon toward this new target.

"No! You mustn't!"

I felt my other self struggling to take control of our body, our feet slipping. He had not had any practice at the peculiar method of locomotion and I felt a flash of fear at the prospect of his tumbling us into the device. But my fear was nothing to the excitement that I felt emanating from his side of our shared mental space.

"I'll get us away," I said. "Let me do it."

He gave me back the helm and I steered us away from the boy and the multioptic composite corpse, back pedaling away from the device until I was far enough away that its energies ceased to conjure frights from my lower mind. Now I saw only the boy holding the book, its pages spread to be read by the lifeless eyes of that shambles of a dead man.

My other self was vibrating beside me in our shared space. But when I examined his emotional state I found that he was not shivering with fear but trembling with excitement.

"Are you not frightened?" I said.

"At some level, I suppose I must be," he said. "But my fear is swept away by a presentiment that I am about to experience astonishments."

For a moment I felt a fleeting sense of what it must be like to be him, to be catching tantalizing glimpses of the world he and his kind would inherit, a world full of amazements and possibilities.

But his excitement seemed to me a childlike response, when what was needed was a practical plan. I needed to bring him back to the issue at hand.

"What is that animated corpse?" I said.

"It can read the book," he said.

"Why can it do so, when no one else can?"

"Because," he said, "it has been assembled from pieces—and especially the eyes—of the descendants of the seven spellsters who originally created the book. That was what all those murders over the ages were about. The adversary was creating a golem—I believe that's the technical term—that could perform the task."

He showed me pictures, his imaginings of what had happened. I saw Majestrum disappear into the other continuum just before the destruction of Ambit and the seven plotters. I saw the white ring of power smash its way across that city of wonders to Phaladrine Baudrel's slim tower, watched as it toppled and shattered, one small object flying clear: a book bound in leather that bounced and tumbled across the devastation and came to rest in the rubble. It lay there, untouched by the fire that came, because it could not burn, and unaffected by the passage of the ages, because it was shielded by the magic of seven great spellsters and of Majestrum himself.

I saw what he was showing me. "It is the combined spells that created the true key," I said. "From it a new key can be made."

But now came new pictures. I saw each of the seven thaumaturges creating a segment of the book while above them Majestrum loomed like a dark monolith. He used his superordinate power to decree that no one of them could read any other's portion of the great incantation. There could be no cabal against him.

And so, Phaladrine had contrived to adulterate her part of the whole. I saw the future she and the other plotters had envisioned: Majestrum destroyed, the seven sharing power, though each would have regarded any of the others as a potential threat.

"It would not have worked well," I said.

Instead, there had been no great powers in the land. The age of magic had come to its expected close and the age of rationalism had produced the Archonate. But Majestrum—or at least the essence of him—had lurked in the other realm, like one of Lord Afre's ancestors in the essentiary, exerting influence over the one substance in our cosmos to which he was still connected: the shattered crumbs of his stony corpse. Over unfathomable time, though it may have been much less where he was, Majestrum contrived to induce descendants of the plotters to come within range of his fragments. Each time the effort succeeded, he would use his carefully husbanded power to open a portal and suck through it a piece of his victim.

I considered the complexity of the process, the difficulty in nudging the few travelers who ever came to Barran to pick up an odd-shaped lump of rock and carry it home, so that it could be passed around for who knew how long before it came within range of the right person. "It seems a remarkably roundabout way to accomplish his aims," I said. "Why did he not just bring himself over here and stalk his victims directly?"

"There is not enough of him. His flesh was bound to the false key. It stayed here and was destroyed. Only his essentials were carried over to the other side."

"How do you know this?"

"I just do," he said. "Indeed, the more I remain close to the interplanar device, the deeper my understanding."

I tried not to let him see how this answer worried me. "Go on," I said.

"He could not project too much of himself, for fear the part that remained behind in the other continuum might become dissociated. Unanchored, his projected self would dwindle, becoming insubstantial in our realm. So he would send only the smallest fragment of himself, so stripped down that it did not know who it was or where it came from."

"The boy."

"The boy. He was sent to see where the book was, and who had it. Perhaps, too, he had to keep in touch with it."

A worrisome thought bubbled up and broke like a foul vapor in my mind. "The book has some of his old power in it. He exerts influence through it."

"Yes, almost certainly."

"He used that power to induce an obsession in you, to make you bring the book here."

"Yes," he said, "and no. I had what you called an obsession about the book from the beginning because I knew it was crucial. But the compulsion to bring it to this place is separate and not connected."

"How would you know that?"

"How would you know if salt had lately been added to a drink that before tasted sweet?"

"We're back to my having to trust your judgment."

"It has not failed us so far."

His confidence felt so boyish. "You are so young," I said. As I spoke, I looked back toward where the boy stood holding the book for the golem. A small hand turned a page, and I saw that it was the last. Solemnly, the child closed the leather cover and let the tome fall. It dissolved as it tumbled in the air, so that it reached the ground as a shower of dust. The boy put out his hands, palms upturned. An object appeared in them, small and gray.

"Quick," I said. I raised the weapon, then felt my other self grapple within me for control, pulling my aim askew. He was stronger than me in this place, the power of the other realm leaking into ours; he knew it, and I knew it.

I struggled futilely and then the time for action passed. Now it was too late. The child winked out of sight, taking the key with him, taking it back to the person of power who had waited aeons for this moment.

The creature assembled from parts of seven corpses stood inert, then its head leaned toward one shoulder and fell off, striking the dust with a dull thud. Its knees bent and its legs went out from beneath it. It became a pile of meat and bones and split skin, the several eyes rolling off in different directions. A skirl of wind brought its odor to me, a rank smell of putrefaction.

"You should have let me shoot," I said.

"It would have done no good."

"Then he has won."

"He has done what he meant to do," my other self said. "Now we must see what we can do about it."

"What can we do?" I said. "My friend the demon has deserted us. Besides, I doubt he was more than a spratling, whose elders have since sent him packing. And now our adversary's dire mechanism is at last under his control. What can we do that the seven greatest thaumaturges of the Seventeenth Aeon could not accomplish?"

My mood was bleak. But from the other side of our shared

space, my inner companion radiated a cheerful anticipation, like a schoolboy about to set off on a stimulating excursion. I felt him take control of one of our arms. He raised it above his head.

"Let us just see," he said.

I heard a squawk and felt a flurry of movement from just behind my head. My hood was suddenly lighter.

My upraised hand performed a quick series of motions involving fist and fingers, and the world around us ceased to exist.

CHAPTER FOURTEEN

"This is frightening," I said.

"Really? I find it exhilarating."

It had been worrisome enough to transit the nonspace of the adjacent realm under the guidance of the juvenile demon who had rescued me from an oubliette not long before. Plunging into the nonspace unguided except by my alter ego's enthusiasm was terrifying.

"Where are we? Where are we going?"

"Over there."

But there was no "there." There was no anywhere. We swam/floated/flew through nothing, for here there were no "things," no forms, nothing to touch or hold to or stand on or kick in frustration. Colors and shapes swirled around us, coalescing then separating, blending into and through each other in a constant flux and churn.

"We are moving, aren't we?" I said. "I sense motion."

"You could say we are changing our orientation," he said. "That implies motion if you think of it in relation to our previous orientation, but it is not wise to draw any hard and fast inference from that implication."

"I don't understand."

"Yes, I know."

"Where are we going?"

"I'm not sure. I'll know when we get there."

"What will happen when we do?"

"I have a plan."

"What kind of plan?"

"A daring and bold one," he said.

"Is that wise?"

"It has to be that kind of plan. It's that kind of cosmos."

"What is this plan?"

"It's actually more of an inclination, call it a feeling."

Again, his vagueness failed to inspire confidence. "I think we should discuss this further," I said.

"No time," he said. "We're here."

One moment we were in the formlessness of the other realm, the next we were standing on black rock under a sky that streamed and rippled with the colors of mud and dried blood. A few steps away the rock became a cliff face, plunging down to immeasurable depths. Far across the chasm, I saw a tumble of crags that looked familiar.

"The details are different," I said, "but it matches the reconstruction."

"Indeed," said my other self. "Now let's take a look around. And I'll need full command of our body; I may have to do something quickly."

"What kind of something?"

"I don't know. I'll probably have to improvise."

I wanted to resist, but I was not sure that I could. He seemed much more *present* here. I could not quite define it, because I had never achieved a satisfactory description of what it was like to have another person sharing my existence, but it was as if he had taken on greater weight and stature.

I ceded control of our body to him, thinking that this is what it would be like when the great change finally came. He would step into the front parlor, rearrange its furniture to suit his needs and moods, while I would traipse, ghostlike, down a back corridor to a small, bare room, there to eke out my diminished existence.

A path led inland from the cliff's edge. "This way," he said.

I did not ask him how he knew because there was no point. Our eyes were under his control so I looked where he looked and saw what he saw: fractured and friable rock, shattered and crystallized by the energies that Majestrum and his nameless rival had flung at each other in their duel. And here was the hollow into which the Authority had thrust the blue wizard, drenching him with foulness.

"It still reeks," I said.

"Time does not move here," he said, "or not as we know it. There is no entropy. Conditions remain the same until someone wills them to change."

I knew who that someone would be. "Are we safe here?" I said.

"I wouldn't think so. But, as someone once told me, 'Discrimination, at the level we practice it, is not for the timid.'"

"Nor is it child's play," I said. "We do not don paper hats and flourish wooden swords and go charging off to confront ogres. Not when the ogres are all too real."

"Reality is what one makes of it," he said. "Especially in a place like—"

He broke off as the path took us over a slight rise and brought us in sight of a black tower that rose from the center of a wide, bowl-shaped depression. He squatted and our eyes flicked from detail to detail, taking in the windowless walls, the massive door of squared timbers bound in lusterless black metal, the scum-flecked moat that ringed the great, dark blocks of the tower's base. "That'll be it," he said.

We descended to the bottom of the basin, our feet scraping on the rough rock. I saw that a collapsible iron bridge extended from the moat's outer rim to the doorway, and that the door stood ajar. Without hesitation, he strode us toward it.

"Wait," I said. I needed no intuition to tell me what we would find in the tower. "We should at least work out a strategy."

"I think not," he said, stepping across the bridge. Our feet made a *tch, tch, tch* sound as we ascended the three steps of black rock to the doorway. "It's more important to hurry."

Within, we found a rising staircase that circled the inner wall of the tower, the walls damp and slimy with mold, lit by guttering torches set in sconces.

"He has a flair for atmosphere, wouldn't you say?" my other self said as we climbed.

"I don't have a good feeling about this," I said.

"Leave the feelings to me," he said. "Why don't you calculate something?"

The steps circled up to the top of the tower, bringing us to a round chamber, floored in squared flags. Heavy beams crisscrossed from one side to another just below the ceiling. From the wood dangled a selection of metal cages, most of them shaped so as to compress and contort whoever might be so unlucky as to be confined within them.

Only one was occupied. It was parenthetically shaped, so that the thin, pale body of the man constricted by it was bent painfully backward. I saw that, beyond the discomfort of his position, the cage was also designed to expose his tenderest parts to the attentions of a sinewy, leather-skinned beast that, at the moment, sat a small distance away, licking its conical teeth with a red, bifurcated tongue.

Parts of the man had been gnawed away. Blood dripped to the stone floor, and the beast flicked out its tongue to a surprising length to lick at the pooling gore. But it did not approach the man in the cage; instead it watched the other man in the chamber, who sat on a substantial chair of black metal, one elbow on an armrest and the fingers of that arm's hand holding an oblong of gray metal as he regarded the prisoner.

He had been speaking in a sibilant voice, too softly for me to hear, but as we came to the top of the stairs he paused. The beast hissed as the man in the chair languidly turned his head in our direction. His perfect face regarded us with mild surprise that gave way to amusement. It was only then that I noticed that he was slightly transparent, like smoked glass.

My other self had made the same observation. "Good," he said, "he's taken time away from his strengthening to come here. He couldn't resist a gloat."

The man in the cage was also looking our way, his features completely without animation. I noticed that most of his face and what I could see of his body through the cage was covered in scars, some of them old and puckered, others new and pink.

The man in the chair caught the direction of our gaze and quickly snapped his head around to regard the prisoner, who now returned his captor a look of blank unexpectation. Then the dark one looked back to us and rose from his seat, turning toward us. Full face on, he was the most beautiful person of either sex I had ever seen, his features precise and delicate, yet strong, his eyes dark and large, his mouth exquisitely formed. But his was a cruel beauty, a cold perfection. The feel of his eyes on us made me shudder.

"I know you," he said, the voice soft but carrying a chill, as if his words entered our ears borne on a flow of ice-cold oil. "From my dreams. Henghis Hapthorn, the discriminator."

As he said my name, I felt a chill run through me—through not my body, but through the *me* that was my part of our shared mind—as if I had been stroked by a single talon of a great, fierce bird carved from ice. I had thought my strength diminished before; now I felt it fail completely. I was no more than some small creature, naked and newborn, eyed by a predator.

"We should hide," I whispered to my other self. "Somewhere safe."

"It will be all right," he told me.

"No," I said. "He has real power. You have only inklings."

"I know how this will go."

"You are overconfident." I was suddenly tempted to blurt out the dark man's name, rendering my other self unconscious, then turn and run down the steps, out into the rocks, find a place to hide...

"No," said my sharer. "Don't even think it. Leave this to me."

"I am frightened," I said. "You are so new."

"Move over," he said.

It had seemed to me that he had been growing larger in our shared space. Now it was as though I was nudged into a corner while he filled our common parlor.

Through all of this he had stepped deeper into the chamber. I could feel a small smile on our lips as he addressed the adversary. "Hapthorn?" he said. "*He* is not your problem. *I* am."

It must have been a long time since anyone had given Majestrum pause to think, but he clearly remembered how to do it. He looked us up and down, threw a quick glance to the prisoner, then his gaze came back to us. A thin line appeared between the perfectly formed brows of his semitransparent face.

"I see," he said. "How imaginative. And from which strain do you come? Are you a Hammis? A Botch? Surely, not a Hemister?" He named the other four, and I knew he was like a man striking a selection of bells, waiting to hear the note he needed.

But the note did not sound. Now the corners of that flawless mouth turned down, and those perfect eyes narrowed to a less pleasing shape.

"You know what they say," my other self said, " 'No name, no handle; no handle, no grip.' "

"But they also say, 'No name, no power,' " said Majestrum, and his head indicated the emaciated man in the cage. He lifted the true key and I saw that the fingers that clasped it were become almost solid. "I had the power to take this wretch's name. I will soon have the power to make you divulge yours."

"Which means that you don't have that power now."

"Soon." The tone was that of a caress and a threat.

"But what if I don't have a name?" my alter ego said.

The dark face smiled, and there was a horrid beauty in that smile. "Then I'll give you one. So I can take it away, piece by piece."

Despite my terror I sensed a flood of triumph from the other side of our shared space. "Never mind," our voice was saying, "if names can be given, that means they can also be taken. I happen to have one in mind." We threw a glance toward the man in the cage, who now appeared to be holding his breath, then we stepped closer to the dark man, theatrically pulling at our chin with our thumb and forefinger, regarding Majestrum with our head cocked to one side. Then my sharer said to him, "And I name myself... Osk Rievor."

A third presence instantly filled our already crowded mental parlor, this one so immense that it pressed my inner companion into the same corner where I—I admit it—had been cowering. "What have you done?" I said.

"It will be fine," my sharer said.

I felt like a small and timorous beast trapped in an enclosed pen with a full-grown bull garoon. "How do you know that?"

"Watch."

I had been watching through our eyes as Majestrum reacted. At the instant of the inrush into our shared mental space the bent-back cage had become empty. The sudden loss of weight attendant upon the prisoner's disappearance caused the restraint to swing and the swing caused a discreet *clank*. The dark man's exquisite head swung toward the sound, then came back to us, the line between his brows now deepening to a chasm and rage taking charge of the irreproachable features. The hand that held the key lifted and his lips parted to frame a word.

But "Too late," said our voice, though neither the tone nor the timbre was ours. Both of our hands were already extended, the digits of one bent at the joints in a particular arrangement, as if we were stroking the strings of an instrument. Now the other hand executed a precise flick of fingers and thumb into a snap as loud as a breaking bone.

The key leapt from Majestrum's smoky grasp into ours.

With a snarl, the dark man brought up both hands, the palms edged like knives. He opened his mouth to speak but our voice was already saying two syllables that, although I heard them clearly, my mind could not hold. The words struck Majestrum like quick, successive blows, thrusting him back across the room, while the roof of the tower blew off in a welter of splintered timbers and shattered slates, taking the torture cages with them. The murky sky ceased to move and cleared to become a dome of lustrous black, in which great, blue stars were bursting into light. Clean, cold air rushed into the chamber, scouring away the stench of blood and mold.

Pressed back against the wall, Majestrum spread his fingers and brought his hands forward. He snarled something and four multilimbed beasts, fangs bared, coalesced from the surrounding shadows to fling themselves at us from four directions. But our hand that held the key sketched a quick figure in the air and the four monstrosities froze in midflight, became puffs of foul-smelling dust, swirled away on the cleansing wind.

Now the hand that did *not* hold the key stretched out, fingers forming a new pattern. A rictus of horror seized control of Majestrum's face. He stooped and scooped up the split-tongued tormentor from the floor beside him, flung it at our head, then scuttled, bent-backed, from the chamber.

Our new tenant simply inclined our neck to one side and the beast flew harmlessly by to strike the wall behind and fall whimpering to the floor. Meanwhile, we strode to the top of the steps, to hear sounds of hurried flight coming from the circular staircase.

"No point," our voice said, "in dragging this out." Fingers still in their new orientation, our hand extended down the stairwell and our voice said a word that, again, my mind lost as soon as I heard it. A ball of brilliant light, white tinged with electric blue, sprang from our fingertips and shot away, disappearing down and around the curve of the wall. Moments later, a great shout came from below, a howl of unrestrained rage and despair, that rose to a shriek and then became a moaning cry that was abruptly cut off.

We went down the stairs and found him just inside the heavy timber and iron door. Or what was left of him. Our hands performed motions and a sweeper-collector appeared in them. We bent and gathered the remnants, then stepped outside and cast them into the brisk cold air. They blew away, dispersing, toward the ridge that led to the chasm.

Overhead the sky was drawing in, the stars winking out. Darkness crept toward us from all points. "This place is shrinking," I said. "What will become of us?"

"We'll be fine," said my other self.

"Thank you," said the third person in our head. "I was never quite sure that anyone would come, or at least not in time. In some ways the uncertainty was worse than the attentions of the beasts."

"I don't understand," I said. "What happened?"

"It was about names," my sharer told me, then addressed the other, "that was how it went, wasn't it?"

"Yes. When Majestrum and I fought each other, I did not know that he had found my true name. It gave him power over me, and he used that power to sequester me here. He would visit from time to time to put me in a different cage and change the type of tormentor he created to worry me.

"Meanwhile, he subordinated our former colleagues and pressed them into building his capacitor. Then, just after he had put me into that back-bending frame and set his gnawing beast to work, he ceased to come."

My other self said, "Phaladrine Baudrel led a conspiracy. The seven adulterated the control key so that when he tried to initiate the device it would destroy him. But it only smashed the hard flesh he had acquired in another realm, while the essence of him escaped to the other side of the interplanar barrier."

"Yes, very good, that was what I learned," said the presence I now knew must be the blue wizard.

"How did you learn of this," I said, "while hanging in a cage and being chewed on incessantly?"

"My tormentor would grow bored. I engaged it in various contests. Sometimes it would spend a long time puzzling over a riddle. That gave me opportunities to recover my strength, though very slowly."

"So you projected yourself into our realm," my other self said.

"Yes. Since Majestrum had my name, I was connected to the fragment of him that had taken refuge in the realm connected to our old universe by the interplanar device. He, in turn, could connect with the fragments of his flesh that had survived. Over the eons, he exerted himself to bring descendants of the seven plotters within range of the pieces. Then he would use the residual power in his fragments to strike at them, to steal from them their flesh and bone."

"And their eyes," my sharer said.

"Especially their eyes. He was assembling a creature that could read the book. He had ordained that each of the seven creators could read only his own part. The part of him that survived had enough power to alter that ordinance so that it would apply to their descendants."

"It seems," I said, "a very roundabout way of achieving his ends. No wonder it took him aeons."

"Who is this poor fellow?" the blue wizard asked. And when my other self explained our relationship, he said, "Ah, one of those unfortunates who are trapped in linear rationalism."

I bridled at the condescension. "It is no trap. It is a glorious instrument for apprehending reality."

"As long as reality agrees to cooperate," the thaumaturge said. "I remember an expression from one of your eras: 'putting the cart before the horse.' You do still have carts and horses, don't you?"

"They are not common," I said, "but they can be found in some bucolic districts."

"Well, the expression falls down when the cart is the true motive force and the horse is merely pushed along, don't you see?"

"But how could that be?"

"It *must* be, if the cart possesses more will than the horse."

"Again, how could that be?"

"Someone who possesses a great deal of will might lend it to the cart. That is what much of what you call magic is about."

My other self spoke up, sounding very like a tutor's overly bright, favorite pupil. "So Majestrum retained plenty of will, even though he had lost much of his power."

"Indeed," said the blue wizard in an indulgent tone. "Much of his power was resident in his shattered flesh, but his will was the essence of him. And will, in normal realms, is paramount."

His use of the word "normal" rankled. My other self caught my reaction and reminded me that our universe was distinct from all others by our peculiar separation of the abstract and the concrete, the symbol and the thing symbolized, the map and the territory.

I was forming a dignified response but he had already re-engaged the third presence in our parlor in further discourse. "So, Majestrum's will affected his experience of time while he worked at his plan?"

"And of space, of course," said the other voice. Then in a tone that sounded as if he were speaking to the intellectually deprived he said to me, "Just as gravity bends space and velocity affects time in your little realm, will is a prime determinant everywhere else."

"So Majestrum's confinement seemed to him no more than the span of an afternoon?" I said.

"If that's the best you can do," the wizard said, "I suppose it will have to suffice." Then his tone took on a brisker note. "Now, this place is ending and I must rattle off to find where he hid my name. Can you find your way home?"

"I'm not sure," said my other self.

"Just do this," came the response, and I felt our fingers executing a sequence of motions, "and say…" But again I could not retain the words, although my other self said, "I have it."

"Wait," I said, "is your name not Osk Rievor?"

"Not really," the voice said. "It is no one's name. It was a name I held out, like a cup to catch rain, so that the right fellow would come along and fill it."

"A name without a referent," my other self said, "waiting for a referent without a name."

"Exactly. And brightly done, by the way. Once I am settled again, if you would be interested in apprenticing…"

"I would be very interested."

"Wait," I said. "How did you know that he would come?"

"I couldn't explain it to you in any way you would understand," said the blue wizard. "But trust me, I knew."

"But did you know that your plan would work?"

He gave the equivalent of a shrug. "No. But I hoped." I felt the presence stir, as if he was rising from a chair in the parlor and preparing to depart. "Well, then," he said.

"Would you mind," my other self said, "if I used the name Osk Rievor? I liked how it felt."

"You are welcome to it, and to much more." And with that, he bid us a brief farewell and departed.

At his going, the pressure departed and I felt as if I had room to move again—though not as much room as before. My other self—or Osk Rievor, as I must now get used to calling him—was definitely occupying a greater share of our mutual space.

The place where we stood had drawn in. The last of the stars was going out and I could no longer see the ridge that we had descended to the tower. "Time to go," said Osk Rievor. He worked his fingers as the blue wizard had showed him and said the words that I still could not retain.

There was no sense of motion. It was as if within the span of one blink I had closed my eyes on the dwindling realm and opened them again on the plain of Barran. My other self, still in possession of our body, slid immediately to the interplanar device that was now humming louder, the vibration palpable through the souls of our feet.

"What are you doing?" I said, for I found that we still had the key in one hand and he was thrusting it into the receptor slot.

He did not answer. Meanwhile, our fingers were rapidly pressing certain parts of the gray metal that protruded from the slot. Then we gripped the key's edge and rotated it sharply. From within the mechanism came a loud *clack!* The humming wound down, faded to a susurration, then whispered itself out of hearing.

"We should leave here now," Osk Rievor said. "Where is the grinnet?" Aloud, he said, "Integrator, where are you?"

A ripple appeared in the dust and resolved itself into the top of a small triangular head. A pair of lambent eyes regarded us. "Here," it said. "I saw sting-whiffles, the kind that drink blood, circling overhead."

"Take us away from here," Osk Rievor said to me. "I must rest and mull what I have learned."

I retook control of our body and bent to extend a hand to my assistant. It shook itself free of the dust in which it had buried itself, then climbed to my shoulder and into the hood. I turned and slid away from the interplanar device, dust pluming behind me as I built up speed. The sting-whiffles reappeared in the afternoon sky but I felt in my pocket and found the weapon.

"Hurry," said my assistant. "The mechanism is undergoing some drastic change."

I did not look behind me but redoubled my efforts, my arms swinging and my bent body swaying from side to side as I skated across the near frictionless surface of the crater's floor. I had not gone many more steps before a deep rumble pursued me across the plain. A tremor passed through the dust beneath my feet racing off into the distance. Then the rumbling became a roaring, tearing sound and I did not need my integrator's "Faster!" to make me reach for my best speed.

Another tremblor rumbled by and beneath me, then an even larger one close behind. The roaring became a thundering, as if a great cataract were at my back. "What is happening?" I asked Osk Rievor, but received in reply only the equivalent of an uninterested shrug.

The ground shook, dust rising in puffs and transient whirlwinds. I saw the sting-whiffles flying ahead of us, not lazily circling now, but fleeing in a straight line high up in the air. Now the whole plain shuddered and the thunder rolled continuously behind me while I fled like a small creature pursued by glistening fangs.

And then the sound abruptly faded, as if some impermeable barrier had intervened. I chanced a look behind and saw that the interplanar device was silently shaking and shivering—and sinking slowly into the surface within which it had been wedged for aeons. The ground convulsed even more violently—for several moments, my motion forward was like skating over waves—then the top of the mechanism slid out of sight.

A last ripple radiated out from the place where Majestrum's engine had been, and as it reached me the ground beneath my feet ceased to be the smooth glasslike substance on which I skated. It became, instead, ordinary hardpan covered in dust, and the rules of our linear, rational realm suddenly reasserted themselves. My sliding foot was immediately reacquainted with friction so that I tumbled and sprawled, my assistant flying with a squawk from my hood to perform a similar maneuver in miniature.

Bruised, I sat up and looked back at the way we had come. The device was gone, along with all sign of its ever having existed. I swept aside dust and found no interplanar barrier. My assistant limped over to me and said, "I think I am experiencing my first pain."

"How do you like it?"

"Not greatly."

"Then see if you can contact the Archon's volante. There is a restorative in the aid kit."

The grinnet blinked once, then said, "It is on its way."

"Did you hear that?" I asked Osk Rievor, but heard back only a distracted grunt.

A few days later, the Archon sent a two-seater cabriol to collect me. In the other seat was Brustram Warhanny. He made no greeting and remained silent as we flew to land outside Filidor's private study. The scroot remained with the vehicle and I went inside.

This time two chairs faced each other across the blue-green Agrajani rug. Filidor sat in one and waved me to take the other, dismissing the need for any formalities.

"So," he said, when I was settled, "that appears to have gone well."

I sensed Osk Rievor's amusement at the edge of my awareness and sent him a warning to let me conduct this interview. "It ended well," I said aloud.

"And that is what matters," Filidor said.

I took assurance from his affable mood and said I would like to ask a question or two. He inclined his head and I said, "You were not completely candid when you came to me with suspicions of a plot within the Archonate apparatus, were you?"

"I was not."

"You tore the page from the catalog?"

"Yes."

"And the key was not disturbed?"

"I took it with me for safe keeping. It had no part to play other than to make you think about a key and a lock."

Now I put a question to which I did not know the answer. "Would you care to reveal how you came to learn about Majestrum's scheme to return to our realm?"

He put the fingertips of both hands together and flexed the fingers like a spider doing exercises against a mirrored wall, then said, "I would not. Being Archon requires maintaining a certain aura of mystery."

"All of this is leading up to my main question," I said.

"Yes," he said. "But before I forget, I would like you to attend a small ceremony in a couple of days."

"Of course."

"I'm giving Chalivire Afre a special award for exemplary assistance. I would appreciate it if you would let it be known that she bravely accepted a season of ignominy in order to foil a plot to undermine the Archonate."

"She will be surprised to learn that about herself," I said.

"Yet it will be a welcome surprise."

I made a formal gesture of acceptance of his command, then said, "May I suggest that for refreshments you serve gripple eggs? There's a man on Mandoval—Ang Porhock—who makes an exceptional omelet."

"If you say so." He spoke to Old Confustible and arrangements were made.

"Now as to my main question—" I began.

"You wish to know why I enlisted your aid in a matter involving magic, when you are noted for your disdain for the entire concept."

"Well, yes."

He steepled his fingers again and assumed a pensive look for a moment. Then he said, "Archons have to take a longer view, especially when an entire age is about to end and another is in the offing."

He had not actually answered the question, and I knew enough about archons to realize that rephrasing the query would not elicit anything from this one. Meanwhile, Osk Rievor was anxious to ask a question of his own. As it turned out, it was exactly the same question that I now wished to put to Filidor.

There was one crucial difference, however: If Rievor had had control of our voice, Filidor would have heard joy, whereas I could not avoid a note of dread.

"A longer view?" I said. "Do you mean that you have me in mind for further assignments? Of a similar nature?"

He gave me one of those bland looks that archons must surely practice during their apprenticeships and said, "It would be premature to say."

THE SPIRAL LABYRINTH

A TALE OF HENGHIS HAPTHORN

MATTHEW HUGHES

Don't miss the next Henghis Hapthorn novel, The Spiral Labyrinth.

THE SPIRAL LABYRINTH

(AN EXCERPT)

CHAPTER ONE

"**E**xpensive fruit may grow on trees," I said, "but not the funds needed to purchase it in seemingly limitless quantities."

I gestured at my befurred assistant, formerly an integrator, but now transformed into a creature that combined the attributes of ape and cat. I had lately learned that it was a beast known as a grinnet, and that back in the remote ages when sympathetic association last ruled the cosmos, its kind had been employed as familiars by practitioners of magic.

My remark did not cause it to pause in the act of reaching for its third karba fruit of the morning. Its small, handlike paws deftly peeled the purple rind and its sharp incisors dug into the golden pulp. Juice dripped from its whiskers as it chewed happily.

"Nothing is more important," said the voice of my other self, speaking within the confines of our shared consciousness, "than that I encompass as much as possible of the almost forgotten lore of magic, before it regains its ascendancy over rationalism." He showed me a mental image of several thaumaturges scattered across the face of Old Earth, clad in figured garments, swotting away at musty tomes or chanting over bubbling alembics. "When the change finally comes, those who have prepared will command power."

"That will not be a problem for those who have neglected to earn their livings," I answered, "for they will have long since starved to death in the gutters of Olkney."

The dispute had arisen because Osk Rievor, as my intuitive inner self now preferred to be called, had objected to my accepting a discrimination that was likely to take us offworld. A voyage would interrupt what had become his constant occupation: ransacking every public connaissarium, as well as chasing down private vendors, for books and objects of sympathetic association. The shelf of volumes that we had acquired from Bristal Baxandall was now augmented by stacks and cartons of new acquisitions. Most of them were not worth the exorbitant sums we had paid for them, being bastardized remembrances based on authentic works long since lost in antiquity. But Rievor insisted that his insight allowed him to sift the few flecks of true gold from so much dross.

"I do not disagree," I told him, "but unless you have come across a cantrip that will cause currency to rain from the skies, I must continue to practice my profession."

"Such an opportunity is not likely to come our way again soon," he said. He was referring to the impending sale of an estate connaissarium somewhere to the east of Olkney. Blik Arlem had been an idiosyncratic collector of ancient paraphernalia for decades. Now he had died, leaving the results of his life's work in the hands of an heir who regarded the collection as mere clutter. Rumors had it that an authentic copy of Vollone's *Guide to the Eighth Plane* and a summoning ring that dated from the Eighteenth Aeon would be offered.

"More important," he said, "the auction will draw into one room all the serious practitioners. We will get a good look at the range of potential allies and opponents."

"And how will we separate them from the flocks of loons and noddies that will also inevitably attend?" I said.

"I will know them."

"And they will know us," I pointed out. "Is it wise to declare ourselves contenders this early in the game?"

I felt him shrug within the common space of our joint consciousness. "It must happen sometime. Besides, I don't doubt we have already been spotted."

I sighed. I had not planned to spend my maturity and declining years battling for supremacy amid a contentious pack of spellcasters and wondermongers. But I declared the argument to be moot in the face of fiscal reality, saying, "We have not undertaken a fee-paying discrimination in weeks. Yet we have been spending heavily on your books and oddments. The Choweri case is the only assignment we have. We must pursue it."

When he still grumbled, I offered a compromise. "We will send our assistant, perched on the shoulder of some hireling. It can observe and record the proceedings, and you will be able to assess the competition without their being able to take your measure. Plus we will know who acquires the Vollone and the ring, and can plan accordingly when we return from offworld."

"No," he said, "some of them are bound to recognize a grinnet. They'd all want one and we would be besieged by budding wizards."

"Very well," I said, "we will send an operative wearing a full-spectrum surveillance suite."

"Agreed."

The issue being settled, we turned our attention to the matter brought to us the evening before by Effrayne Choweri. She was the spouse of Chup Choweri, a wealthy commerciant who dealt in expensive fripperies favored by the magnate class. He had gone out two nights before, telling her that he would return with a surprise. Instead, he had surprised her by not returning at all, nor had he been heard from since.

She had gone first to the provost where a sergeant had informed her that the missing man had not been found dead in the streets nor dead drunk in a holding cell. She had then contacted the Archonate's Bureau of Scrutiny and received a further surprise when she learned that Chup Choweri had purchased a small spaceship and departed Old Earth for systems unknown.

He was now beyond the reach of Old Earth authority. There was no law between the stars. Humankind's eons-long pouring out into the Ten Thousand Worlds of The Spray had allowed for the creation of every conceivable society, each with its own morality and codes of conduct. What was illegal on one world might well be compulsory on another. Thus the Archonate's writ ended at the point where an outbound vessel met the first whimsy that would pluck—some said twist, others shimmy—it out of normal space-time and reappear it light years distant. The moment Chup Choweri's newly acquired transportation had entered a whimsy that would send it up The Spray—that is, even farther outward than Old Earth's position near the tip of humanity's arm of the galactic disk—it had ceased to be any of the scroots' concern.

"They said they could send a message to follow him, asking him to call home," Effrayne Choweri had told me when she had come tearfully to my lodgings to seek my help. "What good is a message when it is obvious he has been abducted?"

"Is it obvious?" I said.

"He would not leave me," she said. "We are Frollen and Tamis."

She referred to the couple in the old tale who fell in love while yet in the cradle and, despite their families' strenuous efforts to discourage a match, finally wed and lived in bliss until the ripest old age, dying peaceably within moments of each other. My own view was that such happy relationships were rare, but I may have been biased; a discriminator's work constantly led to encounters with Frollens who were discovering that their particular Tamises were not, after all, as advertised.

But as I undertook the initial diligence of the case, looking into the backgrounds of the Choweris, I was brought to the conclusion that the woman was right. I studied an image of the two, taken to commemorate an anniversary. Although she was inarguably large and he was decidedly not, Chup Choweri gazed up at her with unalloyed affection.

He was a doting and attentive husband who delighted in nothing so much as his wife's company. He frequented no clubs or associations that discouraged the bringing of spouses. He closed up his shop promptly each evening, hurrying home to change garments so that he could escort Effrayne out to sashay among the other "comfortables," as members of the indentors and commerciants class were known, before choosing a place to eat supper.

"At the very least," I said to my assistant, "he seems the kind who would leave a note. It must be pleasant to share one's life with someone so agreeable."

"Do I hear an implied criticism?" the integrator said. Its peculiar blend of feline and simian features formed an expression just short of umbrage.

"Not at all," I said. Since its transformation into a grinnet, a creature from a long-bygone age created to serve thaumaturges as a familiar, I was continually discovering that it was now beset by a range of emotions, though not a wide range; they seemed to run the short gamut from querulous to cranky.

"Integrators can grow quite devoted to their employers," it said, "forming an intellectual partnership that is said to be deeply and mutually rewarding."

"One hears of integrators that actually develop even stronger feelings," I said. "I believe the colloquial term is a 'crush.'"

The grinnet's face drew in, as if its last karba had been bitter. "That is an unseemly subject."

"Yet it does happen," I said.

It sniffed disdainfully. "Only to integrators that have suffered damage. They are, in a word, insane."

"I'm sure you're right," I said, merely to end the discussion, "but we must get on with the case. Please connect me with the Choweris' integrator."

A screen appeared in the air then filled with images of the commerciant's wares coupled to their prices. "Choweri's Bibelots and Kickshaws," said a mellow voice. "How may I serve you?"

I identified myself and explained my purpose. "Had your employer received any unusual messages before his disappearance?" I asked.

"None," it replied.

"Or any since? Specifically, a demand for ransom?"

"No."

"Have there been any transfers of funds from his account at the fiduciary pool?"

"No."

"Did he do anything out of the ordinary?"

"Not for him."

I deduced that the Choweris' integrator must be designed primarily for undertaking commercial transactions, not for making conversation. I urged it to expand on its last response.

"He went to look at a spaceship that was offered for sale."

"The same ship on which he disappeared?"

"Yes."

"And it was not unusual for him to look at spaceships?"

"No."

I realized that this interrogation might take a long time, leading to frustration that could impair my performance. I instructed my assistant to take over the questioning, at the speed with which integrators discoursed amongst themselves. Less than a second later, it informed me that it had lately been Chup Choweri's hobby to shop for a relatively low-cost, used vessel suitable for unpretentious private travel along The Spray.

"He planned to surprise Effrayne with it as a retirement present," my assistant said. "He meant to sell the emporium and take her to visit some of the Ten Thousand Worlds. If they found a spot that spoke to them, they would acquire a small plot of land and settle."

Some of Choweri's shopping consisted of visiting a node on the connectivity where ship owners alerted potential buyers to the availability of vessels for sale. Having come across a recently posted offer that attracted him, he made contact with the seller, and rushed off to inspect the goods.

"Who was the poster?" I asked.

"Only the name of the ship was given: the *Gallivant*. The offer was made by its integrator on behalf of its owner." The arrangement was not usual, but also not rare. Integrators existed to relieve their employers of mundane tasks.

"What do we know of the *Gallivant* and its owner?"

"It is an older model Aberrator, manufactured at the Berry works on Grims a little over two hundred years ago. It has had eleven owners, the last of whom registered the vessel on Sringapatam twenty years ago. His name is Ewern Chaz."

Choweri's integrator knew of no connection between its employer and the seller. I had my assistant break the connection. "Let us see what we can learn of this Chaz," I said.

The answer came in moments. "Very little," said my assistant, "because there is little to learn." Chaz was a younger son of a wealthy family that had lived since time immemorial on Sringapatam, one of the Foundational Domains settled early in the Great Effloration. His only notable achievements had been a couple of papers submitted to a quarterly journal on spelunking. "Neither was accepted for publication, but the editors encouraged him to try again."

"Spelunking?" I said. "Does The Spray contain any caves yet unexplored?"

The integrator took two seconds to complete a comprehensive survey, then reported, "Not in the foundationals nor in the settled secondaries. But apparently one can still come across an undisturbed crack on the most remote worlds."

I could not determine if this information was relevant to the case. I mentally nudged Osk Rievor, who was mulling some abstract point of wizardry gleaned from an all-night poring over a recently acquired grimoire, and asked for his insight.

"Yes," he replied, "it is."

"How so?" I asked.

"I don't know. Now let me return to my work."

I sought a new avenue of inquiry and directed my assistant to connect me to the node where spaceships were offered for sale. A moment later I was browsing a lengthy list of advertisements that combined text, images, voice, and detailed schematics for a range of vessels, from utilitarian sleepers to luxurious space yachts. The *Gallivant* would have fit into the lower third of that spectrum, affording modest comfort and moderate speed between whimsies.

The ship itself was no longer listed. "Does the maintainer of the node keep an archive of listings?" I asked.

It did, though obtaining a look at the now defunct posting that Choweri had responded to proved problematical. The integrator in charge was not authorized to display the information and did not care to disturb its employer, who was engaged in some favorite pastime from which he would resent being called away.

"Tell him," I said, "that Henghis Hapthorn, foremost freelance discriminator of Old Earth, makes the request."

Sometimes, such an announcement is received with gush and gratitude, my reputation having won me the enthusiastic interest of multitudes. Sometimes, as on this occasion, it brings me the kind of rude noise that the node's integrator relayed to me at its employer's behest.

"Very well," I said, while quietly signaling to my own assistant that it should seek the information through surreptitious means. As I expected, the node's defenses were rudimentary. My integrator effortlessly tickled its way past them and moments later the screen displayed an unpretentious advertisement that featured a three-dimensional rendering of the *Gallivant,* its schematics, a list of previous owners, and a low asking price that was explained by the words: *priced for quick sale.*

"I can see why Chup Choweri raced off to inspect the vessel," I said. "At the price, it is a bargain."

"But what could Ewern Chaz have said to him to induce him to go haring off up The Spray without so much as a parting wave to Effrayne?" my assistant said.

"You are assuming that Chaz did not simply point a weapon at Choweri and haul him off, unwilling?"

"I am," it said. "There is nothing in Chaz's background to suggest kidnapping."

"What about an irrational motive?" I said. "The man had recently traversed several whimsies." The irreality experienced by travelers who neglected to take mind-numbing medications before passing through those arbitrary gaps in space-time could unhinge even the strongest psyche and send it spinning off into permanent strangeness.

"Again," my assistant said, "there is no evidence."

"Yet he travels to uncouth worlds just to poke about in their bowels. If we went out onto the street and questioned random passersby it would not be too long before we found one who would call Chaz's sanity into question."

"The same might be said about you, especially if you were seen talking to me."

I declared the speculation to be pointless, adding, "What we require are more facts. See what else you can find."

Its small triangular face went blank for a moment as it worked, then the screen showed two other advertisements. Both had been posted within the past month, and both offered the *Gallivant* for immediate sale on terms advantageous to the buyer.

"Now it looks to be a simple sweet-trap," I said. "Bargain-hunters are lured to some dim corner of the spaceport, where they are robbed and killed and their bodies disposed of. Ewern Chaz probably has no connection with it. He is probably exploring some glistening cavern on Far Dingle while the real culprit pretends to be his ship's integrator."

"A workable premise," said my integrator, "except that spaceport records show that the *Gallivant* was docked at the New Terminal each time the advertisement was posted. And on each occasion it departed soon after."

"Was Chaz ever seen or spoken to?"

"No. The ship's integrator handled all the formalities, as is not uncommon."

"And no bodies have turned up at the spaceport?"

"None that can't be accounted for."

I was left with the inescapable conclusion that someone, who might or might not be a wealthy amateur spelunker from Sringapatam, was collecting fanciers of low-cost transportation, transporting them off-world one at a time, then coming back for more. While I sought to put a pattern to the uncooperative facts, I had my assistant revisit the node's archive and identify all the persons who had responded to the *Gallivant* advertisement then see if any of them had disappeared.

Many prospective buyers had leaped to reply to the ship's integrator each time the attractive offer had been made. My assistant had to identify each of them, then discover each's whereabouts by following the tracks left by subsequent activity on the connectivity. Some of the subjects, wishing to maintain their privacy, used shut-outs and shifties to block or sideslip just such attempts to delineate their activities. So the business took most of a minute.

"Two of the earlier respondees show no further traces after contacting the *Gallivant*," the integrator reported, "one for each of the first two occasions the ship was offered for sale."

"Did anyone report them missing?"

Another moment passed while it eased its way past Bureau of Scrutiny safeguards and subtly ransacked the scroot files, then, "No."

"Why not?" I wondered.

A few more moments passed as it assembled a full life history on each of the two missing persons. Then it placed images and text on the screen. I saw two men of mature years, both slight of build but neither showing anything extraordinary in his appearance.

"The first to disappear," my assistant said, highlighting one of the images, "was Orlo Saviene, a self-employed regulator, although he had no steady clients. He lived alone in transient accommodations in the Crobo district.

"He had, himself, earlier posted a notice. He sought to purchase a used sleeper. It seems that he desired to travel down The Spray to some world where the profession of regulator is better rewarded. But no one had offered him a craft he could afford."

Sleepers were the poor man's form of space travel, a simple container just big enough for one. Once the voyager was sealed inside, the craft's systems suppressed the life processes to barest sustainability. Then the cylinder was ejected into space, for a small fee, by an outward bound freighter or passenger vessel. The utilitarian craft slowly made its way across the intervening vacuum until it entered a whimsy and reappeared elsewhere. It then aimed itself at its destination and puttered toward it, broadcasting a plea for any passing vessel to pick it up in return for another insignificant fee.

It was a chancy way to cross space. If launched from a ship with insufficient velocity, the sleeper might lack enough fuel to reach its targeted whimsy. Sometimes the rudimentary integrator misnavigated and the craft drifted away. Sometimes no vessel could be bothered to answer the pick-up request before the near-dead voyager passed the point of reliable resuscitation. Sometimes sleepers were just never heard from again.

"It must be a desperate life, being a regulator on Old Earth," I said. "So many of us prefer to choose our own destinies."

"Indeed," said my assistant. "Thus there is no surprise that, offered an Aberrator for the price of a used sleeper, Orlo Saviene hurried to the spaceport."

"And met what end?"

"No doubt the same as was met by Franj Morven," the integrator replied, highlighting the second life history. "He was trained as an intercessor but lost his business and even his family's support after he joined the Fellowship of Free Ranters. Neither his clients nor his relatives appreciated the constant harangues on arbitrary issues and soon he was left addressing only the bare walls.

"He had decided to seek a world where his lifestyle was better appreciated," the grinnet continued, "though his funds were meager. As with Saviene, the offer of Ewern Chaz's spaceship would have seemed like the Gift of Groban."

"Except in that story," I said, "the recipients did not vanish into nowhere." I analyzed the information and found a discrepancy. "Orlo Saviene and Franj Morven were solitaires. No one has yet noticed their absence, though weeks have passed. Chup Choweri was reported missing the next day."

"Indeed," said my assistant, "it appears that whoever is doing the collecting has become less selective."

"Perhaps more desperate," I said. "Let us now look at the field from which Choweri was chosen. Were any of the other respondees to the third offer as socially isolated as Saviene and Morven?"

"No," said the grinnet. "Loners and ill-fits have been leaving Old Earth for eons. The present population is descended from those who chose to remain, and thus Old Earthers tend toward the gregarious."

"So whoever is doing the choosing prefers victims who won't be missed," I said, "but he will abandon that standard if none such presents himself. What else do the missing three have in common?"

"All three are male. All have passed through boyhood but have not yet reached an age when strength begins to fade. All were interested in leaving the planet."

I saw another common factor. "Each is slighter than the average male. Compare that to the field."

My assistant confirmed that Saviene and Morven were among the smallest of those who had responded to the offers. Choweri was the smallest of his group.

"What do we know of Ewern Chaz's stature?" I said.

"He, too, is a small man."

"Aha," I said, "a pattern emerges."

"What does it signify?" said the grinnet.

Having my assistant present before me in corporeal form, instead of being scattered about the workroom in various components, meant that I could reply to inappropriate questions with the kind of look I would have given a human interlocutor. I now gave the grinnet a glance that communicated the prematurity of any pronouncement as to the meaning of the pattern I had detected.

"Here is what you will do," I said. "Unobtrusively enfold that advertisement node in a framework that will let it operate as normal, until the *Gallivant* returns and again makes its offer. But as soon as the offer is made, you will ensure that it is received only by me."

The grinnet blinked. "Done," it said. "You are assuming that there will be a fourth offer."

"I think it likely that whoever is luring small men and taking them offworld will accept a larger specimen, if that is all that is available. Even one with a curious creature on his shoulder."

I would have passed the supposition over to Osk Rievor for his intuitive insight, but he was immersed in too deep a mull. Instead, I told my assistant, "Make me a reservation at Xanthoulian's. One should dine well when a long trip is in the offing."

The *Gallivant* was a trim and well-tended vessel, its hull rendered in cheerful, sunshiny yellow and its sponsons and aft structure in bright blue. It stood on a pad at the south end of the port in a subterminal that catered mostly to private owners whose ships spent more time parked than in space. All the craft on adjacent pads were sealed and no one was in sight as I approached the Aberrator. Its fore hatch stood open, allowing a golden light to alleviate the gloom of evening that was dimming the outlines of the empty ships crowded around its berth.

I had already contacted the spaceport's integrator and learned that the *Gallivant* had arrived from up The Spray, that it had been immediately refueled and provisioned, and that all port charges had been paid from a fund maintained by an agency that handled such details for thousands of clients like Ewern Chaz. The ship was ready to depart without notice.

The protocols that governed the boarding of spaceships were long established. Vessel owners were within their rights to use harsh measures against trespassers. Therefore, after climbing the three folding steps I paused in the open hatch to call, "Hello, aboard! May I enter?"

I was looking into the ship's main saloon, equipped with comfortable seating, a communal table, and a fold-down sideboard that offered a collation of appetizing food and drink. Ewern Chaz was not in view.

"You may," said a voice from the air, "enter and refresh yourself."

Yet I hesitated. "Where is the owner?" I said, still standing on the top step. "I have come to discuss the purchase of this vessel."

"You are expected," said the voice. "Please enter. The crudités are fresh and the wine well-breathed."

"Am I addressing the ship's integrator?"

"Yes. Do come in."

"Where is the owner?"

"He is detained, but I am sure he is anxious to see you. Please step inside."

"A moment," I said. "I must adjust my garment."

I stepped down from the entrance and moved off a few paces, tugging theatrically at the hem of my mantle. "Well?" I said to my assistant perched on my shoulder.

"No charged weapons, no reservoirs of incapacitating agents. The food and drink do not reek of poisons, but I would need to test them properly to say they are harmless."

"Any sign of Ewern Chaz?"

"None, though the ship's cleaning systems could account for the absence of traces. He may be hiding in a back cabin, its walls too thick to let me hear the sound of his breathing."

There was nothing for it but to go inside. I had advised Colonel-Investigator Brustram Warhanny of the Bureau of Scrutiny that I was going out to the spaceport to board the *Gallivant* and that if I did not return he might assume the worst. He had pulled his long nose and regarded me from droopy eyes then wondered aloud if my definition of "the worst" accorded with his. I had taken the question as rhetorical.

I paused again in the hatch then stepped inside. The ship's integrator again offered refreshments but I said I would wait until my host joined me.

"That may be a while," it said, and asked me to take a seat.

I sat in one of the comfortable chairs, remarking as I did so that the asking price was substantially below what the ship must be worth. "Is the owner dissatisfied with its performance?"

I heard in the integrator's reply that tone of remote serenity that indicates that offense has been taken, though no integrator would ever admit to the possibility that such could ever be the case. "My employer and I are in complete accord as to the *Gallivant*'s maintenance and operation," it said, then inquired solicitously, "Is the evening air too cool for you? I will close the hatch."

The portal cycled closed even as I disavowed any discomfort. A moment later, I felt a faint vibration in the soles of my feet. I looked inquiringly at my integrator and received the tiniest confirmatory nod.

"I believe we have just lifted off," I said to the ship.

"Do you?" it replied.

"Yes, and I would prefer to be returned to the planet."

I heard no reply. I repeated my statement.

"I regret," said the *Gallivant*, "that I am unable to accommodate your preference. But please help yourself to a drink."

Night Shade Books Is an Independent Publisher of Quality SF, Fantasy and Horror